CANDLELIGHT

"ZANE, YOU'RE INSATIABLE."

His hands stroked her body as if to memorize every line. "Ashley, I don't think I could ever get enough of loving you. Now, let's get those sheepskin rugs. I've fantasized about this for days. Now I want the real thing."

"But, Zane," she protested with a shaky laugh, "haven't you had enough? I don't think I can . . ."

The fiery glimmer in his eyes halted her words. "Is that a challenge, my sweet captive? Do you think I can't make you want me again, and again, and again—as I want you? I burn for you, Ashley. You will feel that heat too, until the fire's so hot within you you'll beg to be taken."

CANDLELIGHT ECSTASY SUPREMES

FIRE
IN PARADISE

Betty Henrichs

A CANDLELIGHT ECSTASY SUPREME

Published by
Dell Publishing Co., Inc.
1 Dag Hammarskjold Plaza
New York, New York 10017

Dell ® TM 681510, Dell Publishing Co., Inc.

Candlelight Ecstasy Supreme is a trademark
of Dell Publishing Co., Inc.

Candlelight Ecstasy Romance®, 1,203,540, is a
registered trademark of Dell Publishing Co., Inc.

ISBN: 0-440-12519-7

Printed in the United States of America

First printing—December 1985

To Kent, who is my paradise.

To Our Readers:

We are pleased and excited by your overwhelmingly positive response to our Candlelight Ecstasy Supremes. Unlike all the other series, the Supremes are filled with more passion, adventure, and intrigue, and are obviously the stories you like best.

In months to come we will continue to publish books by many of your favorite authors as well as the very finest work from new authors of romantic fiction. As always, we are striving to present unique, absorbing love stories—the very best love has to offer.

Breathtaking and unforgettable, Ecstasy Supremes follow in the great romantic tradition you've come to expect *only* from Candlelight Ecstasy.

Your suggestions and comments are always welcome. Please let us hear from you.

Sincerely,

The Editors
Candlelight Romances
1 Dag Hammarskjold Plaza
New York, New York 10017

CHAPTER ONE

Ashley Buchannan looked from Monica Bennett, the owner of the *Honolulu Daily News*, to Ray Wyatt, her editor. "I've seen naked men before," she insisted. "That's not my objection to this assignment."

An hour later, Ashley's gray eyes sparkled with excitement after she'd finally accepted the new assignment. "A daily column with my own byline! Who would have believed it!" she said as she returned to her desk.

Sitting down, she raised her empty coffee cup in a silent toast. *Butcher, maybe you were worth it after all.*

Before she could question this sentiment too deeply, Jake, one of the photographers on the newspaper, dropped a package of black and white pictures on her desk.

"Here's today's shoot, Ashley. If you like football jocks these should really turn you on. By the way, I just heard the news. Congratulations on your new assignment. You'll get a kick out of following the Hawaiian Kings." He grinned. "Women covering sports! The ol' NFL may never be the same." With a friendly wave, he turned to go. "Be a pal and don't lose these photos." he said over his shoulder.

"They aren't labeled yet. See you Sunday at the game."

Ashley glanced through the first set of pictures, but instead of seeing the Kings football players battering tackling dummies, unwanted images of her ex-husband Butcher flooded her mind. As memories best forgotten surfaced to blunt her happiness, the exhilaration she'd experienced over her unexpected promotion deflated like a day-old balloon.

How in the world had she ever let herself get into this mess? Interviewing half naked athletes in the locker room; watching grown men crash into each other, playing a game instead of working for a living; dealing with giants whose egos were bigger than their biceps. Hot tears gathered in her eyes as she stared down at Jake's pictures. She'd sworn she'd had enough of football players to last a lifetime, but now in a mad moment of weakness she'd let Monica and Ray convince her to get involved with them all over again. Talk about being a fool! Hadn't twelve disastrous years with Butcher taught her anything?

As Ashley shook her head in disbelief, a curling tendril of black hair escaped from her neatly coiled chignon. No! She wasn't going to think about the past anymore. Angrily, she wiped away the tears with her hand. She'd cried enough, endured enough hurt, suffered enough regrets. No more! The memories of Butcher, of that day, that game, the instant that had shattered everything, had haunted her long enough!

With a determined thrust of a bobby pin she shoved the fallen lock of hair in place and forced her thoughts back to the exciting assignment Monica had unexpectedly offered her. Her own column! It was something she'd always wanted. Admitting that made her face the truth. It wasn't a momentary weakness or stupidity that had made her dare to accept this job. Ambition had been the culprit, and she wasn't sorry.

Ashley's chin rose. So what if this new assignment involved a bunch of jocks? She didn't have to get involved with them. She just had to write about them—and that might be fun. She certainly knew football, both the good and the seamy side. That especially made good copy. Firmly burying the memories of Butcher away where they belonged, she pulled out her mirror to repair her smeared mascara.

As Ashley glanced back down at the pictures, her smile returned. Now the only problem she had was thinking up some attention-grabbing topic for her first column. What had Monica said? Ashley's smile broadened, remembering the words. Okay boss, she thought, if you want a real "hell-burner" to kick off the new column, that's exactly what you're going to get!

She waved her hands above Jake's pictures as if casting a spell and began flipping through the next set. "Okay do your stuff. Inspire me!" she murmured.

They didn't. Jake had done a series of shots of the two lines crashing together. He'd captured all the sweat and brawn of battle, but unfortunately he hadn't captured her imagination. The third batch wasn't any better.

Ashley sighed and picked up the next set. Her eyes widened as she stared at them, and she carefully laid out the pictures. Jake had obviously clicked off three fast frames. They were all of the same football player and all were taken from the same angle, behind the man. In the first, with his head down, no pads or helmet, a man standing alone isolated against the green of the mountains behind, he seemed almost poetically at one with nature. She had no idea who he was, couldn't even see his face, but still his image intrigued her. The man was big and brawny, reminding her of Butcher, yet instead of conveying savage force, the weary set of his shoulders lent a touch of vulnerability that appealed to her, reaching out to her, touching her as no other had.

In the next two pictures the mood changed. Jake had caught the player bending and stretching like some young warrior ready to do battle, flexing muscles bulked for strength, for physical force, not for grace. This time as her gaze wandered from picture to picture no memory of Butcher intruded to cloud her response to the man.

For the first time in a long time Ashley felt her blood warm. The player's blond hair, ruffled by the breeze, skimmed shoulders so broad they strained the seams of the practice shirt. The T-shirt was cropped short, revealing the ripple of muscles across his back. As her eyes searched longer, his image, like the caress of the Hawaiian sun, heated her skin, then the heat flowed inward to bring a smile of pleasure.

Mirroring her rising good spirits, delightfully wicked thoughts tickled her mind as she looked at the pictures.

Hmm, that's what I call a great tight end! What a fabulous backfield in motion.

A chuckle escaped at the thoughts. She smiled, savoring the sensations flowing through her. Her eyes lingered on the player's heavily muscled legs. More blond hair, curly and thick, covered muscles built for power.

14

"Ah, unfair." She giggled softly to herself as another football allusion popped into her consciousness. That's unnecessary roughness . . . *but what enticing roughness!*

Suddenly her palms began to itch, and she had the wildest impulse to run her fingers over those corded muscles, to trail them through that lush roughness, to feel—

With a gasp Ashley shook away the disturbing thoughts. Her heart, a second ago thudding with pleasure, now pounded with fear. How could she find any man who even remotely resembled her ex-husband appealing? Her reaction to the man in Jake's pictures was so immediate, so physical, so sensuously intense it frightened her. It reminded her of the first time she'd met Butcher—and look where that had led!

She glanced down again and shuddered. When would she learn? If anything, instead of warming her blood, this blond giant should send chills through her, chills of warning. Remember Butcher! Football players are bad news! Hadn't she learned that sad lesson over and over again?

Deliberately Ashley took a deep, steadying breath. She was simply overreacting to the excitement and the pressure. First Monica unexpectedly gave her the column when half a dozen guys in the sports department were as qualified, then she told her the first preseason game was only a day away, which gave her very little time to prepare. Who wouldn't get flustered with all that tossed at them in one afternoon? Yes, that had to be the answer. She refused to believe that her reaction to the blond player might have something to do with any real longing.

Casually, as if proving they had no power to

15

touch her, she gathered up all of Jake's pictures, locked them in her desk drawer, and headed out to her car. The last rays of the sun were just disappearing as Ashley sped past Pearl Harbor toward her beach house, tucked in a tiny secluded cove along the Waimae coast. Only a sandy trail cut between the towering palms hinted that a house nestled beyond.

Home. The place of her childhood usually brought a smile when she pulled the car to a stop and got out to hear the pounding surf, but tonight it failed her. Still disturbed far more than she wanted to admit by the new assignment—or could it be by the pictures of the blond?—Ashley stopped a minute to let the tranquillity soothe her. It didn't work. Instead, the scene that was usually so friendly betrayed her, the jutting rocks reminding her of shoulders straining shirt's seams; and the golden tropical moon glinting off the waves, of blond hair tossed by the wind.

Ashley clenched her hands with a muttered "Damn him!"

Without looking back she marched into her beach house. She tossed her blouse onto the sofa in the living room, the skirt fell on the polished mahogany floor in the bedroom, and everything else ended up on the bathroom tiles. A quick twist of her wrist brought a cascade of water. Praying the water would pound away all the disturbing feelings, Ashley stepped into the icy spray.

Sunday morning the insistent shrill scream of a hungry sea gull pulled Ashley out of a restless sleep. For a second her eyes, gritty and tired from all the background reading she'd been doing, fluttered open, then just as quickly shut, blotting out the bright tropical sun streaming in through the window. She pulled the sheet over her head with a groan, but it was useless. Even though she'd been up almost till dawn doing research on the Kings, sleep wouldn't return.

Yawning and stretching, she threw back the sheet. The warm water of the Pacific welcomed her as she greeted the day with her usual morning swim. She dived through the breaking waves and with sure strokes headed out into deeper water. As always, the warm sun on her back, the sea mist touching her face, the swells gently rocking her as she swam made her feel at peace. She refused to let the thought of the football game ahead and of the memories it would awaken darken her good mood.

Four hours later, Ashley hesitated a moment as she put her hand on the doorknob of the press box. Life-style section to sports page was quite a leap. It had happened so late Friday most of the other reporters had already left for the day. What would their reaction be when she walked in? Monica had handed her the type of choice assignment any one of them would have loved to have had. Would they be angry, resentful? Or would they simply ignore her?

There was a defiant tilt to her chin as she pushed open the door. But she need not have worried. Instead of jeers, the men greeted her with smiles. If any of them felt resentment he didn't show it. Ashley was so relieved she didn't ask herself whether it was because they liked her or because they feared Monica's notoriously acid tongue.

Abe, the statistician for the *News*, gestured to the empty seat next to him. "We flipped a coin and I won. I get the beautiful lady next to me."

Ashley dropped into her seat and returned his

smile. "Wrong. I'm the one who's won. Yesterday I read everything I had time to read on the Kings, but the details are still sketchy. I'll probably be asking you questions all during the game."

"Ashley, you wound me." Dave Jenkins, the senior sportswriter for the *News*, said gravely with mock offense. "I've cranked out reams of copy on the Kings. I've been writing about them for months. Didn't you read any of my articles on the NFL expansion plans?"

"Sorry." She laughed. "After Butcher and I got divorced I reserved the sports page for the sole honor of decorating the bottom of my cockatoos' cage. Maybe they read them. I'll ask Kanani and Kaipo when I get home."

His retort was drowned out by the organ flourish introducing the national anthem. As the crowd cheered wildly, the Kings kicked off. Thirty seconds later it was the L.A. Raiders six, the Kings zero after the receiver ran back the opening kickoff for a touchdown. When the halftime whistle blew, the score was Raiders twenty-one, Kings zero.

Abe threw down his pencil in disgust. "What a yawner! I've seen more exciting high school games."

Dave shook his head. "Ashley, if you can get a good column out of that, you're a better man—I mean, *writer*—than I am. As for me, if nothing better turns up I'm going to write about the cheerleaders. Their shaking around in those short hula skirts is certainly a lot more exciting than anything that's happening on the field."

By late in the fourth quarter, when the score hit thirty-five to nothing, Ashley really began to fidget. Frowning, she glanced down at the few notes she'd made. How in the world was she ever going to get a

18

hell-burner out of this mess? A sudden loud roar from the fans drew her attention back to the field.

She tapped Abe on the arm. "Who is that prancing around in the backfield?"

"Oh, that's Bubba Pirrs, the linebacker. He started doing that war dance in college. He always does it when he sacks the quarterback."

Bubba's antics ignited both himself and the crowd. Their loud cheers reverberated around the stadium when on the second play from scrimmage Bubba stopped the Raiders fullback dead at the line. On third down and ten, as the Raiders quarterback dropped back to pass, Bubba broke through the line again. Like a locomotive out of control he charged at the quarterback. By this time the fans were jumping and screaming in excitement as he chased him out of the pocket to the left. A yard away from another sack, in a collision so loud the microphones on the sidelines picked it up, Bubba crashed to the grass. He never saw the Raiders blocker who blindsided him.

As he lay writhing on the turf, Ashley felt as if someone had kicked her in the stomach. She felt his pain, she knew his agony—she knew it all too well. A knee was so fragile, it was almost as easily broken as a marriage.

"Hey, Ashley, are you all right?" Dave asked. "You're white as a ghost."

"I'm fine." She forced the words through clenched teeth as she watched them carry Bubba off the field on a stretcher. "I just hate to see anyone get hurt."

Dave shrugged. "It comes with the territory. Those jocks get paid damn well to take hits. You know that."

Ashley closed her eyes, blotting out the pain. Yes, I know that, but I *won't* think about it.

"Hey gorgeous, I'm sorry. I forgot about you and Butcher."

Ashley forced herself to look at him. Dredging up a smile, she said casually, "Forget it. I have."

"There he goes!" Abe yelled, watching the field below.

Ashley looked up to see a Kings player flat on his face while the Raiders running back galloped toward the end zone.

Dave shrugged. "Just proves why a backup is a backup. Bubba never would have let anyone run over him like that. Who is that clumsy lummox anyway? He's as big as the side of a mountain, and obviously about as mobile."

Abe ran his finger down the roster. "Zane Bruxton, from USC. He played a couple of years in Canada. Ever heard of him?"

"Zane?" Dave laughed, poking Ashley in the ribs. "Doesn't exactly inspire fear, does it? Linebackers should be named things like Killer or Jaws."

"Or Butcher?" Ashley asked with a sad smile.

"You have to admit, gorgeous, he was one of the great ones."

Before she had time to answer, the two-minute whistle sounded. Surprisingly, with less than a minute left, the Kings drove in for a score. But even that wouldn't furnish a hell-burner of a column.

At the final whistle Dave stood up and stretched. "Now the fun starts! And I can't wait!"

"What have you been waiting for, a cold beer?" Ashley asked, gathering up her sketchy notes. "I know that's what I'd like after that fiasco."

"Nope." He rubbed his hands together eagerly. "What I can't wait to see is the reaction when you

20

walk into that locker room for the postgame interviews. It'll give ol' Clyde a stroke!"

For an instant she frowned. "Clyde? Oh, you mean Clyde Winston, the owner of the Kings."

"Yep, the old macadamia nut mogul himself, as cantankerous, conservative, and chauvinist a multimillionaire as you'd never want to meet." Dave held out his arm. "Come on, gorgeous, the naked men await."

The tunnel under the stadium was crawling with fans as they tried to push their way through to the locker room.

Dave shook his head. "After that game today I'm surprised the Kings have any fans at all."

Ashley dodged a little kid intent on finding his mother. "Football players are always popular with kids and women. Just not for the same reason," she commented with a trace of bitterness.

"I'll bet!" Dave chuckled, throwing an elbow to clear a path for them. "Someday over a brew you'll have to tell me if all those wild stories I heard about Butcher were true."

"They were," she muttered with a grimace as they reached the closed door at the end of the hall.

As she reached for the knob a burly guard stepped in front of her. "Hey, lady, you can't go in there. That's the men's locker room."

She calmly looked at the hulking brute in her path and said, "Who says I can't?" She tapped the badge pinned to her blouse. "I'm Ashley Buchannan. As you see I have a press pass issued by your office. If you have a problem take it up with them."

He looked around desperately for help. "Look, lady I don't care if you have a pass from King Kamehameha himself, you can't go in there!"

"Want to bet?"

Dave, who had slipped into the background to enjoy the confrontation, came forward now to lend his support. "That's telling him, gorgeous."

The guard ignored him. "Lady, have a heart. Mr. Winston will have my badge if I let a woman into his locker room."

"Someone should have thought of that before his office issued my press pass. Now it's too late, so get out of my way."

The door behind the guard suddenly opened and a handsome gray-haired gentleman emerged from the locker room.

"Mr. Winston, thank goodness you're here." The guard pointed to Ashley. "This lady insists I let her go into the locker room."

"That's quite impossible!"

"Why?" demanded Ashley.

"Only authorized reporters are allowed in."

"I am an authorized reporter."

"Only authorized male reporters are allowed in."

Suddenly a commanding feminine voice cut through the argument, silencing everyone. "Ashley, what's the problem? Why are you out here instead of in there?"

Ashley turned to see Monica Bennett. Elegantly dressed in a pale peach silk suit with diamonds sparkling at her ears, neck, wrists, and from at least half her fingers, she looked completely out of place in the grimy hallway.

Ashley welcomed her support with a smile of greeting, but Monica was glaring at the guard. "Young man, move! My reporters have a story to cover."

"You stay right where you are!" Clyde countered.

"Surely you aren't going to deny access to your locker room to one of my reporters."

"Damn it, Monica! You know I won't allow—"

"I don't give a damn what you allow," Monica snapped. Her eyes, already cold, became pools of blue ice. "You may be the owner of the Kings, but you can't tell me whom to assign to cover your precious football team. You've had your way in this town long enough! That's going to change."

The grim look on her face didn't soften a bit as she turned to Ashley. "You're going to get in there and get that story if I have to call the police and have them bust down the door."

Clyde folded his arms. "I'd like to see you try, Monica. As you know, I am not without influence in this town."

"Neither am I. Shall we see who holds the most power, you and your nuts or me and my newspaper? Care to venture a guess?"

Ashley looked from Monica to Clyde in confusion. Their anger ran too deep, their barbs were too sharp, for this to be just an argument over her entering the locker room. There was a lot more going on between them, but Ashley didn't have a clue what it was.

She raised her voice to interrupt Clyde's denial. "I don't mean to be rude, but could we finish discussing this later? Right now I have a story to file, and it's due in less than two hours." She looked directly at Clyde. "If I can't enter the locker room and get the story I'd planned to write, then I have no alternative but to use your refusal to let me cover your team as the basis for my exposé on sexual discrimination. And you know as well as I do, that's something the NFL strongly disapproves of."

"Exposé! Discrimination!" Clyde sputtered. "Now look here, young woman, you can't—"

"Not only can she, I'll personally see that she

does." Monica smiled sweetly. It was a smile that didn't reach her eyes. "I believe they call this checkmate, Clyde darling."

Clyde Winston was speechless. "I admit you've won this round, Monica, but this isn't over! Don't forget that!" He turned abruptly on his heel and slammed through the door.

Now that the moment was finally here, Ashley hesitated. It was one thing to bravely insist on your right to walk into a room full of men, no doubt in various stages of undress. It was another thing entirely to do it.

Monica smiled, unaware of her reluctance. "That charge of discrimination was brilliant. Now get me that hell-burner of a first column I want, and the day will be perfect."

"Come on, gorgeous, don't worry. If any of those hunks tries to tackle you I'll protect you," Dave promised.

She looked at him—skinny, balding, with wire-rimmed glasses—and smiled grimly. "My hero?"

"So what if I don't know karate? I can always stab them with my pencil. Remember, the pencil is mightier than the brawn."

"I don't think that's the way it goes, but thanks for the thought." She laughed, grateful for his humor, which helped to bolster her courage. She took a deep breath. "Okay, I'm ready if you are."

Dave opened the door, and immediately she wished with all her heart she hadn't taken that deep breath, as the sickly-sweet odor of stale sweat assaulted her. But that wasn't the only thing that assaulted her senses. Ashley gulped at the sight of so many half clothed and unclothed men—so many magnificently built unclothed men. A hot flush scalded her cheeks, but she refused to give in to her embarrassment. She'd known what she was walking into.

The room was foggy with the steam pouring out of the showers, and for a moment no one noticed she'd entered. Then suddenly one of the men yelled, "Holy sh— uh, holy *cow,* there's a broad in here!"

His warning triggered such comical responses, amusement overcame Ashley's twinge of embarrassment. Three of the men dived for cover. One, cowering behind the plastic shoulder pads he strategically clutched in front of him, backed quickly away from her as if she had the plague. Most of the others greeted her with catcalls and wolf whistles.

A more specific message came from the Kings center. "Hey babe, hey you from the press, come over here," he invited, flipping the towel wrapped around his waist suggestively at her. "Have I got a *tale* for you!"

"That's enough of that!" Clyde's commanding voice silenced the taunts. "I don't like this situation any better than you do, but we're stuck with it. It's called freedom of the press, so forget she's a woman and treat her like any other reporter."

Ashley tried to smile a thank you at him, but he deliberately turned his back and walked away. With a shrug, Ashley flipped open her notebook. After a moment of indecision she headed toward the training room, where she saw a trainer working on Bubba before they moved him to the hospital. Nothing else exciting had come to mind; maybe an interview with Bubba on how it felt to go from his sack dance to crutches in one hit would grab the sympathetic interest of the readers. It wasn't great, but she didn't have anything else.

As she approached the table, the big burly trainer

turned and saw her. Letting out a whoop, he lifted her in his arms, he spun her around. "Ashley Buchannan, I don't believe it! What in blue blazes are you doing here?"

"Hi, Sammy. I didn't know you'd joined the Kings," she said, smiling breathlessly when he put her back on her feet.

"Had to. That old arthritis of mine has been acting up, so I thought I'd try some sun-and-sea therapy."

As Sammy turned back to Bubba he said, "I suppose you want to interview our wounded hero here, but you'll have to wait a minute. I want him to remain absolutely still while I pump up this air cast to immobilize his knee. Then you can ask all the questions you want."

While he worked, Ashley glanced across the room at the whirlpool, catching her breath at the sight of the player rising from the churning water. Blond hair curled by the warm mist, water dripping off a body bronzed by the sun, shoulders so broad they had to belong to the player she'd seen in Jake's pictures. Then he turned. Somehow she knew his face would be just as full of strength as his body.

For a second she just gazed at him, intrigued by the interesting mix of angles and planes. High jutting cheekbones accented blue eyes so dark they looked almost black. His cheeks, lean and hollow, swept down to an uncompromisingly square chin. Only his mouth, with its full lower lip, lent any softness to his face. As he became aware of her inspection, one corner of his mouth curled up in a grin, and he winked before wrapping his towel more firmly around his waist and walking out of the training room.

He acts like a swaggering pirate, she thought to

herself, displeased that she'd let herself be distracted by him.

Yet as she turned her back on the whirlpool, something about the image nagged her. Suddenly she smiled. No, he didn't look like a pirate. She had the wrong ocean. He reminded her of a Viking. Fierce, proud, with an intriguing whiff of the primitive, she could visualize him sweeping in from the foggy North Sea to pillage and plunder. Yes, she could easily see him in that role. He was so strong, no captive could resist if he decided he wanted her.

Abruptly Ashley snapped off the thoughts. What a wild imagination! Vikings, captives, ravishing and plundering—the steam must be fogging her brain!

"Ashley, I'm done." When she didn't answer, Sammy raised his voice. "Earth to Ashley, come in, please. Are you there?"

"Sorry, Sammy, I guess I was just thinking about something. Tell me, who was that blond guy who just stepped out of the whirlpool?"

"Hey baby, he's nobody," Bubba interrupted. "I'm the star here. I thought you were going to interview me."

"Sorry, Bubba, she'll have to visit you in the hospital. The ambulance is ready to leave." Bubba started to protest, but Sammy shook his head. "Dr. Thomason is waiting. The sooner we get that knee into surgery for some arthroscopic magic, the sooner you'll be back doing your sack dance."

As he watched them wheel Bubba out of the training room, he sighed, "This sure is a lousy way to start the season. I'll bet Mr. Winston is about ready to spit nails."

"Why? Because his starting linebacker went down?" asked Ashley.

"That, plus the fact it must be damn embarrassing to see your nephew fall flat on his face in front of fifty thousand people."

Ashley's gray eyes lit with excitement. "Nephew? I read all the clippings on the Kings and I didn't see anything about the owner's nephew being on the team," she said, sensing she might have found her story.

Sammy shrugged and started packing up the rolls of tape. "Maybe no one else knows. I happened to stop by Mr. Winston's office the day Zane signed his contract, and he introduced us. He didn't say anything about it being a secret."

Ashley snapped her fingers. "Are you talking about that second-string linebacker who came in for Bubba, the one who missed the tackle in the fourth quarter and let the Raiders score that easy touchdown? What was his name? Oh, yes, Zane Bruxton."

Suddenly Sammy looked uneasy as he glanced over his shoulder. "Maybe I wasn't supposed to let that particular cat out of the bag. It could make Mr. Winston mighty angry. He's got a temper that makes the Kilauea volcano seem tame."

She kissed him on the cheek. "Don't worry, I know how to protect my sources. No one will ever know you gave me this scoop. Now I've got to go. I've got one hell-burner of a column to write."

Returning to her office, Ashley flipped on the word processor to do her column and sat for a minute staring at the empty screen. Then a happy smile touched her mouth as she typed her headline: ISN'T NEPOTISM A WONDERFUL THING?

CHAPTER TWO

"Get up! Get up, sleepyhead!"

At the words Ashley woke with a start. "Will you be quiet!" she muttered groggily, pulling the pillow over her head. "The alarm clock hasn't even gone off yet."

"The sun's up, sleepyhead! Get up."

Ashley rolled over and slowly opened her eyes. "I knew I shouldn't have let you stay last night, but I wanted to celebrate. Now if you're going to share my bedroom you'd better be quiet. Understand?"

With one last warning frown she settled back under the sheet. As soon as her head nestled on the pillow her eyes closed, only to suddenly fly open when her companion insisted, "Time to eat, sleepyhead."

"That does it!" she bolted upright in bed and glared. "One more word out of you and what I eat will be cockatoo stew!"

Her warning elicited a shrill squawk and a wild flutter of wings in the rattan cage across the room. Before she could soothe the ruffled cockatoos, the phone rang.

She picked it up. "Yes what is it?" she snapped.

"I know it's early, but is that any way to talk to your editor?" Ray Wyatt asked.

"Ray, I'm sorry. It's been a wild morning. Is there

a problem at the *News*?" Ashley asked, rubbing her sleepy eyes to clear them.

"We need you down here, right away."

"But why?"

"Ashley, don't ask questions. Just get down here!" Ray ordered.

"Okay, but I've got one errand I have to do on the way."

"Make it snappy. This can't wait."

Before she could respond, he hung up. A worried frown furrowed her forehead as she dressed. What could she have done? Was something wrong with the column? Maybe Sammy had been wrong. Maybe Zane wasn't Clyde Winston's nephew. A hundred questions, a hundred doubts, bombarded her as she fed Kanani and Kaipo, her two white cockatoos, and rushed out to the car. She made a quick stop on her hurried way to Honolulu.

When she walked in, the newsroom fell strangely silent, as everyone stopped what they were doing to look at her. Ashley's knees began to tremble, but she marched to her desk. In the editor's glass cubicle, she could see Ray and Monica talking.

Monica looked up, spotted her, and immediately charged out. When she arrived at Ashley's desk and leveled a finger at her. "Ashley, I have only one thing to say to you."

Ashley swallowed nervously, waiting anxiously as Monica paused. "That article of yours was fabulous! I wanted a hell-burner and you delivered." She raised her voice imperiously. "Ray, bring that champagne. Bring a couple of bottles." She threw her arms wide to embrace the whole staff. "Everyone, join us. We're going to celebrate!"

After the other reporters had drunk their champagne and drifted back to their desks, Monica asked, "How did you ever dig up that wonderful dirt?" She rubbed her hands together, obviously relishing the thought. "You really stuck it to them." Before Ashley could answer she went on. " 'Raiders Score as Owner's Nephew Falls on Face!' How delicious! I can just see Clyde. If I know him he's pacing across his office right now, absolutely blowing his top!" Her harsh laugh grated. "Then do you know what he'll do? He'll yell at his secretary that the coffee's not strong enough."

"It sounds like you know him pretty well," Ashley observed, sipping the last drop of champagne from the paper cup.

As if a switch had been clicked, Monica's smile froze. Totally ignoring Ashley's observation, she commented, "Your first column was an excellent start. I expect nothing less in the future." She glanced at her diamond-studded watch. "I have to leave for a meeting with the mayor. Keep that last bottle of champagne for a more private celebration."

Ashley stared at her back in confusion as Monica marched out of the newsroom. Then she shrugged. As Ray always said, the rich can afford to be different.

With a happy sigh she turned her attention to Monday's copy of the *News*. Once she found the sports section she spread it out on the top of her desk. Her smile widened. She had it all, the lead left-hand column, her picture above the eye-catching headline, and best of all, her own byline.

Her fingertips traced the headline lightly, as she savored a success that tasted even better than the champagne. Suddenly, without warning, a motorcycle helmet crashed down onto her desk, obliterating the words. She gasped, her gaze flying up to

31

meet blue eyes so dark with anger they seemed almost black. Ashley blinked.

"I want to know what the hell happened to objective journalism!"

She gulped, trying to find words. But all she could think about was how he'd looked stepping out of that whirlpool bath, water dripping off shoulders so wide they seemed to fill the room.

Before she could stop it, the question teasing her mind slipped out. "Were your ancestors Vikings?"

"Vikings? What in the hell are you talking about? Aren't you Ashley Buchannan?"

She didn't say anything. Cold sapphire-blue eyes swept disdainfully over her. "Of course you are. I recognize you from the locker room. Brother, does that show how wrong first impressions can be! When I saw you, I thought, there is one great-looking chick! I should have known with hair so black you'd turn out to be as shrill as a crow and about as appealing!"

Stunned by Zane's attack, Ashley didn't say anything as he grabbed the bottle of champagne. "Is this how you celebrate your brand of sleazy reporting?" he demanded, slamming it back down so hard it was a wonder it didn't break the desk.

The word *sleazy* finally snapped her out of her daze. Ashley's eyes glowed like hot coals. "Now hold it right there," she snapped. "I assume you're Zane Bruxton, or you wouldn't be bellowing at me."

"You know I am. And I demand—"

"Do you deny you're Clyde Winston's nephew?"

Ashley, disturbed more than she wanted to admit by his looming presence, hit back before any more unconscious thoughts about marauding Vikings popped out.

32

"No, but—"

"Do you deny you missed the tackle and let the Raiders running back score?"

"No, but I—"

"Do you deny that wasn't the only tackle you missed?"

"No, but *look*—"

"Do you deny being the owner's nephew sure helps at draft time?"

Zane slapped his hand down so hard on the desk Ashley jumped, her chair scooting backward. "You're damn right I deny that! I was drafted because I know how to play middle linebacker, and not because—"

"It sure didn't look like it yesterday," Ashley retorted, carefully drawing her chair back to the desk. She wished Zane wasn't so *big*. She was tempted to stand up, to look him right in the eye, but she didn't want to give him the satisfaction of seeing that he had the power to ruffle her.

He started to speak, but she interrupted him again. "I write news. I don't write fiction. If you want to quarrel with my column you'd better review the game films first."

"I have no quarrel with some of what you wrote. I don't deny that I played a lousy game, but I do deny your charge of nepotism. Did you do any research before you shot off that broadside? Did you know I was voted the Pac Ten linebacker of the year my senior year? Did you know I started in the Blue-Gray game? That's why the Kings drafted me, not because of who my uncle is!" Zane jabbed his finger down on the desk. "And don't you forget it!"

Before she could answer, he grabbed his helmet. "Next time check your facts before you stick your pretty neck out there, or you may get it chopped off! And I wouldn't mind being the one to do it."

Ashley let out a long sigh as she watched him stomp out of the newsroom. She should be furious, yet the tiny jabs her conscience was delivering dulled her anger. She had checked the files before she'd written the column, but since Zane wasn't on the first string and the Kings were a new team, the background material was sketchy. She knew he'd graduated from USC and played a couple of years in Canada, but that was about all.

Before she could decide how she felt about what he'd said, Ray stopped beside her desk. He gestured toward the door, which had just slammed shut. "Who was the beach bum? He looked like he was giving you a rough time."

"Beach bum?" A smile touched Ashley's lips. Dressed in faded jeans and a wild Hawaiian shirt with his motorcycle helmet tucked under his arm, she supposed Zane did look like a typical Waikiki surf bum. He even had the physique for it. Yet in her mind she still saw a primitive rampaging Viking, not a modern surfer.

"That 'beach bum' was Zane Bruxton. Needless to say he wasn't very happy with my column today," she explained.

"Your job is to keep our readers happy and interested." He gave her a fatherly pat on the shoulder. "Don't worry about some dumb jock who's had his ego bruised. By the way, Monica just phoned. The switchboard is flooded. Your column's a hit. You just keep hitting, and hitting hard. What are you writing about today? I need it early, so get it to me as quickly as you can."

"Ray, give me a break." Ashley protested, laughing. "You roust me out of bed to come down here for champagne and celebration. Then I get attacked by some hulking brute who doesn't appreciate my honesty. And before I can even get a chance to breathe, you want my next column delivered to your desk immediately, if not sooner."

"Not immediately. Three this afternoon will be fine." He grinned. "What's the big deal? Just go back to your inside source. I know you can do it." With a wave of his hand he went back to his office.

Ashley pulled out her notebook. She'd just begun jotting notes about Bubba's sudden fall from sack dance to crutches when her phone rang. She answered it, and a hushed voice whispered, "The box just arrived. How in the world did you ever remember what brand of cigars I like? Thanks."

"Why all the cloak-and-dagger stuff? I can hardly hear you, Sammy."

"You're not exactly popular around here this morning, so I just thought I'd play it safe and keep it low."

"My column isn't going to get you in trouble, is it?" she asked, frowning.

"Hell no, no one knows where the inside info is coming from. Besides, I'm enjoying this. That column really set things hopping around here." Sammy chuckled. "You should have seen Mr. Winston this morning. He came charging in snorting like a bull. But the funny thing was, he seemed more angry at that owner of yours, Ms. Bennett, than at you."

"Monica acted strange this morning too," Ashley admitted. "She was delighted at the success of my first column, but I got the feeling a boost in circulation wasn't what she was interested in. I wonder if—"

Suddenly a harsh noise erupted through the

35

phone. Ashley moved the receiver a safe distance from her ear, but she could still plainly hear the sounds of a scuffle, and the accompanying string of shouted obscenities.

"Ashley, I've got to go play referee before somebody gets killed. No, wait a minute, Coach Mitchell just arrived. He's got it stopped," Sammy explained.

"What's going on there?" Ashley asked, flipping her notebook open to a new page. "It sounded like World War Three had erupted."

"Naw, it was just Razor and Micky getting into a brawl."

"Razor and Micky?" she replied, quickly trying to place the names.

"Yeah, you know, Ralph 'the Razor' Williams, the starting quarterback, and his backup Micky Jones," Sammy reminded her.

"What were they fighting over? Who's going to start the next game?" Ashley asked, beginning to make notes.

"No, Razor has a lock on that. But he's got a hot temper and he doesn't like to lose, not even at Ping-Pong. And he especially doesn't like to be beaten by his backup."

"You mean they started trading punches over a Ping-Pong game?" Ashley demanded.

"Actually, the first fist didn't fly until after Razor threw his paddle at Micky's head. The kid's got a great arm. It'll probably take me three or four stitches to close the cut."

"Sammy, I owe you another box of cigars. This will make a great column for tomorrow!"

"Make it a bottle of Scotch and you've got a deal."

She hung up the phone and sat staring at her

36

notes a minute before turning on the word processor. Typing quickly she wrote her headline: THE GREAT PING–PONG WAR.

Tuesday morning Ray was waiting at her desk when she arrived. He waved her column at her. "Monica has already called to say that newsstand sales have jumped three percent since your first column hit the stands yesterday and orders for new subscriptions are coming in this morning."

Ashley smiled. "I have to admit I'm enjoying covering the locker room a lot more than all those society teas I had to endure when I was assigned to the Honolulu Life-Style section. Those who-is-wearing-what-by-whom articles are a real bore."

"So now we know what makes your pen sizzle." Ray winked. "You just like naked men better than overdressed women. I guess Monica knew that when she insisted you should be assigned to cover the Kings. By the way, she also said Clyde Winston has already been burning up her telephone line this morning in protest over your column on his precious quarterbacks."

"Does she want me to back off?"

"You must be kidding!" Ray laughed. "She thrives on controversy. The last thing she said to me was, 'tell Ashley to keep the hell-burners coming.' Now all I need is three more columns and you can call this week a wrap. So get to work."

"Slave driver!" Ashley called after him, grimacing, as he hurried away.

By Thursday afternoon, when Ashley turned in her last column for the week, about a wide receiver already singing the familiar "Play Me or Trade Me," she felt drained.

Driving home that night she hummed a happy tune, looking forward to the two days off before

Sunday's game, but by the time she'd finished her lonely dinner, her contentment had disappeared. As always when troubled Ashley pulled on her bikini and headed outside. The moon turned the ocean into a sea of silver as she dived under a crashing wave and headed out past the breaking surf. Swimming around the point she could see the lights of Honolulu casting a golden glow on the distant sky.

People, noise, excitement—maybe that's what she needed tonight, instead of the solitude of her beach house. She just didn't know. She turned over onto her back and let the ocean rock her, trying to understand her mood. Looking up at the full moon, which seemed to mock her unhappiness with its bright light, she frowned. The full moon! Of course, that was it. There had been a full moon the night her divorce became official three years ago. Three years of rebuilding her life. Three years of being alone. Three years of hurting. Three years was enough!

Ashley flipped over angrily and swam toward shore. She waded out of the surf onto the beach, touching her face. Was it the sea or tears she felt? She didn't know. But she did know if it was tears, they were the last she'd ever shed for Butcher and the past.

She had nothing more exciting to do during the day Friday than clean Kaipo and Kanani's cage, but the evening held a special treat for her. Ashley started humming happily as she got ready for the concert. Music had been her solace through many rough times in the last couple of years, and now that she could spend her money any way she wanted, she'd bought season tickets to the symphony.

She first reached for the beaded white silk suit

38

she usually wore to the concerts, but then changed her mind. Inspired perhaps by the evening's program of romantic chamber music, she dug through her closet until she found the silver and lace dress she'd bought to surprise Butcher. Ashley still remembered his reaction. He'd refused to let her wear it, claiming it was too flashy and too daring for *his* wife. So like so many other things, she'd packed it away with her dreams. But tonight she'd dress to please herself.

With a defiant toss of her head, she slipped on the dress. Turning to look in the mirror, she smiled, liking the way the scooped neckline plunged deeply, exposing the soft rounded curve of her breasts. As the light caught the silver threads woven through the lace, the shimmer made her hair look even darker and echoed the gray of her eyes, enhancing their mystery. Finally, instead of twisting her hair up into its usual functional chignon, she let it fall loose and full below her shoulders like a dark cloud, in keeping with her romantic mood.

As usual when she got to the concert hall, Mrs. Perkins was already there waiting for her. Ashley had struck up a friendship with her during the three concerts they had already attended, maybe because the frail older woman reminded her of her grandmother back in North Carolina.

After they exchanged hellos, Mrs. Perkins observed as she nodded to the empty aisle seat next to Ashley, "I see our mysterious concert-goer isn't here again tonight. I'd been hoping he'd turn out to be your Prince Charming. I've been busy concocting all sorts of matchmaking schemes."

Ashley laughed, patting Mrs. Perkins's hand. "It's nice of you to care, but at thirty-three I'm too old to believe there's a Prince Charming out there for me."

"Why, that's the biggest piece of nonsense I've ever heard! You're never too old to fall in love. Besides, you can't fool these old eyes. If you'd given up hope you wouldn't have worn a dress like that. Once the men get a load of you, I'll probably have to call the ushers to keep them away."

Ashley sighed, thinking of the emptiness that filled her nights. I don't want hordes, but one interested man sure would be nice.

Not wanting to worry the older woman with her loneliness, she changed the subject. "Are we going out for a drink together after the concert as we usually do?"

"I wouldn't miss it! I always say the best thing about Hawaii are the mai tais!" Mrs. Perkins opened her program and squinted at it. "These old eyes just aren't what they used to be. What are we hearing tonight? I can't make it out."

Ashley turned her back to the aisle as she scanned Mrs. Perkins's program and read the introduction. " 'An evening of harpsichord and flute music spiced with a touch of the Baroque.' I think that will be—"

Mrs. Perkins's sharp jabs on her forearm silenced her. "Prince Charming!" the older woman hissed.

Ashley's back stiffened as she heard the seat next to her creak with the man's weight. Suddenly her senses were enthralled with a scent so provocatively masculine it robbed her of breath for a moment. Their mysterious concert-goer had arrived.

"Turn around for heaven's sake!" ordered Mrs. Perkins. "You can talk to me anytime."

Slowly, not wanting to seem curious, Ashley shifted in her seat, casually glancing at the man beside her.

When their startled gazes tangled, Zane slapped his hand down so hard on the armrest the whole row vibrated. "Damn it! Can't I go anywhere without running into you? This is just great! I can see the headlines now, 'Linebacker Turns Out to be Artistic Wimp!' Harpsichord and flute! If it had been Wagner, I might have lived it down, but this—never! I'll never survive the locker-room jokes, and my death will be on your hands. What damn luck. At least I don't have to stay here and watch you laugh at me!"

He started to rise, but before Ashley even realized what she was doing, her hand reached out to stop him. As her fingers curled over the muscles rippling up his arm, sensations so delicious they should have warned her this man was dangerous raced through her. Before she could stop herself, she said, "Don't go. Loving beautiful music doesn't make you a wimp, if I must use that horrible word." As she looked at him, she felt herself being drawn by those incredibly blue eyes of his. They beguiled her senses, making her wish the moment would never end. She smiled at him, unconsciously increasing the pressure of her fingers. "There won't be any headlines about tonight. Your secret's safe with me. I promise."

"And what do you want in return?"

"Nothing."

He raised a skeptical eyebrow. "Nothing? That's quite a switch." He stared at her for a long breathless moment, as if trying to see into her soul. Then he smiled. "But somehow I believe you." She caught her breath as she saw his shoulders flex and relax. "Shall we call a truce? The thought of that is suddenly very appealing."

Ashley felt the warmth rise in her face. It was not

41

the warm flush of embarrassment, but the heat of desire. It shouted a warning, a warning she ignored. Before she could change her mind she told the truth. "I can't think of anything I'd like more."

He gave her a charming grin that captured her heart. "I'd shake hands on it, but you're still grabbing my arm. Not that I have the least objection, mind you, when a beautiful woman wants to hang on to me. It could become addictive, especially since you are that beautiful woman. It makes me even sorrier I had to miss the first three concerts because of training camp."

"No wonder they call you a linebacker. You've got quite a line," she teased.

Flustered, she tried to pull her hand away, but Zane was quicker. He trapped her fingers beneath his, his grin broadening to reveal dimples deeply carved into his cheeks. "Who says it's a line? I'm just being selfish. The concert wouldn't be nearly as interesting if you deserted me now. It's your punishment for that charge of nepotism."

"Since I didn't do anything wrong I shouldn't be punished," she retorted, wiggling her fingers free. They felt suddenly chilled, but she firmly resisted the temptation to nestle them back in his grasp. Before he had a chance to say anything else, the lights dimmed and the orchestra began to play its first selection.

Normally the beautiful music would absorb all her thoughts, transporting her to another world, to another age, but not tonight. All of her emotions were captured by the man sitting next to her.

Zane shifted in his chair, casually brushing his arm against hers, and the bolt shooting through her felt like an electric charge. This is insane! she thought, carefully moving her arm away from the disturbing sensation. One touch and I act like a sixteen-year-old who's never been kissed. She didn't like it—or did she?

Ashley glanced at him through lowered lashes, frowning. He seemed completely lost in the music. Yet he sensed she was looking at him and turned to smile at her. "Hope you've got season tickets too," he whispered. "Do you?"

"Shh," was her only answer. Yet without realizing it, she returned his smile.

During the third musical selection, Zane, obviously feeling cramped in the narrow seat, threw his arm across the back of her seat. The warmth of his touch, flowing through the thin lace of her dress, awakened embers that she'd thought long dead. Forgotten sensations stirred, and Ashley shifted uneasily in her seat. She felt betrayed by her senses, reacting when she didn't want to, yet at the same time she loved those feelings he evoked too much to pull away.

When the lights came up for intermission, Zane stretched, turning to her. "Don't you dare tell anyone I told you this, but I love chamber music. As it plays, do you know what I always see?"

"Okay, I'll bite. What do you see?"

"Lords and ladies swirling across the polished floor of a ballroom in one of those fabulous English castles."

Ashley blinked, hardly believing his words.

Zane's smile faded. "I knew you'd think that was stupid."

Her hand reached out to touch him again. "No, I don't think that's stupid. It just surprised me, because that's exactly what I always see."

"I guess we're just a pair of incurable romantics."

He glanced down at her hand resting on his arm. "I knew you couldn't resist me for long."

Ashley pulled her hand away as if it had been burned. How in the world had it gotten there? She hadn't even been aware she'd reached for him again. This was definitely getting to be an irritating habit that she'd have to break right now!

"There's nothing to resist, because there's nothing to attract," she retorted, reaching for her purse and standing up. "If you'll excuse me, I want to get a glass of wine."

Remembering the woman beside her, she turned to Mrs. Perkins. "Shall I get you one?"

"Brother, do you lose the mood of the music fast," Zane complained. "Maybe the music didn't inspire you, but it did me. Here I was all prepared to pretend to be a smitten lord, like some knight of old, setting out on his quest to fetch the fair maiden of his dreams her nectar of the grape and you won't join in the spirit."

"I don't think that's necessary. I am perfectly capable of—"

"Go to your quest, young man," Mrs. Perkins ordered, grabbing Ashley's hand and pulling her back into her seat. "I'll keep the fair maiden here for you."

Zane winked at her. "Thanks for the help. Even us knights sometimes need help with these stubborn damsels."

As soon as he was gone, Mrs. Perkins sighed. "I told you you'd find Prince Charming."

Ashley shook her head, trying to clear her thoughts. "Well, you're wrong! That man's a football player, and that's about as far as you can get from Prince Charming. Believe me, I know. Besides, he's too young for me. I'm not into robbing cradles."

"Balderdash! This is the eighties. That type of thinking went out with the Edsel."

"Look, it's silly to argue about this," Ashley insisted. "I am not, repeat *not*, interested in Zane Bruxton! Or for that matter any other football player. I was married to one once, and never again. Let me tell you what they're really like. Under all that brawn is an ego the size of a football stadium. That ego makes them crave adoration. To be happy they must always be in the limelight. Believe me, there is no power on this earth that could force me to get involved with another man like that. I mean it."

Mrs. Perkins smiled as Ashley's tirade wound down. "Sounds like you're trying to convince yourself as much as me. That's one great-looking man who's off playing your gallant knight. Trust an old lady. Don't throw him back into the sea just because the last fish you had was rotten."

Ashley was just as adamant as Mrs. Perkins. "Trust someone who knows. This fish goes back!"

Before either could say anything else, Zane returned. A moment later the lights dimmed.

Drinking the glass of wine was a mistake, Ashley soon decided. The music and the man beside her were intoxicating enough! The wine just made it worse.

As the music began weaving its magic around her, she couldn't stop thinking about what Zane had said. Images of lords and ladies, all beautifully dressed in silks and satins, swirled through her mind. Somehow it seemed so real she felt she was actually there, hearing the music, seeing the dancers. Her breath quickened as, suddenly, she saw

45

him. A sapphire-blue velvet coat spanning shoulders so broad they filled the doorway, buff-colored britches molded tightly over muscled calves, through the dancers he came. Seeing no one but her he came. Inevitably he came. He came for her.

As the music ended, the illusion shattered. Ashley rubbed her fingers hard against her eyes, trying to erase the images that had danced there.

There's only one explanation, Ashley my friend. You've been alone too long. Yet even as she told herself that, in her heart she knew that wasn't the whole story.

As if drawn by a magnet Ashley had no power to resist, her glance stole back to him. She quickly looked away when she found him gazing just as intently at her.

"You've been rubbing your eyes. Is there something in them?" he whispered.

"No, I'm fine," she muttered, deliberately turning away.

But his strong fingers wouldn't let her escape. He tilted her face back to look searchingly at her. "If you don't have anything in your eyes, maybe you're looking into the future and hardly believing what you see."

"That's ridiculous. Now shh! I want to enjoy the music."

His confident smile flashed through the darkened theater. He turned in his seat to face the orchestra again, but under his breath he murmured, "That's not the only thing you're going to enjoy, fair maiden."

CHAPTER THREE

When the lights came up after the final piece, Zane stretched his cramped muscles. He noticed her looking at him and grinned. "These seats just aren't designed for us giant economy–size packages. And what this package needs right now is to be fed. Where do you want to go to dinner?"

"Dinner?" Ashley asked, surprised at his unexpected invitation.

"Yes, dinner. You didn't think I'd let this evening end this early, did you? After all, I've got my reputation to consider. You know us jocks. We work hard and we play harder."

"I know that entirely too well, and that's why I'm not going to have dinner with you," she insisted in a weary voice.

"Okay, so you don't want dinner. I'm flexible. How about going out for a drink?"

Ashley bravely met his gaze as she agreed. "Yes, a drink is always enjoyable after a concert. That's why I already have plans to sample some mai tais with Mrs. Perkins."

"Child, you must be daft," the older woman commented, joining their conversation. "I'm much too old to go running around bars at night."

Ashley looked at her pleadingly. "But we always go to—"

"Sorry, child. The only place I'm going tonight is to bed." She smiled at Zane. "You might see that Ashley does the same thing." With a cheerful wave she turned to go. "See you both next Friday."

"Ashley, shame on you. Did you really expect that nice old lady to run interference for you? Besides, why worry? I certainly wouldn't try to tackle you in a public place. I have to agree she's right about one thing, though." Zane's blue eyes sparkled mischievously. "You should be in bed. But how about a drink before we follow her advice?"

Ashley tapped her foot impatiently on the carpet. "Do I have to spell it out for you? I won't have dinner with you. I don't want to have a drink with you. And I'm not worried about any tackle you might throw—I've fended off the best. Good night!"

She turned to pick up her purse, but Zane grabbed her hands. With effortless ease he held her, forcing her to look up at him. "No dinner. No drink. No interest in my tackles. Hmm, you are an unusual woman." His voice grew low as he murmured, almost to himself, "An unusually exquisite woman."

The warm touch of his hands enfolding hers did such disturbing things to her heartbeat that she tried to pull away, but he wouldn't let her. Half exasperated, half afraid if he kept holding her she'd give in, she demanded, "Why are you being so persistent when I've already said no twice?"

"For a bright lady that's a dumb question. Look in the mirror. What man wouldn't want to spend the evening with you?"

Ashley tried to tug her hands free again, but it was useless. "Don't I have a choice about this?"

"Not really." Zane grinned at her. "I always get

what I want, so why fight it? In the first place, I'd like to apologize for flying off the handle earlier this evening. I misjudged you, and I'm sorry. In the second place, and most important, you intrigue me. I want to get to know you better."

"The feeling isn't mutual!"

"Ah, such spunk! I never could resist a spirited woman."

"Well, I can resist you. I've developed a powerful immunity to football players."

His smile faded. "You'd better not have, at least not to *this* football player."

Before she could object he shifted both her hands into one of his. Gently he traced the soft shadows under her eyes with the fingers of his free hand. "You know, you have the most unusual eyes I've ever seen. They're like the ocean, always changing. Just then, when you snapped at me, your eyes turned the chilly gray of a London fog. The other day at the *News*, when you were angry, your eyes looked like a storm-tossed sea. Then tonight, listening to the music, they became dreamy, letting me see the softness in your soul." He paused to waggle his eyebrows rougishly at her. "But best of all I liked the way they looked in the locker room."

Ashley's face flamed as the image of him emerging dripping wet from the whirlpool bath burned again in her mind, but she refused to give him the satisfaction of admitting that she remembered— that she remembered entirely too vividly for her own good. Her chin lifted. "I have no idea what you're talking about."

"Ashley, you're not a very good liar. I'm not vain, but I've seen that look before. At that moment you were as intrigued by me as I am by you right now."

"It must have been temporary insanity. Everyone

49

should be allowed one moment of weakness. It won't happen again."

"Want to bet?" he challenged. "All I have to do is find the one thing to offer you that you can't resist, then you'll go out with me tonight. Ought to be simple."

Afraid to give into the impulses his touch stirred, she tried to joke. "I promise you, it won't work."

Zane's grin deepened his dimples. "Quiet. You're about to get the famous Bruxton treatment. I can divine weaknesses you don't even know you have. Now, let's see what one thing will seduce the stubborn Ashley Buchannan into spending the rest of the evening with me."

She started to say something, but he placed a silencing finger across her lips. "You shushed me all evening. Now it's my turn. What is the one thing you can't resist?" He gazed intently into her gray eyes, then suddenly snapped his fingers. "I've got it. Ice cream!"

Ashley gasped. "Zane, how did you— I mean . . ."

His laugh echoed loudly in the rapidly emptying auditorium. "I knew I'd get you." His fingers returned to gently caress her lips. He closed his eyes. "Now let me guess what flavor."

"I don't believe this!" she mumbled under his touch. "Somebody told you I love ice cream. Who's your inside source?"

Suddenly his eyes opened to look at her. "Inside sources are your specialty. I don't need one. I rely on instincts, and my instincts tell me we're going to be spending a lot of time together. Don't you believe I can know what you're feeling, what you're thinking?"

"Not unless you're psychic, and I don't think you are."

His eyes grew serious. "It's something much simpler than that, Ashley. I know what you're feeling because I'm feeling the same thing."

"Do you know what I'm feeling right now?" she asked, half afraid he might really be able to tell how much his presence, his touch, disturbed her.

"Of course I do, fair maiden." He paused as he smiled down at her. "You're feeling hungry for some coffee ice cream dripping with hot fudge and topped with almonds."

Ashley laughed. "All right, I give up. I don't know how you did it, but you've discovered my deepest secret. I never could resist ice cream, especially coffee ice cream with hot fudge and nuts."

Zane winked at her. "If you're real good I'll even add a double serving of whipped cream."

He tucked her hand into the crook of his arm, but didn't move. "I knew I'd find your weakness." His blue eyes, darkening to deepest sapphire, left her breathless. "I'm going to enjoy discovering what other things you can't resist."

"There's nothing else to discover. Overindulgence in ice cream is my only vice," Ashley insisted, uncomfortable with the suggestiveness beneath his words.

His smile flashed. "I wouldn't bet money on that!" Before she could reply he started walking with her down the aisle.

Ashley's eyebrows raised in surprise when they stopped beside a battered blue van. "I thought the nephew of Hawaii's macadamia nut king would drive something a lot fancier. I expected a Jag at least," she teased.

He threw open the door with a flourish. "This *is*

fancy. Be thankful I'm not asking you to climb onto the back of my motorcycle. That's how I usually get around." His gaze raked over her slim hips. "Come to think of it, I'm sorry I didn't bring my bike. Watching you climb onto the back in that tight skirt could be *very* interesting." He winked. "Not to mention how great it would feel to have your arms wrapped around my waist. Oh, well, I guess those are treats that will have to wait for another day."

Ashley shook her head. "How do you know there'll be another day?"

"There will be."

Once in the van, Ashley looked around at the scuba tanks and snorkeling gear tossed on top of his surfboard, commenting with a laugh, "I see why you need a van. It's so you can carry around all your toys. And I thought you bought it just because it matched your eyes."

"Toys?" Zane glanced back at the scuba equipment. "I guess some people might call them that. I don't."

"Ah, I see I've fallen in with a serious hobbyest. But I don't blame you. I love the ocean too."

He started to say something, but she interrupted. "Zane, before I let you buy me that ice cream, there is one thing I'd like to explain. I did check your file before I wrote that column, and I hate to deflate your ego, but there wasn't much in it. It said you went to USC and that was about all. It didn't even say what your major was." She reached across to pat his biceps. "But I bet I can guess. You majored in physical education with a minor in weight lifting."

Zane pulled the van to a stop at a red light and turned to look at her. "Is that really what you think I am," he asked without a smile, "just some dumb jock whose IQ equals his shoe size?"

52

Ashley swallowed, sensing his hurt. As she stared into his eyes, she saw the formidable intelligence sparkling in the cobalt blue depths. "I'm sorry I said that. I was just being flip. That's not what I think at all. And I am curious. What did you study at USC?"

His easy grin returned as he shifted the van into gear. "What else, I studied fish."

"Fish?" She giggled. "Be serious. Nobody studies fish, unless they want to be a chef."

"Ichthyologists do. Actually I had a double major. I combined that with oceanography. If things go as I plan, I'll start some graduate courses after the season."

Remembering all the silly things Butcher and his friends did to fill the empty hours until training camp started, Ashley missed the seriousness in Zane's voice when he talked about his studies. "That should keep you busy until football starts again."

A similarity suddenly struck her. "I might have known you'd like fish," she said, laughing. "It must be my destiny to become involved with men who are enamoured of the scaly things. You studied them. Butcher spent all his free time fishing trying to catch them." She wrinkled her nose. "I got so tired of eating those blasted things I used to sneak out at night just to have a hamburger."

Zane's eyes narrowed as he glanced quickly at her left hand, where an aquamarine had replaced her wedding band. "Who's Butcher? I thought I had a free track when you showed up at the concert alone."

Ashley twisted her hands tightly together. "I was married to Barry 'Butcher' Buchannan for—for longer than I care to remember," she admitted.

His low whistle echoed through the van as he

53

pulled into a parking lot near Waikiki Beach. After he stopped, he turned in his seat to look at her. "I'd heard that ol' Butcher was married to a real stunner. The man must have taken one too many blows to the head to let you get away. Why'd he do it?"

She bravely met his incredulous gaze. "It's simple. I grew up."

He was shaking his head in confusion as he came around to open her door. "You're going to have to explain that remark someday. But not tonight. Tonight I don't want any other man in your thoughts." He grabbed her hand. "Come on, the night is young, the moon is full, and the ice cream's waiting."

Ashley made one feeble attempt to free her hand and gave up. Zane was so much stronger than she was it was useless to struggle against him. At least that was the excuse she gave herself for letting her hand stay nestled warmly in his.

The outdoor café he led her to had tables scattered at the edge of the sand. They ordered, and Ashley gazed out at the ocean, smiling. "I live on the beach, and yet I never get tired of hearing the sound of the sea or watching the moonlight sparkle off the waves."

Zane gently squeezed her hand. "The waves aren't the only thing touched by the moon. I think it's being extra beautiful just to bless this night." With his other hand he cupped her chin and drew her face around. "I love the way it warms your skin to golden, like the richest honey, and glints off your hair like a shower of diamonds." One fingertip traced her cheek, and looking into her eyes, he murmured, "I'm glad, I'm very glad you finally admitted you're as involved with me as I am with you."

"I didn't admit any such thing," she said, yanking her hand out of his.

"Oh, yes, you did. A few moments ago you said it was your destiny to become involved with men who are fascinated by fish."

"Zane you know that I didn't mean . . . that we would be . . ." Ashley protested, flushing with embarrassment. "It was just a figure of speech."

With a carefree laugh he leveled a finger at her. "Gotcha!" His endearing grin made him look like a kid. "I love to see you ruffled," he teased. "It isn't a sin, you know. You've got to learn to loosen up. And speaking of loosening up, I like your hair down." He reached across the table and ran his fingers through the long sweep that fell below her shoulders. "It makes you look less formidable."

She tried to pull away from the disturbing touch, but he wouldn't let her escape. "Don't worry," he joked, "I'm not going to bite you—at least, not here in public. In private, I make no such rash promise."

Before she could say anything, their triple sundaes arrived. "I'm glad the ice cream finally got here," she insisted after the waitress had left. "Maybe it will cool you off."

One side of his mouth turned up in a challenging grin as he dug his spoon into the whipped cream. "Are you sure you want that? Believe me, if I'm hot it will be a lot more fun for both of us."

She was ready to scold him, but when he wagged his eyebrows up and down at her, begging her to "Think about it" he looked so adorable she laughed instead. Suddenly Ashley realized how good it felt to laugh, to smile. It had been so long since either had come easily.

She looked at Zane eagerly devouring his heaping dish of ice cream. The whole thing was crazy!

He was not only too young for her, but he should be everything she despised. Yet watching him happily licking the whipped cream from his upper lip, she couldn't help but smile.

Why deny it? For one evening it felt good to laugh again. Ashley rested her chin in her palm. As she looked at him, his provocative words echoed in her mind. A flicker of warmth ignited as she remembered how he'd promised to find other "things" she couldn't resist. To her surprise the warmth pleased her as much as the laughter. Yes, it lifted her spirits to have a man look at her, see a flame kindle in his eyes. Naturally, she silently assured herself, she had no intention of fanning that flame, but after Butcher's desertion it was nice to feel that other men still found her attractive.

After spooning up the last drop of ice cream Zane glanced at her. "Hey, what's wrong? You're not eating."

"I was watching you," she confessed. "I don't think I've ever seen anyone attack a sundae with such enthusiasm."

"Around you I get enthusiastic about a lot of things. But we can talk about that later." He picked up her spoon, dug out an enormous bite of ice cream, and held it out to her.

"I can't eat all that!"

"Sure you can. Open wide."

With a giggle Ashley obeyed, then obeyed again when he scooped up another spoonful. When the bowl was empty, Ashley laughed. "I can't believe you made me eat all that. I'll have to swim two miles tomorrow to work it off."

He reached across the table and covered her hand with his. "I can think of a few other ways to

56

work it off, and I promise you they'd be a lot more fun than swimming."

Her smile faded, not at what he'd said, but because of the sudden bolt of desire that burned through her at his words. Frightened by these feelings she had no power to control, Ashley stood up. "The ice cream's gone. I think it's time to go home."

Zane's confident grin told her her confusion delighted him. But before she could repeat her request, he was beside her. "Nope, you're wrong. It's not time to go home yet." Unexpectedly he dropped to his knees. "Kick off your shoes. We're going wading."

"Now?" Ashley glanced down at her lace dress, then at his suit. "Dressed like this?"

"Sure, why not? That moon's too romantic to waste."

"You know you're crazy!" Yet even as she complained, she stepped out of her shoes.

As they walked out onto the beach, he put his arm around her shoulders. Neither spoke as they strolled along the edge of the surf. There was no need. The golden moon, the sound of the breaking waves, the rustle of the palms as the breeze blew through them was enough.

Ashley sighed, savoring the feel of the warm water lapping over her ankles as they walked. "I love it here. I never wanted to live anywhere else, and what happened? Butcher dragged me through five NFL cities in about as many years." She shuddered. "Green Bay was the worst!"

Zane stopped. Warm hands held her gently as he turned her to face him. "I don't want to hear about Butcher. I don't want to hear about your life with him. I don't want to think about you with another man. Ashley, please don't let regrets from the past spoil this moment."

"Zane, I—"

"Shh, my fair maiden," he murmured, and bent his head to her.

At the touch of his lips, Ashley tried to draw back, but his hand, slipping behind her neck, held her still. All the months alone had left her vulnerable, yet she couldn't really blame her response on that. No, when Zane's kiss possessed her it was like nothing she'd ever experienced before. Soft, like the lightest breeze from the sea, his lips caressed hers, not demanding but almost begging she not turn away. The kiss seduced her will to resist with its gentleness. Butcher had always been an impatient lover, so Zane's slow arousal left her unprepared for the smoldering fires it kindled. Those fires burned hotter within her than any she remembered, as the kiss spun on and on, slowly drugging her senses with its beauty.

She knew it was madness to give in to the feelings stirring within her, yet the need to be closer to him smothered any warning. And for that moment she didn't care! With only the glittering moon above to witness her defeat, Ashley wound her arms around Zane's powerful neck and relaxed against him.

The warmth of his lips moving over hers sent tingles of sensation spiraling inward, turning the fire into a raging blaze. Knowing only that she needed more to ease the throbbing within her, she was the first to part her lips, she was the first to run her tongue over the valley guarding the secrets of his mouth, she was the first to explore the moist sweetness within. Zane gasped as her velvety thrusts found his tongue, but his response was immediate as he met each stroke with one of his own.

His embrace tightened, bringing the length of her body hard against his.

Through the lace of her dress she could feel the ripples of muscle as he pressed his chest against her breasts. It was those sensations that finally shattered the fog of desire shrouding her common sense.

With a frightened shudder she pulled away. His eyes fluttered open as he felt her retreat. In the moonlight the blue of his eyes glittered like the rarest diamonds, but as he saw the pain and doubt in her gaze, the glitter died. His breathing trembled unevenly with desire suddenly denied, but he didn't try to force her back into his embrace.

"What's wrong, Ashley? One moment you're kissing me, making me feel things I've never felt before, and the next you're drawing away as if it never happened. Was I dreaming?"

Two emotions battled within her. Embarrassment at her passionate response to his kiss warred with her fear. She couldn't let this happen. She just couldn't! Unable to look at him any longer, Ashley glanced down at the sand. "Maybe we both were," she confessed. "I don't know. But if it was a dream, it's time to wake up."

Strong fingers forced her chin back up. "No, it isn't! How can you let so beautiful a dream slip away so easily? I don't want it to end. Stay with me tonight, Ashley. Let the dream become real."

Sadly she shook her head. "Dreams never can be real."

"Right now, wanting you feels *damn* real, and that's no fantasy!" When she started to argue he interrupted, "And don't try and tell me I was the only one dreaming. I didn't force you to kiss me that way."

Ashley, afraid to admit how powerful her desire had been, tried to make joke of it. "Then I guess I'll have to blame my momentary weakness on the moon. That's why they call it lunacy. People are bewitched by the full moon into doing all sorts of foolish things. Not only did we have the moon, we had the seductive rhythm of the surf playing on our senses. No wonder we both got a bit carried away."

He flung his hands out impatiently. "A bit carried away? Bewitched into doing foolish things? That's a bunch of garbage! That's not what happened to us, and you know it!"

Ashley shrugged, trying to appear untouched. "Well, whatever it was, it's over. I think it's time you took me back to my car."

"Why are you afraid of me, Ashley?" he demanded, refusing to move.

She ignored his question. "Are you going to drive me back to my car or do I have to walk?" she inquired coolly.

"You don't have to walk," he muttered. "It goes against every instinct I possess, but I'll take you."

Ashley turned to go, but Zane's hands curling over her shoulders stopped her. "We aren't finished with this, you know."

She shook her head. "You really are persistent, aren't you?"

His grasp tightened. "Damn right I am, especially about things that are important to me. And I've got a real strong hunch you're going to become a *very* important part of my life."

"No I'm not. I'm not going to play any part in your life." She twisted away from his grasp. "We might as well get this settled right now. I'm sorry I let you talk me into that ice cream and I'm even sorrier I let you kiss me. As I said, blame it on the moon. Everything about this is wrong. In the first place, I'm older than you are."

"So what? If I don't care why should you? Besides, don't you remember that song? 'Older Women Make Better Lovers.'"

"Zane, will you be serious!"

"I am serious. I'm always serious about my love affairs."

"There's not going to be a love affair. In the *second* place, it would be a professional disaster for me to get involved with someone I have to cover. I might as well toss objectivity out the window, and I can't afford to do that. This column means too much to me."

"If that's all that's bothering you, then don't write about me. My ego can stand my remaining an unknown."

"Oh come off it," she scoffed. "You'd hate that. All football players live to see their names in print. Butcher kept a closet full of scrapbooks, dating all the way back to grade school and—"

Zane's hands descended onto her shoulders again, but this time no gentleness softened the touch. "Ashley, I am not Butcher! I'm me!" he said, grinding out each word. "Will you please get that through your head? Don't compare us!"

"Look, Zane . . ."

"No, you look. I'm sorry you were hurt, but don't make me pay—don't make yourself pay—for what another man did to you. I enjoyed being with you this evening. And I sure as hell enjoyed holding you in my arms and kissing you. Be honest, tell me you don't feel the same way."

"It doesn't matter what I feel. I'm not getting involved with another football player! I'm not!"

Zane's grasp turned to a caress, and he began to

61

massage her shoulders. "Want to bet? You can fight, you can run, you can lie to yourself, but I'm not going to let you say good-bye." His voice softened to a seductive rumble. "You can count on that."

Before she could resist, he leaned toward her and brushed a soft kiss of promise against her lips. "I don't care what you say, this isn't the end, it's just the beginning. Nothing that feels this right can be wrong."

CHAPTER FOUR

"Hey, Ashley!" Dave waved as she entered the press box on Sunday. "What unlucky stiff is going to feel the sharp edge of your pen today?" She sat down, and he swiveled his seat around to face her. "I hate to admit it, but those columns of yours have really been smokin'. Maybe my chauvinist streak is showing, but I didn't honestly think a woman could have such insight into football."

Ashley smiled without answering. She heard Dave's words, but her thoughts weren't on her column. In her mind she saw the locker room, where she knew Zane was changing. She wished with all her heart she couldn't visualize the scene, but she could. Shoulders broad and powerful, hardly needing pads to make them square, muscles rippling over a chest that tapered to a trim waist, and finally his legs, those legs more massive than graceful, yet still fascinating. Yes, she could see it all. Damn it, why hadn't he stayed in that whirlpool bath? Damn it, why couldn't she forget?

She closed her eyes, but that didn't help, as the memories of Friday night crowded in. Every moment they'd spent together remained etched in her mind. Every taste, every scent, every sound . . . every sensation stirred by his kiss replayed over and over. And it wasn't just her magical response to his

63

touch that had made the night so special. She had never felt so at ease so quickly, or laughed so easily, as she had with Zane. Yet even as he'd leaned in through her car window to kiss her good night, she knew in her heart it must be good-bye.

With the promise to forget the madness of the moments she'd spent with his arms wrapped tightly around her, she'd driven home. But nothing worked. She'd walked on the beach, trying to find peace, yet the moon above only reminded her of the beauty of the night. The sound of the surf was the sound she'd heard during their embrace. It should be so easy to forget him. Over and over again she told herself Zane had it backward. There were so many things wrong it couldn't be right, yet a tiny part of her heart didn't want to listen to her mind.

As the emotions battled within her, she hardly heard Dave's voice. "Might want to borrow some pads yourself before you walk into that locker room after the game. Razor Williams, the quarterback you skewered in that column, sure wasn't happy when I talked to him. If you aren't careful the next time he throws a Ping-Pong paddle it'll be at your head. Makes me glad I'm writing the straight sports news. I make fewer enemies that way. By the way, I hear Clyde Winston, too, is really out for your scalp. Take some advice from an old pro and watch it. He's a very powerful man."

His last words finally penetrated. "Hmm, what did you say? I'd better watch what? They haven't even kicked off yet."

"Didn't you listen to anything I said? I was just saying Clyde Winston is out for your blood, so watch it."

"He's not the one I'm worried about," she murmured.

Dave glanced sharply at her and saw the faraway look in her eyes. He shrugged. "Well, don't say I didn't warn you. Looks like they're about ready to flip the coin. Let's hope it's a better game than last week. It's hard making copy out of rank mediocrity."

Ashley's throat was parched as the teams lined up for the kickoff. The Kings had won the toss and elected to receive. The whistle blew, the ball sailed into the air, the return man shot through the first line of defenders. As a roar went up from the crowd, he dodged the last tackler, and there was nothing but green all the way to the goal line. It was a spectacular run. Ashley saw none of it. Instead, without thinking, she scanned the sidelines until she found the one man who refused to leave her in peace.

When she realized she'd missed the touchdown, she angrily collected her wandering thoughts. She was acting as moony as a kid, not like a thirty-three-year-old woman!

After the kickoff, she heard the announcer say over the PA system, "First down and ten yards to go."

She shook her head. The truth was she and Zane had *no* yards to go. As she stared down at the field painful memories assaulted her. Zane might be a gorgeous hunk of a blond Viking, but unfortunately he was also a football player, and she knew only too well what that meant.

Ashley's gaze returned to her pad and she wrote in big block letters EGO. That was the first problem. It wasn't just Butcher. She'd known a lot of players and they were all the same. The game always came first. Their ego needed it to survive. Football came before even their wives and their children. Butcher was always saying they'd start their family next year, only "next year" never came. She needed a man, not some boy who played games.

With disgusted jabs of her pen she scratched out the word EGO and wrote WOMEN. That was the second problem. Most women found athletes irresistible, and what man wouldn't take advantage of something offered so freely? Before all the bitter memories of the nights Butcher hadn't come home could swamp her, she quickly scratched out WOMEN and wrote TRADES.

How she'd hated the constant moving! Ashley looked over the walls of the stadium to the lush green mountains beyond. Hawaii was her home and nothing would tempt her to leave again. And then there was always the chance of injuries. She winced as she wrote the word, but she forced herself to remember. One hit, one blown knee, and not only was Butcher's career over, so was their marriage.

She scribbled through both words, hesitated, then wrote one last thing: SIX YEARS. It was a gap she had no power to close, a gap of time making any relationship with twenty-seven-year-old Zane impossible. Ashley looked at the paper and sighed with relief. Writing down all the negatives somehow put everything in perspective. Suddenly she felt free of the momentary insanity that had made Zane seem appealing.

She smiled and looked down at the field where the Kings were huddled, feeling nothing—well, almost nothing. She did have to admit that when he bent over to hear the call, it showed off his cute rear end, and she liked the way his blond hair curled out from below his helmet, but that was all. Deciding the problem was finally solved, she crumpled up the sheet of paper and tossed it aside. Now all she had to do was concentrate on the game and come up with another hell-burner of a column.

The Kings lost again, but their play had improved so much that the locker room crackled with high spirits when she walked in. Her arrival caused as much stir as the first time, but for a very different reason. Most of the players had apparently decided her column was attracting so much attention they wanted their names included, so instead of being ignored Ashley found herself in the middle of a group of men, all eager to be interviewed. All but Clyde, who took one look at her, scowled, and stomped out of the locker room.

One of the few who didn't try to approach her was Zane. She spotted him coming out of the shower, dressed as before in only a towel. But this time, to her delight, her pulse only fluttered a little instead of racing wildly, as it had when she'd seen him step out of the whirlpool. Ashley tossed him a casual wave, knowing she had her emotions under control, and turned to listen to the starting quarterback brag about how he got the nickname Razor.

Monday the team had the day off. She half expected Zane to call, but while she got a lot of phone calls none came from him. As the hours rolled by she told herself she was glad, but that didn't stop her from streaking for the phone every time it rang.

The setting sun was busily painting the sky brilliant shades of orange and red as she pulled up in front of her house. For a long moment she stood, savoring a beauty that never failed to thrill her. Inside, vaguely unhappy but unwilling to admit she was disappointed Zane hadn't called, she opened the door of the cockatoos' cage. Immediately Kaipo flew out to land on her shoulder. "Hi, gorgeous!

Give me a kiss," he chattered, gently pecking her cheek.

Ashley ran a hand over his feathers and smiled. "I'm glad at least you're happy to see me."

He rode on her shoulder as she went into the kitchen. Turning on the radio, she opened the refrigerator to see what she might throw together for dinner. Reaching for a head of lettuce, she heard the announcer warn of a tropical storm brewing in the Pacific. Suddenly she froze.

It sounded like a Chopin piano concerto, but that was crazy! She glanced quickly at Kanani, wondering if she'd suddenly developed a hidden talent, laughing at once at the absurd idea. That was ridiculous. Still she thought she heard Chopin, but how? Ashley frowned. Her house was so isolated she knew the music couldn't be coming from a neighbor's house. Could it be the wind playing tricks on her? She wandered out into the living room and listened. No, it *was* Chopin, and it was coming from the beach.

Ashley returned the birds to their favorite perch and pushed open the screen door, letting it swing shut behind her. "I might have known!" She laughed. "What are you doing here?"

Zane waved, holding up a half gallon of coffee ice cream. "What am I doing here?" he repeated. "Foolish question, fair maiden. I'm here to seduce you. Look, I've brought everything I need. Romantic music to get you in the mood, ice cream to weaken your will—even a blanket to keep the sand out of your gorgeous hair after my kisses have made you powerless to resist me. Now if the moon would just hurry up and rise everything will be perfect for the big seduction scene."

Ashley stood with her hands on her hips and

68

shook her head. "I don't believe this. You're impossible!"

"Yep, that's me." He thumped his chest proudly. "I'm impossibly good, if all the women in my lurid past are to be believed. Must be my Viking blood. I could give you references if you have any doubts."

Ashley choked with laughter. "Sure, I can just imagine what that would be like." She held an imaginary telephone receiver to her ear. "Hello, Miss Jones? There's a man here named Zane Bruxton who's trying to seduce me and he gave me your name as a reference. He did? I don't believe it! On the back of his motorcycle? On the fifty yard line, during the Super Bowl? No, you don't mean it. On a float during the Rose Bowl Parade too? I'm surprised he has any energy left to pester me!"

Zane rose from the blanket with a grace that was surprising in a man so large. "Pester you?" he asked, approaching her. "Me? Never!" He held out his hand. "You can't possibly resist after that glowing recommendation good ol' Miss Jones gave me."

"Glowing recommendation, ha!" she teased. "It sounds to me like you're a public exhibitionist!"

Zane's fingers closed about hers. "It's *very* private here."

The sudden blaze in Zane's eyes as he looked at her jumbled her heartbeat. But he seemed deliberately to put a brake on his emotions, and his gaze cooled. He grinned. "Come on, Ashley, have a heart. I can't eat a half gallon of ice cream by myself. Please." As he tugged on her hand his eyes grew soulful, like a little boy about to have his treat denied him. The plea proved irresistible.

"I ought to tell you no," she insisted.

His grin of victory flashed. "But you're not going

69

to, are you?" He chuckled. "Hurry up, the ice cream's melting."

She glanced at him sideways as they ran hand in hand to the blanket. He had the most expressive eyes she'd ever seen. One minute they challenged with all the swagger of a Don Juan. The next he pulled that whipped-puppy look that made her want to gather him up in her arms and never let him go.

How had he done it? With one smile, with one touch, he'd made all those logical reasons she'd written down, why she shouldn't see him again seem unimportant. Her mind told her she ought to wrap her heart in a protective layer of ice, yet his smile had the power to melt that ice as easily as the Hawaiian sun would have. The man was dangerous, there was no doubt about that.

Zane pulled her down to the blanket beside him, and pried off the lid of the carton. When he handed her the spoon she hesitated. "You know I'm only doing this because I can't bear to see ice cream go to waste."

"Sure, whatever you say," he scoffed gently, obviously not believing a word of her nonsense.

She started to dip into the ice cream but he stopped her. "Before I let that ice cream start to work its wicked wiles on your willpower, there's something I want to get straight right now. I'm not a fortune hunter."

"What?" Ashley looked blankly at him. "Why would I suspect that? I don't have a fortune."

His eyes widened in innocent surprise. "You don't? Rats!" He grabbed the carton. "Well, I guess I'll be going." He jumped up, holding the ice cream away from her.

Ashley laughed, joining the game. "You bring that ice cream back here before I change my mind

70

and write that column on Zane Bruxton, lover of harpsichord and flute." She glanced at his tape recorder. "Even Chopin isn't very macho. Guess I'll have to include that damning information as well."

"Okay, okay, I give up. You can have the ice cream." He waggled his eyebrows at her. "And anything else of mine you want. But I'm still curious," he commented, sitting down again and putting the carton on the blanket in front of her. "I haven't been in Hawaii very long, but even I know you don't have beachfront property, especially not any as nice as yours, without a lot of money."

Ashley dug her spoon into the ice cream. As the cool sweetness filled her mouth she gazed at her home. Large and rambling, with a deep veranda to shade the interior from the fierce Hawaiian sun, the house looked like it belonged on a plantation instead of on the beach. After another spoonful she glanced back at Zane.

"Have you ever read James Michener's novel, *Hawaii*?"

"Sure but—"

"Remember those stiff, pompous, proud missionaries who came over here and put clothes on the happy carefree natives? Well, they were my ancestors. This property has been in my mother's family for almost a hundred and fifty years."

Zane studied the architectural style. "Let me guess," he said, his glance sweeping from the heavy white rattan furniture on the veranda to the columns in front. "I'll bet the house looks more antebellum than Hawaiian because those missionary ancestors of yours came from the South."

"You're right, but it could be worse. If they'd been from Boston no doubt they'd have built a saltbox and covered it in clapboard. At least the

71

veranda helps keep the house cool. When my parents decided to move back to Dad's home in Missouri, they gave it to me." She smiled. "I love it here! It's the main reason I never want to leave Hawaii again."

Zane shrugged as he scooped up another giant spoonful of ice cream. "I guess I can understand that feeling."

"You guess?" Ashley asked, perplexed.

"It's hard for someone who's never had a home to understand roots." He saluted. "You're looking at a true navy brat."

"The navy, huh? That explains it. I knew something had to turn you into such a pest!"

He ignored her. "You said something funny when I came charging into your office. You asked if my ancestors were Vikings. Actually they were, they were from Denmark. If the legends are to be believed they sailed and plundered all over Europe." He winked, "Pillaging's not very nice but it's certainly *profitable.*"

A sudden shudder racked her at the thought. The scene blazed brightly in her mind. A coastal village, an attack at dawn, women torn from their beds to be thrown over broad shoulders and carried off, never to see home again.

Unconsciously Ashley's gaze wandered over the breadth of Zane's shoulders. It wasn't hard to imagine him as a conquering Viking. What would it feel like to be carried away by him? What would it feel like to belong to him, to have a pitching longboat for their bed as she lay beneath him, powerless to refuse him anything he wanted? She could almost see his blue eyes flame with desire as he gazed at his prize. She could almost feel his hands strip the clothes from her body, then stroke his brand of

72

ownership onto her bare flesh. She imagined feeling the weight of his body pressing her deeper into a mattress of straw, forcing her to respond to the hard thrusts that made his conquest complete.

Her heart pounded at the thoughts racing through her. As she looked at him, bronzed and blond, it was so easy to envision him the conquering Viking—and herself his prize, his possession, to do with as he wished. The images evoked feelings so real, stoked a desire so hot, she shuddered again— and not from fear.

Frightened by the intensity of her feelings, Ashley blinked, deliberately forcing the disturbing fantasy from her mind. Luckily Zane didn't notice the warm flush rising in her face as he continued. "Anyway, that Viking blood seems to run deep in our family. That same lure of the sea pulled my dad from one navy post to the next. I saw the world, but I never had a place to call home." He shrugged as if to push away the bad memories. "I guess I shouldn't complain. *I* can't fight it, either. It's probably that same salt water in my veins that makes oceanography the only thing I want to study."

She'd been so absorbed in his tale and her powerful response to it that she didn't realize how quickly the ice cream was disappearing until her spoon scraped the bottom of the carton. "You're dangerous!" she muttered, dropping the spoon in disgust. With an effort she forced a light note. "If I'm not careful you're going to turn me into a coffee ice cream junkie!"

"Yeah," he agreed, happily licking his lips, "but what a sweet way to go!"

To her intense relief, Zane gave her his usual boyish grin, and the image of the rampaging Viking faded and the scowl left her face.

He touched her lips with one fingertip. "I'm glad to see your smile come back. It means my seduction strategy is really beginning to work." He licked his lips again. "But I forgot one thing. I forgot that ice cream makes you thirsty. I wish I had brought a bottle of wine. Then we could toast the rising moon, and everything would be perfect."

Suddenly, a delicious idea struck her. Quickly, before she could change her mind, Ashley rolled over and stood up. "Wait here. I've got just the thing we need. In fact, maybe it's poetic justice that we share this," she added mysteriously. "In a way, we've both earned it."

She returned with the well-chilled bottle of champagne Monica had given her and two glasses on a tray. "Not that I'm complaining, but just how did I earn this?" Zane asked, lifting one eyebrow.

Ashley looked slightly guilty as she poured two glasses of the pale dry wine. "I guess you earned it by being Clyde's nephew. Monica was so pleased with that first column I wrote about you that she gave me this to celebrate." She handed him his glass. "Still want some?"

"Why not?" he asked, taking the offered glass. "My scars, made by your poison pen, have healed. In fact, I think we should make a toast to that first column. If you hadn't written it we might not have met. And if we hadn't met we wouldn't be here in the middle of this great seduction scene." He took a big sip, then saluted her. "I love the way you're really getting into the spirit of this thing. It's going to make my night."

"Zane, I'm not!" she protested, wishing she'd never thought of the champagne. The gesture had obviously given him ideas she had no intention of fulfilling. "I just thought—"

He leaned nearer and stopped her protest with a kiss, then drew back a fraction to scold her gently. "That's the trouble with you, Ashley, you think too damn much." His hand stroked through her long dark hair. "Feeling is much better," he murmured.

"Not if it feels wrong," she whispered.

Before she could protest he took the champagne glass from her fingers and placed it on the sand beside his. With an infinitely gentle touch his hands ran up her arms to settle on her shoulders. His fingers curled possessively about her, drawing her nearer until her breasts brushed against the muscles of his chest. In a husky voice he demanded, "Does it feel wrong to be in my arms?"

Her lips parted to answer but his kiss descended to steal the words. There was no barrier to stop him, but Zane didn't try to force a response from her. His lips moved softly over her mouth, and he drew away again. "Does it feel wrong to taste of desire with our kisses?"

With gentle pressure he eased her back until she was lying on her back. As his body followed hers to the blanket, he whispered, "Does this feel wrong?"

He felt her tremble beneath him as he began to drop light kisses against the pulse beating wildly in her throat. Ashley's indrawn breath became a gasp as his touch moved upward and his warm breath blew a message of desire in her ear. His tongue traced the fragile shell and teased the sensitive interior with moist thrusts that pulled a shuddering sigh from her.

He raised himself up on one elbow so he could look at her. Through her blouse his free hand gently caressed her breast with teasing strokes, until her nipple hardened beneath his palm. A satisfied smile curved his lips as his caress stilled. "I can feel your heart beating just for me." With one fingertip he again began tracing the outline of the taut peak. "I touch you and that beat becomes a throb. Look at me and tell me what you're feeling right now is wrong."

"Zane, I—"

He laid a finger across her lips. "Ashley, please don't say no. Friday night was one of the most magical times of my life. And no matter how much you try to deny it, I know you felt that magic too. Words can always lie, but never your kiss. I want to recapture those feelings. I want to kiss you again."

His breath caressed her cheeks as he bent even nearer. "Tell me you haven't dreamed of our walk on the beach. Tell me your lips haven't felt desolate and deserted because they aren't touching mine. *Tell me. . . .*"

A hot blush crept across her face. His words so accurately revealed how she really did feel—but shouldn't. "Zane, *don't,*" she whispered as the pain she'd suffered with Butcher warned her not to admit the weakness. "Please don't say things like that."

"Why, Ashley? Because they're true?" He shifted his weight until she lay more intimately beneath him. "I want you, and the desire couldn't burn this hot if I wasn't responding to the same fire within you."

The stormy gray of her eyes revealed her confusion. "Why me? Why are you doing this to me?"

"Because I want you."

He eased away just enough to caress her face with his fingertips. As he traced the sculpted planes he confessed, "But what I feel is more than just desire. You touch something inside me no other woman has ever reached, and you touch it on so many

76

different levels I can hardly believe my luck in finding you."

He delicately stroked her forehead with his thumbs, framing her face with his big hands. "There are so many things that make you special. I admire your clever wit and the courage you have to write columns you know are going to make enemies for you. I love the way your gray eyes soften and go misty when you listen to beautiful music. It lets me see your vulnerability." His fingertips traced the shadows under her eyes. "Then when I kiss you, these dreamy eyes burn with a passion equalling the blaze within me." He smiled. "And I love how you lick your lips happily after eating ice cream. It reminds me of a little girl who hasn't had enough fun in her life." He bent to place a reverent kiss on her lips. "Ashley, you touch my mind, my soul, my heart, my desire. What more could any man want?"

Once, twice, he brushed kisses across her lips, then drew away. "Are you going to tell me to stop?"

Ashley gazed into his blue eyes, eyes she knew possessed the power to rob her of both common sense and willpower. "Zane, please stop," she whispered, closing her eyes in an effort to fight their force.

"Look at me. Tell me that's really what you want. Is that what you want?" he repeated.

She hesitated a long moment, and at last let her heart speak, instead of her mind. "No . . . it isn't," she whispered as her arms wound around his neck.

"Good, the night is too beautiful to spoil with any more words," he murmured, and his kiss claimed her.

Resistance was useless. She couldn't fight him any more than she could fight herself. Why lie? It did feel good to have the weight of his body pressed against hers. It did feel good to have his caresses stir embers long asleep. It did feel good to relax, to let the velvety rasps of his tongue part her lips and find the warm mysteries within.

With the surf pounding an accompaniment to the Chopin in the background and the moon casting its silvery glow, they found the magic once again. The kiss spun on and on, his tongue meeting hers, and they danced the ancient dance of desire, her blood heating until it felt like the surf was pounding inside her and the glitter of the moon came from within.

As in her fantasy she seemed powerless to stop him from doing what he wanted . . . anything he wanted. For this was what *she* wanted!

CHAPTER FIVE

The moon was high before Zane drew away from the sweetness of her mouth. His smile mirrored his satisfaction. "For someone . . ." he began to say in a voice raspy with desire. He cleared his throat and began again. "For someone who only came out because she hated to see good ice cream go to waste, you've certainly gotten into the spirit of this seduction scene."

Ashley, more shaken than she wanted to admit by the ease with which he'd conquered all her resolve, tried to joke away the confusion. "It must be that Viking blood of yours. Women know it's useless to resist you because you're a master of the two Rs, ravishment and rapture."

Zane's hand gently cupped her breast. "I know you're only teasing, but in a way you're right." His usually smiling eyes were serious as he confessed. "You do tempt me to take what I want, but I could never hurt you."

When he eased away from her Ashley felt the hardness of his desire. She blushed. He touched her face, one fingertip moving along her flushed cheeks, his smile a little sad. "I guess it's no use lying. You can tell how much I want you. I want to be inside you. I want to drive you to the edge of sanity with the passion we'll ignite together, but only when you're as hungry as I am."

Ashley gazed at him, not certain what she really felt in her heart, what she really wanted. The moonlight made him even more compelling, turning his blond hair to silver and casting fascinating shadows across his rugged features. As she looked at him, felt the warmth of his body touching hers, the heat of her own hunger flared hotter. Yet even as her lips longed to taste his again, part of her knew it was sheer madness to feel anything for this man.

The confusion battling within her jumbled her words. "I don't . . . Zane, I'm not . . ."

He gently kissed the words away, lifting his head after a moment to read the doubt behind the desire firing her eyes. "You don't need to explain. I know tonight is not the night to make you mine. I want you, but I won't rush you." His easy smile returned. "I'm greedy. When you lie naked beneath me I don't want any doubt cooling your passion."

Powerless to draw away without one last touch, his hand lingered over the lush softness of her breast. When he felt her response, a response she had no power to still, he chuckled in eager anticipation. "And I don't think I'm going to have to wait long!"

"Zane!" she fussed, protesting his cocky presumption.

"Don't scold me. Can I help it if I'm a hopeless optimist?"

As he pulled her to her feet her body brushed against his, and it felt like a sparkler had ignited inside her. One touch from him and suddenly it was the Fourth of July! If she didn't get a grip on her emotions, he was right—it wouldn't be long. And worse, she honestly didn't know if her weakness at his touch frightened her . . . or thrilled her.

"You bring the tape recorder," he ordered, taking the champagne and the glasses. "We'd better polish this off inside before the moonlight and the sound of the surf convinces me to let my Viking lust win over my honorable insanity."

As they walked toward the house she curled her fingers around his and gave them a gentle squeeze. "I don't think there's anything insane about caring."

He stopped walking and looked at her. "You're right. I am beginning to care an awful lot, Ashley, and whether you admit it or not, you are too."

She shook her head, dropping his hand. "Maybe I am, but I shouldn't. You're still a football player and if anything in the world should make me run as fast as I can in the opposite direction, that's it."

"I think it's time we talked about Butcher. He's not even here, yet he's standing between us like a steel gate. I can feel his presence every time I take you in my arms, and I don't like it."

"It won't do any good. Talking about Butcher won't change anything." She smiled sadly. "What's the expression? Once bitten, twice shy."

"Hey, give me a chance. You might learn to like the way *I* bite." With his free arm he swept her against him to demonstrate. "First I'd start with a light nibble on the neck. Like this."

As his lips danced over the sensitive flesh of her throat, Ashley whispered, "I thought you wanted to talk." Yet even as she protested she tilted her head, allowing his kisses to travel over her neck.

"We can talk later," he murmured, gently nipping her throat where her pulse was beginning to beat wildly in answer to the caress of his lips. His kiss traveled upward. "See, biting can be fun . . . if you know how," he whispered, blowing the words softly into her ear. His teeth closed over the lobe, and his gentle tugs shot a bolt of fiery sensation directly to the core of her desire, which began to throb with a need hard to deny.

Ashley sighed, as the delicious sensations ignited by his kiss stilled every cautious voice within her.

"You see, my biting isn't making you shy," he whispered.

He was right. His breath blowing in her ear, the rasp of his tongue as he traced the delicate shell and plunged within to stir the fire didn't make her feel shy. Instead it released the brazenness in her soul. She twined her arms about his broad back, wriggled deeper into his embrace. Needing to feel more of his muscles, more of his warmth, she arched against him, unconsciously moving her hips tantalizingly to experience the rebirth of his desire.

Finally it was Zane who pulled away. Even in the moonlight she could see his blue eyes glittering with the heat of his wanting her. "Ashley, I warn you," he muttered. "One more touch like that and I will let go of my integrity and give in to my need. And I have a feeling you'd be a willing victim." Smiling, he searched her cloudy eyes. "Shall we see?"

He leaned nearer, but Ashley's hands came up against his chest to hold him off. One more kiss and she knew she was lost, and there were still too many doubts to let that happen.

"Let's not," she countered. "You made your point. I wasn't shy about that kind of biting, but demonstration time is over. My ear can't take any more. Besides the champagne's getting warm."

"It's already warm. If you wanted cold cham-

82

pagne you shouldn't have spent so much time frolicking with me on the beach blanket."

"You make this whole thing sound like it's my fault," she protested, pulling out of his embrace.

"Well, it is." Zane chuckled. "If you weren't so damn desirable I wouldn't want you so much, and there'd have been no need for this champagne to get warm."

Somehow Ashley couldn't come up with an argument for that. "Bring it inside. I'll get some ice," she muttered.

She had forgotten that the cockatoos were flying free, and so failed to warn Zane as they opened her door.

"What the hell!" he yelped as the two birds dove at him, one landing on each broad shoulder.

Ashley's giggle turned to laughter at Kanani's shrill wolf whistle. "Pretty boy," she said sincerely.

Before Ashley could say anything, Kaipo added, "Time for bed. Time for bed."

Zane glanced at the bird perched on his left shoulder. "Those are my feelings exactly, but she won't cooperate. Maybe you can talk to her." He looked at Ashley. "I don't want you to think I'm a coward, but are your friends here housebroken? I'd hate to have to explain to the dry cleaner how I was attacked by two sex-crazed cockatoos. By the way, we haven't been properly introduced. What are their names?"

"The one with the crush on you is Kanani, which means 'the pretty one' in Hawaiian. I got her first, and then I bought her a mate. I called him Kaipo, the sweetheart, but I think after tonight I'll change his name to Nui Waha, 'big mouth.'" She snapped her fingers and the two birds flew to her. "You get the ice while I put them in their cage. I think you

83

have enough scandalous ideas without Kaipo offering you more."

He winked. "I didn't know cockatoos were so smart. You have to admit he made an excellent suggestion. Maybe we should take his advice."

Her only reply was a muttered, "Get the ice while I silence these two pests. Three against one is more than I can handle!"

She pulled the cloth down over their cage and returned to find Zane standing just where she'd left him. "I thought you were going to chill the champagne."

His glance wandered over the two chintz-covered sofas, done in soft peaches and grays, and the large overstuffed chair where she'd tossed one of the two sheepskins her parents had brought back on their last trip to New Zealand.

"I like this room. It's kind of soft and friendly." He grinned. "Just like you." He trailed his fingers through the second sheepskin, thrown over the back of one of the sofas. "Hmm, this gives me some wonderfully wicked ideas!"

Ashley shook her head in reprimand, but when she saw how his eyes lit up as he stroked the lush wool, she couldn't help laughing. "Oh, you and your ideas. I'm going to get the ice. Maybe that will cool you off!"

"I doubt it." He chuckled again as she left the living room to go to the kitchen.

Zane was sitting on the other sofa when she returned. He noticed her raised eyebrow, and explained, "I had to get away from temptation. The vision of you lying naked on that sheepskin stirred up that hot Viking blood of mine." His smile faded. "I meant what I said, I think it's time we talk."

Ashley nestled the champagne bottle in the silver

ice bucket and joined him on the sofa. Tears glittered against her dark lashes as she confessed, "It's not much fun to talk about failure, immaturity, stupidity, betrayal—the list is endless."

Zane's fist clenched. "Damn Butcher! How any man could hurt you is beyond me," he muttered, carefully wiping her tears away.

Not really aware of what she was doing, her fingers twined with his, seeking comfort from the pain. "I don't think he did it deliberately. But times change, people change, and what we had somehow just slipped away. I should have seen it coming. Maybe I just didn't want to."

"Avoiding the truth is something we all do sometimes," Zane said soothingly. "Don't blame yourself."

Ashley shook her head. "I have no one to blame but myself. I should have seen the truth about Butcher from the beginning, but I didn't. I was too dazzled by *what* he was to see *who* he really was."

Zane squeezed her hand. "Is that where the immaturity comes in?"

"Yes. I'll never forget the day I met him. Kelly, my roommate, had a brother on the football team. It was the last practice before they left for the Sugar Bowl in New Orleans, so we went down to the field to wish Jed good luck. He brought over the captain of the football team to meet us." With a sad laugh she admitted, "I was so excited when Butcher started flirting with me. Imagine a freshman catching the eye of the biggest big man on campus around. Before leaving he jokingly suggested Kelly and I come to New Orleans for the game, and on a whim, we did."

"I've been to New Orleans. Jazz, Bourbon Street,

85

those lethal Hurricanes . . . it can be a very romantic city."

Ashley smiled at the memories. "It was. Everything seemed perfect. Butcher was even named Most Valuable Player. I came back blindly in love. But thinking of it now, I honestly don't know if it was Butcher I loved or if it was that he was the man every girl on campus wanted, and he wanted only me. Anyway, we dated the rest of that semester and got married right after he graduated. We didn't even have time for a honeymoon because he wanted to report early to the Chiefs' training camp." She wrinkled her nose. "I should have known right then what our marriage was going to be like, but I didn't. Maybe if I'd been older, wiser . . . But I wasn't."

"I told you he was a fool!" Zane teased, trying to bring back her happy smile. "You'd never catch me passing up a chance to honeymoon with you."

That did produce a tiny twitch at the corners of her mouth, but she didn't make any other response as she poured them each a glass of champagne. "To wisdom," she said, clinking her glass against his.

Zane offered a toast of his own. "To Butcher's stupidity and my good fortune."

The cool wine eased some of the pain. "No, don't misunderstand," she continued. "Butcher was a lot of things—egotistical, obsessed with football, a womanizer—but he wasn't stupid. He walked away because I wasn't the kind of woman he needed to be happy."

"Ashley, that's crazy! You're every man's fantasy. Intelligent, beautiful, witty, sensual, you love music, and you have an incredible figure! What else could Butcher possibly want?"

"Worship. He wanted me to worship him the way I did when we first met. His ego demanded that kind of total adoration to survive," she explained, taking a sip of champagne. "After we were married, I guess you could say I grew up, and the blinders came off. I saw the flaws beneath the superstar, but that didn't mean I stopped loving him. I was even relatively happy until . . ." She shuddered at the memory, hesitant to relive those awful days.

"Until what?" Zane squeezed her hand, urging her to continue. "Tell me what happened?"

"I'll never forget that horrible game. Butcher had been traded to Green Bay." Ashley shuddered again. "Believe me, for someone raised in Hawaii the weather there was hell for me. Anyway, the Packers were playing the Jets. When Butcher went up for a pass, he came down off balance, and one of the Jets slammed his helmet into Butcher's knee." Tears flooded her eyes again. "You should have seen him when the doctors told him he'd never play again. As far as he was concerned his life was over. In a very real way it was, I suppose, and so was our life together. After he got out of the hospital, the real trouble started."

Zane put his arm around her and drew her against the protective warmth of his shoulder. "Let me guess. He couldn't stand being out of the spotlight. And that's why he found someone who'd give him the kind of no-questions-asked homage you did when you first met."

Ashley nodded. "Her name's Jerrie. They've been married a year and she just turned twenty."

She pulled out of his embrace. "Can't you understand why I don't want to go through that kind of pain again? That's why it's insane for me even to let you get near me, let alone touch me. I don't want to get hurt! I've been hurt enough."

He tried to draw her back into his arms, but she shook her head. "Zane, don't."

"Ashley, don't you know I would never hurt you?"

"Even if you meant that with all your heart it could still happen so easily. You could get bored with my 'damn stubborn independence,' as Butcher put it. You could get traded." Her hands twisted together. "I've watched what football does to people. The game becomes everything. It gets in your blood like a drug until you can't live without it. What if you got hurt? I couldn't bear to watch anyone I cared for go through that hell again. This time it would probably destroy me as well."

"Damn it, Ashley, I'm not Butcher! Don't lay his hang-ups on me. So I play football. That doesn't mean I'm like every other jock in the game. I'm different." The look in his eyes made her think of a hurt puppy. "Give me a chance to prove it. That's all I ask," he pleaded.

That look already had the power to steal her heart, but even as she felt herself weaken she deliberately thrust another problem between them. "I'm also older than you are. Don't forget that—and women age faster. In a couple of years you'd probably be ready to toss me on the trash heap and find someone Jerrie's age, like Butcher did."

"So you're a couple of years older. Big deal!"

She wanted to shout that six years was more than a couple, yet something held her back. Zane charged on. "I think experience makes a woman a hell of a lot more attractive. It adds character to beauty."

Before she could resist he drew her back into his embrace. One fingertip tracing her lips, he murmured, "I don't want an empty-headed teenybopper. I want a woman, the woman who's in my arms right now. And I'm not going to give up until you know this is as right as I do."

He bent to place a kiss on her lips. It was a kiss of promise, not a kiss of passion. "You said you were dazzled by *what* Butcher was, not *who* he was," he reminded her. "Don't make the same mistake with me. I am a football player. It's what pays the bills and enables me to have the other important things I want in life, but that doesn't mean anything else about me is like Butcher. Learn who I am before you shut me out of your life."

It made sense, yet the hurt she'd endured when Butcher had walked out on her made her afraid to believe him. The questions, the doubts, whirled like a raging storm through her mind. She looked at him, remembering his kiss, the touch of his caress, and felt more strongly drawn to him than any other man she'd ever known. But when she remembered why he had such muscles, such broad shoulders, fear tarnished the allure.

She stirred uneasily in his arms, but before she could say anything his mouth quickly covered hers, as if he knew she was about to tell him to go. She tried to resist, to turn her heart to ice, but the gentle warmth of his lips moving over hers melted all her resolve to fight the attraction flaring between them. When he felt her soften, his caress deepened. Again and again his tongue brushed irresistibly across her lips, until they parted to allow him the entry they both craved. Slowly, as his kiss plundered its willing captive, the doubts slipped away, leaving his allure as compelling as ever.

After Zane left, Ashley walked out onto the beach. Heavy clouds, the harbinger of the approaching storm, had moved in to obscure the moon. She glanced up at the darkening sky, a sad smile touching her lips. "Well, Mr. Moon," she muttered to herself, "you're in as much of a fog as I am."

With a sigh she sank down onto the sand, drawing her knees up to rest her chin on them and staring out at the pounding surf. As the soothing sound of crashing waves echoed in her ears, she tried to sort out her muddled feelings. The explosion of sensation she experienced in Zane's arms shocked her with its intensity.

Her thoughts drifted back over the last years, remembering how the bitterness of her divorce seemed to stifle all the emotion within her. Many men found her attractive with her dark hair and mysterious eyes, and she had no trouble filling her empty evenings, yet their kisses left her cold. Nothing seemed to have the power to touch her heart or arouse her desire. Then suddenly with those first pictures, that first glimpse of Zane rising from the whirlpool, from his first kiss all those sleeping feelings had exploded into life.

Even now, thinking about how he looked dripping wet in that towel, Ashley felt the fire begin to burn within her. She stroked a fingertip over her sweetly bruised lips, then suddenly the tears came. As they splashed silently down her cheeks, the questions raged. Damn it, why did it have to be Zane—a football player—who made her feel again? Why, when there were so many problems with the relationship? Wouldn't it be better to end it now before his touch drove all caution from her mind and his possession became complete? In her heart she knew it could end in a hundred ways. Wouldn't it hurt much more if they became lovers?

Slowly other thoughts came, pushing away the

doubts. Remembering his compassion while he'd listened to the sad tale of her marriage, thinking about the hurt in his eyes when he saw her own hurt, recalling the gentle way he waited for her willing response before his kiss burned hotter, the tears quietly dried. As she walked back to the house the smile was back on her lips, only this time no sadness dimmed its happy glow.

CHAPTER SIX

After the emotional whirlwind of the evening before, Ashley slept late. It was after ten when she walked into the *News*. She hadn't been at her desk five minutes when Jake came sidling over. He glanced over his shoulder twice as if someone were on his trail, and whispered, "Your inside contact called. He wants a meeting. The Hukilau on Kamehameha Highway at noon. Be there." Quickly he turned to go before anyone saw him.

"Jake, what is all this cloak-and-dagger stuff?" she protested with a laugh. "I'm covering the Kings, not taking part in international espionage."

She saw his shoulders relax as he turned back to her. "Hell, how was I supposed to know? You weren't here. Your phone was ringing off the hook and I couldn't let just anyone answer it. What if it was your mysterious lover?"

"Mysterious lover?" Her blush betrayed emotions her words refused to acknowledge. "I don't have a lover, mysterious or otherwise."

"Don't you? You could have fooled me. For the last week you've been positively glowing. I almost need sunglasses when I come near you. And I should know. Kakalina's the same way."

A dreamy smile lit Ashley's face at the thought of the joy of others, a joy denied to her. "She should be. She's carrying your baby. When is the little one due?"

Jake whisked imaginary beads of sweat from his forehead. "Within the month, and it can't come too soon for me! This father-to-be business is wearing me down. Oh, by the way, Kakalina has a yen for *laulaus* tonight, and told me to invite you."

"I'll bet she wants to pump me about my mysterious lover who doesn't exist." Ashley laughed, knowing her friend's inquisitive nature all too well.

Jake shifted from one foot to the other. "Ah, well . . . I did happen to mention you looked unusually radiant lately. Come on, Ash, have a heart. She's as big as a hippo and is about as uncomfortable. Humor her. Come to dinner tonight. Since she quit her job here she misses you."

Ashley laughed. "What she misses is the gossip, but I promise I'll come. I wouldn't miss Kakalina's Hawaiian cooking for anything."

"Great!" He leaned nearer conspiratorially. "Care to tell me who your inside source is? Everyone is dying to know." His eyes narrowed. "Are you shacking up with someone on the Kings? Is he feeding you all this inside stuff?"

"The answer is no and no. And furthermore, my source stays covered." Her smile turned serious. "Jake, he's a friend, no more, no less. Turn that news-hound nose elsewhere. Okay?"

"Sure, Ash, whatever you say. You may not be able to trust the rest of these bums, but you can always trust me. See you at six. Oh, don't forget your raincoat. The news just came over the wire. That tropical storm is now officially a hurricane. We shouldn't get hit with the high winds but it's bound to blow up a mess of squalls." With a friendly wave he left.

93

Ashley had just flipped on her word processor when her phone rang. It was Ray, wanting her in his office. There was a huge bouquet of gardenias, white plumerias, and orchids on his desk. "Looks like you've got a secret admirer. Or are you surprising your wife with flowers?"

"Neither. These just came for you." He shoved the flowers across the desk at her. "Maybe they're a bribe from Clyde Winston to ease up in your columns. From what I hear, every time he picks up the sports page and reads your latest, he hits the ceiling." He rubbed his hands together. "I have to admit Monica was right when she insisted you get the assignment."

Ashley reached for the card. Remembering the passion of the night before she smiled, assuming the flowers were phase two of Zane's seduction strategy. Idly wondering why he hadn't had them sent to her home, she tore open the small envelope containing the card.

A huge smile spread across her face as she read it. "Well, aren't you going to tell me who's sending you posies?" Ray demanded when she didn't say anything.

She tossed the card onto his desk. "Read it yourself. It's from our illustrious leader."

"From *Monica?*"

Ashley grinned with delight. "It seems our boss is very pleased with my columns. To quote, I am to 'keep the punches flying. With luck Clyde Winston has a glass jaw.' " The vehemence of Monica's card suddenly struck her. "It sounds like she has a personal vendetta against Mr. Winston. Got any idea why?"

Ray shifted uneasily in his chair. "I have no idea," he muttered, refusing to meet her gaze. "Of course,

Monica always enjoys taking potshots at the rich and famous. And the owner of the Kings is certainly both of those."

His evasive answer aroused Ashley's reporter instincts. There was definitely more going on here than Monica enjoying taking potshots at Hawaii's rich. And unless her feelings were very wrong, it was something personal between Clyde and Monica. Ashley was about to probe a little deeper when she happened to glance at the clock. It was after eleven. If she was going to be at the Hukilau by noon the questions would have to wait.

She rose and picked up the fragrant bouquet of flowers. "If you talk to Monica, give her my thanks."

"What's tomorrow's column on?"

"I'll let you know this afternoon. I'm having lunch with my 'friend.' "

Ray chuckled. "An inside pipeline to the Kings! You are one lucky reporter, Ashley. Keep that friend of yours happy so those fabulous scoops keep rolling in, and I promise there'll be a raise to go along with those flowers."

"I'm going to hold you to that." She laughed happily. "I can use the extra money."

Ashley put the flowers on her desk and hurried out to her car, taking one of the gardenias with her. Leaden gray clouds heavy with rain obscured the sun as she turned onto Kamehameha Highway. She pulled into the restaurant parking lot as the first splatters of rain hit the windshield. She tried to hold her hair with one hand, wishing she'd put it up in a chignon, as the blustery wind whipped it wildly around her face as she hurried into the crowded restaurant.

Sammy, waiting in a corner booth, waved his cigar at her. She reached the table and leaned over to pin the gardenia to his lapel.

He glanced down at it, then back up at her. "Does this mean we're going to the prom?" he kidded, sniffing the fragrant blossom.

"Nope. I just wanted to share the thank you I got from my boss with you," she explained, sliding into the booth beside him. "You've earned it." She patted his gnarled hand. "And I want you to know I appreciate it. The stories you've given me have been great! By the way, this lunch is on me."

"If I'd known that"—he laughed—"I'd have picked a more expensive restaurant."

"I was a little curious about your choice. Why are we meeting way out here by the airport? Are you planning to skip town?"

"Naw, I just figured no one from the Kings would spot us here."

Ashley frowned. "Are you sure feeding me inside information isn't going to get you in trouble? I don't want you losing your job because of me."

He thumped his chest. "They can't afford to fire me. I'm the best trainer in football and they know it, so stop worrying your pretty head about it. Besides I'm not giving you any information you couldn't get from someone else, if you dug deep enough." He smiled at her with fatherly concern. "After the way Butcher treated you—or mistreated you, I should say—you deserve a break. If I can help you make a success of this assignment then I'm going to do it, and no one's going to stop me."

"Thanks, Sammy. You're a good friend."

After they'd ordered, Ashley pulled out her notebook. "Okay, what's the scoop? Did Razor throw a tennis racket at his backup quarterback this time?"

"Naw, this is better than that. Ol' Clyde has sicced the F.B.I. on the Kings."

"What?" Ashley's fingers trembled with excitement. "Does he suspect a point-shaving scam? Now, that really would be headline news!"

"It's good, but I'm afraid it's not that good." Sammy leaned his beefy arms on the table. "Here's the deal. Clyde has hired this guy, Edward Armstrong, to handle the security for the team. According to the information they're releasing to the press he's supposed to make sure playbooks aren't stolen, no one disturbs the team when it's on the road, check to see no one is spying on the practice —stuff like that. They're not bothering to mention he's ex-F.B.I."

Ashley frowned, confused. "So what's the big deal?" she asked as their abalone arrived. "Why does Clyde need a former F.B.I. man to handle routine matters like that?"

Sammy clapped his hands together. "Give the little lady a gold star. That's the point, he doesn't. What Edward the Gumshoe is really supposed to do is snoop around and make damn sure no betting scandal, drug deals, or anything else heavy touches Clyde's precious team." He paused to take a bite of the abalone, which was delicious. "You know the only person who tries harder than Clyde to have a goody-goody image is the Pope. Sometimes I wonder if he really cares about the Kings, or just wants a squeaky-clean team that won't tarnish his vaunted name."

Ashley raised her glass of iced tea to him. "I owe you another box of cigars for this one, Sammy."

Three hours later Ashley tossed her finished column on Ray's desk.

"Hot damn!" He chuckled with glee as he read

her headline: KINGS UNDER EX—F.B.I. MAN'S WATCH-
FUL EYE.

" 'Kings players beware, Big Brother is watching
you. Clyde Winston, your owner, has hired F.B.I.
heat to be sure his team is clean—and stays that
way,' " Ray read aloud.

He glanced up at Ashley for a moment and held
out his hand. "The raise is yours. This ought to
send Clyde right through the *roof!* Monica will be
absolutely delirious with joy!"

That pang of instinct nudged her again. "Why
would Monica be delirious that my columns are
sending Clyde through the roof?"

This time Ray met her gaze. "Hell-burners of
columns, as Monica calls them, raise circulation."
He opened his desk drawer and removed a computer printout. "In fact, this just came in. I thought
you'd enjoy seeing it. Since your column started
running, circulation has jumped eight percent."

Ashley took the paper from him. "Wow!" she
whispered in delight when she saw the figures.

Ray came around his desk to pat her on the back.
"As I said, you've earned that raise. Keep it up and
more will come. Now, why don't you knock off early
and get out of here? This storm is going to raise hell
with the rush hour traffic."

It was only when she was driving through the
lashing rain to Jake and Kakalina's home that she
realized Ray still hadn't answered her question
about what was going on between Monica and
Clyde.

Kakalina greeted her at the door with a chilled
mai tai and a hug of welcome. Ashley looked at the
tall statuesque woman, now round with child, and
smiled. "I've missed having you at the *News,* but I

98

can see what you're doing right now is more important."

Kakalina laughed. "I didn't think so when I was suffering with morning sickness! And Jake was not the least bit sympathetic. All he cared about was getting his breakfast." She shuddered. "I can't tell you how awful a fried egg looks first thing in the morning to a pregnant woman. Thank heavens that's over."

"Now all you get is cravings. Jake told me you were hungry for *laulaus*," Ashley teased, following her into the kitchen.

Kakalina licked her lips, thinking of dinner. "Of course they won't be as good as the ones my grandmother made by digging a pit, burning the wood down to coals, and then putting *laulaus*, wrapped in taro leaves, in the *imu* to steam; but aluminum foil and the oven doesn't do a bad job."

Ashley stood a moment listening to the rain beating with savage fury against the windows. "On a night like this, be thankful for the oven," she observed. "Can you imagine what it would be like out there on the beach in this weather, trying to uncover your pit so we could eat?" Kakalina laughed at the picture. "I know they can be made lots of different ways. What kind of *laulaus* are we having tonight?" Ashley asked.

"My favorite. *Mahimahi, 'ula, pāpa'i,* and *'ōpai*, steamed in *hala kahiki waiūpaka*. Sounds scrumptious, doesn't it?"

"Whoa, my Hawaiian's a little rusty. I recognize the *mahimahi*, that's fish, but I sincerely hope there isn't eel hidden somewhere in there."

"Don't worry, my friend. What we're having is a mixture of fish, lobster, crab, and shrimp, steamed in pineapple butter."

"Sounds like it might be edible," Jake observed from the doorway. "The Cubs are playing baseball tonight. Hope dinner is over by seven."

Ashley looked at Kakalina. Kakalina looked at Ashley. As one they said, "Men!"

Then Kakalina moved across the kitchen to give Jake a hug. She patted her rounded stomach. "From the way he kicks I think your son is going to be a soccer star, not a baseball player. But yes, dinner will be over by seven so you can get to your Cubs game. Why don't you put on some music while I toss the salad? Then we'll eat."

Jake tuned the stereo to a classical music station and returned to the kitchen to help Kakalina take the heavy pan of *laulaus* from the oven.

"Mmm, those smell heavenly," Ashley said sincerely as Kakalina tore open the foil to let the pineapple-scented steam escape.

She had just forked a piece of shrimp when Chopin's Piano Concerto Number One started playing on the stereo. Unaware her fork had stopped halfway to her mouth, Ashley smiled, remembering the music, the moonlight, and Zane. Only when Jake snapped his fingers in front of her eyes did the spell break.

"Hey, are you all right?" Kakalina asked with concern.

"I told you she's been going around with that goofy look on her face lately," Jake teased.

"It's not goofy, it's dreamy," Kakalina argued. "Care to tell me what man put those stars in your eyes?"

Ashley ignored the question. "Did I tell you Monica was so pleased with my columns on the Kings that she sent me a huge bouquet of flowers, and on top of that, Ray gave me a raise? Tonight we should celebrate."

"Ash, that's great!" Jake said warmly. "Those columns of yours have really been singeing some tail feathers. You deserve the raise."

After dinner, with Jake settled down in front of the television, Ashley helped Kakalina clear the table. When everything was in the dishwasher, Kakalina looked at her friend. "All right, the dishes are done, Jake's not here, I can see the happiness in your eyes, but I also see something's troubling you. What is it?"

"I guess I could use some advice," Ashley admitted, sitting down at the kitchen table. "I've got myself in an awful mess."

"Don't tell me he's married."

"Worse! He's a football player. Really dumb, isn't it?"

"Maybe. Maybe not."

Ashley laughed. "You're a lot of help." She rested her chin in her palm. "You know, I've heard about women who do this. There's even a course offered at the university called Not Making the Same Mistake Twice. So why am I crazy enough to think about walking right back into the same type of relationship that brought me such grief? At nineteen I wasn't wise enough to see trouble coming. What's my excuse now? Good heavens, I'm thirty-three! I should have learned something over the years."

"Why? Love makes fools out of geniuses every day," Kakalina observed with a knowing smile. "By the way, what's his name?"

"Zane Bruxton."

"Oh, you mean that gorgeous blond! I've seen pictures of him. There's something primitively

101

powerful about him. He sort of reminds me of a Viking."

"Me too, but that doesn't change anything. He says he's different, but I've told you about all the problems I had with Butcher and his career. Well, it could all happen again with Zane, *and* there's one more tiny detail. I'm six years older than he is."

Kakalina shrugged. "So what? That's old-fashioned thinking."

"Is it? I don't think so. Butcher married a girl a lot younger than he is and everyone said, 'How romantic!' If I get involved with Zane everyone will wonder why he needs a mother figure. That's just the way it is."

"Why do you care what anyone else thinks? Love's more important than other people's opinions!" Kakalina's large brown eyes grew misty. "I should know. No one in my family wanted me to marry Jake."

Ashley looked at her friend with sympathy. "I didn't know that. What's wrong with Jake? He's a great guy."

That observation brought back Kakalina's smile. "I agree. That's why I married him. But my family's proud of our pure Hawaiian blood, and Jake's Irish through and through. But the baby seems to have smoothed things out a little. So let's get back to your problem. I'm concerned about you. I've never seen you this confused and uncertain before. What happened to old levelheaded Ashley, the woman who always knew exactly what she wanted."

"I honestly don't know. Where Zane's concerned I'm a mass of conflicting impulses. I sure wish I could figure out why I find him so damn attractive, when I *know* I shouldn't."

"Maybe the answer lies in your heart, not your head. Search there and you may find the truth."

Ashley frowned. "I've tried, but . . ."

Suddenly from the living room the jarring bleep of a weather warning signal interrupted her words. They hurried in just in time to hear a voice intone, "Hurricane David has taken an unexpected turn northward. It will hit Oahu, but if it keeps on its present course it will spare Honolulu, coming ashore somewhere north of the city. Those in that area are advised to take the proper precautions."

As Ashley grabbed her purse, Jake asked, "Do you want me to come with you? Your home is in that area."

"No, the cove will protect me. The house is sheltered. It's withstood blows stronger than this. You stay with Kakalina. Even in Honolulu the weather could turn ugly."

"Are you sure?" he insisted. "I don't like the idea of you out there all alone. There aren't even any neighbors nearby."

"Jake, I'll be fine. That house has stood for a hundred and fifty years. It will survive the night."

"Ashley, I wish you'd stay here with us," Kakalina begged. "You'd be safer."

"I told you, I'll be all right," Ashley insisted. "My ancestors knew what they were doing when they built that house, but I do have to secure things." She saw the concern clouding Kakalina's eyes. "Believe me, I'll be fine," she repeated.

An hour later she wasn't so sure, as she tried to drag the rattan settee into the house. The wind lashed the rain into her face until it was almost impossible to see as she struggled with the heavy piece, trying to pull it to the french doors. Suddenly

103

it was wrenched out of her hands. With a startled gasp she looked up into Zane's furious eyes.

"Damn it," he muttered, easily lifting the settee onto his broad shoulders as if it weighed nothing. "Why didn't you call me? I had to hear on the radio you were in trouble. I'll get the rest of this furniture in. You start shuttering the windows."

Zane was carrying in the last chair when she bolted the last shutter. She turned to look at him. "Thank God my ancestors were originally from the Cape Hatteras area. They knew how to secure a house against any storm."

His eyebrows went up and down. "You're not the only one with ancestors. Just think what *mine* knew how to do," he murmured.

A fiery blush scalded Ashley's face at the thought of the disturbingly erotic fantasies she'd had of him as a Viking, but she refused to let him see how powerfully he affected her. "You're dripping wet. I'll go see if Dad left anything here you can change into."

"No wait, there's something I have to do," he said, starting for the front door.

Watching him go, an unexpectedly desperate protest was forced from her. "You aren't leaving me, are you?"

"Just try and get rid of me." He laughed. "This is one storm we're going to ride out together. But I left something in the van I need to get. You hold the front door open while I bring it in."

Ashley flinched, watching bolt after bolt of lightning streak to the ground as she held the door. The wind howling in her face made it hard to see what Zane was carrying toward her through the driving rain, but it looked like a big rectangular box covered with a sheet.

Inside, Zane set it on the coffee table. "I didn't want to leave my little friends in my apartment in this storm," he explained. "I live in a high rise and was afraid the windows might blow in, and they'd be hurt."

Ashley took a step backward. "You don't have rattlesnakes in there, do you? I remember reading about one of the Cowboy quarterbacks keeping pet rattlers in a box like that."

With a flourish Zane whipped off the sheet. "It's not a box. It's an aquarium."

The instant he uncovered the aquarium the cockatoos started screeching wildly.

"Your friends wouldn't last a minute if Kaipo had his way. Cockatoos love fish, and not because they're pretty. I'll go cover their cage, or they'll never shut up."

When the birds had quieted down, Ashley came to kneel beside him and watch the brightly colored fish gliding through the tank. "Oh, Zane, they're gorgeous!"

His hand stroked her damp hair. "Not as gorgeous as you are. And they sure can't keep me warm on a stormy night."

"What you need is some dry clothes and a hot toddy," she commented, ignoring the suggestive undercurrent of his words. "I'll go see what I can find."

She rummaged around in the back of the closet in her parents' room and finally found an old terry cloth robe her father had left. Returning to the living room, she tossed it to Zane. "Here, put this on while I go change. Then I'll brew us up a couple of rum toddies. Sipping those will be a perfect way to ride out the storm."

"I can think of something a whole lot more perfect than rum toddies. Too bad I didn't have time to stop for some coffee ice cream," he teased. "But I think if we put our minds to it we can still have a seduction scene, even without the ice cream to weaken your resistance. What do you think?"

"I think if you weren't already dripping wet I would tell you to go soak your head," she said, laughing.

Zane winked. "Since you're going to change anyway, why don't you slip into the proverbial something more comfortable. I'll be waiting."

106

CHAPTER SEVEN

Ashley searched through her closet, smiling when she found what she was looking for. Slipping the loose-fitting cotton muumuu splashed with bright red and pink hibiscus on over her head, she muttered, "This ought to be comfortable enough."

She walked back into the living room, and at the sight of Zane instantly wished her father was a larger man. The robe covered him, but Zane's chest was so broad it gaped wide, allowing her to see a disturbing amount of his rippling muscles and blond curly chest hair. Her fingers twitched with a sudden desire to stroke those muscles, to tangle in the curly crispness of that hair, but she deliberately slammed a brake on the desire.

She pirouetted, showing him her muumuu. "I'm very comfortable," she said, sweetly, glancing provocatively over her shoulder.

"That's not exactly what I had in mind, but you'd look as seductive as hell in anything. Or better yet, nothing." He held out his hand. "Come, I've made a fire. I'll bet it's not often you can enjoy your fireplace in Hawaii, but tonight is definitely one of those rare times."

"I'll get the toddies while you throw another log on. It's going to be a long evening."

His gaze raked over her. "I certainly hope so!" he murmured.

When she returned from the kitchen with the hot buttered rum she found him sitting on the sofa with his arms thrown back along the bolsters. He had a faraway look on his face she'd never been before. She sat down beside him. "Do you often dream, Ashley?" he asked, his gaze wandering back to her.

"That's a strange question. Of course, I dream," she asserted, taking a sip of the warming drink. "In fact, I dream in color."

"No, I guess I should have asked, do you day-dream?" He paused. "Listen to that howling wind, the rain lashing against the shutters, the sound of the surf pounding against the shore. Those are the sounds my ancestors heard as they sailed the seas." He gazed off into space again. "Sometimes I imagine what it must have been like on those longboats, lying off some distant coast, waiting for the dawn and the attack. I wonder how they felt, knowing some wouldn't return, as the sea spray stung their faces. It must have been exciting . . . and terrifying at the same time."

She gazed at him, and the words slipped out before she could stop them. "I wish you hadn't told me your ancestors were Vikings. I've been having the most disturbing fantasies."

"You have?" Zane murmured, moving closer. "That's interesting. So have I."

The savage rain driven by the hurricane winds beat against the shuttered windows, echoing the rising storm within her. She looked at him.

"You know what the Vikings did. They took what they wanted," he explained.

"But, Zane . . ."

"Shh." He laid a finger across her lips. "Let the

108

fantasy become reality. It's what I want. And it's what you want, otherwise you wouldn't be dreaming about those two Rs you joked about earlier."

Looking around the room, his glance fell on the two sheepskins. "Aha, just what a lusty Viking needs." He grinned, rising to toss them onto the floor in front of the fireplace. "We don't have a longboat, so we'll have to improvise." He quickly crossed the room to take the candelabrum from the sideboard. Fetching a twig from the fire, he lit the ten candles, carefully placed the candelabrum on the floor to light the sheepskins, romantically, and turned to look at her, smiling. "We want to get this scene right and I know the Vikings didn't have electricity," he said, clicking off the lights.

"Zane, this is crazy!" she protested with a laugh.

"Is it? I don't think so. Maybe it's the old pillaging blood stirring, but tonight I feel every inch the conquering Norseman." He moved toward her, holding out his hand. "I want you. Tonight I won't be denied. Tonight you'll agree it's what you want too." Slipping into the role of the all-powerful Viking, he challenged her. "Come, wench, you've been vanquished. Come to me. Come accept your fate."

The reality of what she was tempted to do battled with her common sense. She shouldn't give in to him, yet when he moved nearer she had no thought of escape.

Grabbing her, he hauled her to her feet and dragged her into his embrace before she could protest. "Now you will be mine," he vowed, scooping her up in his brawny arms.

Ashley knew she should say no, yet it felt so right, so good to be held by him, desired by him, she remained silent as he carried her to their bed of love.

The wool of the sheepskins felt like the lushest velvet as he laid her down and with one grasp tore the cotton muumuu away from her body.

"Zane, are you crazy?" she protested.

"Shh, I'll buy you a dozen more. Right now just feel," he murmured, lowering his body to cover hers. "Pretend this is real. Pretend I am the Viking and you are the prize."

Maybe it was the raging storm outside, isolating them from the rest of the world, maybe the exotic fur beneath her. Maybe it was her fantasies, fantasies she could now make real, but whatever the reason, it was easy to let reality slip away. "The conquered prize?" she whispered.

"Yes. The prize that must do as her conqueror bids, must do *everything* her conqueror bids," he insisted. His voice grew soft. "Ashley, I can't spend another night without you."

She closed her eyes. Why fight when her body had already surrendered? She wriggled against the lush wool. "Does the vanquished have a choice?"

"Only if she agrees. You know what I want?" His hand moved down over her bare breast to complete the conquest. "I want you open to me. I want to know, to possess, every gorgeous inch of you. I want you to give me pleasure in a dozen ways, as I will you."

Ashley shuddered as Zane continued, "I want to see you naked beneath me as you are now. I want to see you writhe at my touch. I want to hear you beg for mercy as my desire drives you to the edge where the passion is so sweet it makes you want to cry. I want you to love me with every ounce of passion

110

that is within you. Don't make me force you, for you know I can."

He traced a fingertip across her forehead. "I know your mind tells you no." His hand moved to seek her breast again through her tattered clothing. As the peak hardened and thrust hungrily against his palm, he murmured, "Yet your body says yes. Which are you going to listen to?"

The fiery response burned too hot to ignore as she whispered, "Tonight I'll listen to only what I want. Let tomorrow care for itself."

"A Viking you wanted, my love, a Viking you shall have. And I promise the surrender will be the sweetest you've ever known."

Zane's breathing rasped harshly. "Ashley, spread your legs for me," he gently ordered. "I want to feel how much you want me."

In the crackling firelight Zane looked every inch the conqueror, and at that moment there was nothing she wanted more in the world than to be conquered by this man, to belong to him, to experience the pleasure she'd lived without for so long.

Refusing to let any doubt sneak in she complied with his wish, as his caress slipped down over her stomach, and lower, to move between her thighs and strip away the silk guarding her last treasure. As his fingers plunged into her, her hips rose unashamedly to meet his thrust. A moan escaped her as Zane teased her, pulling his pleasurable touch away before plunging deeply again and again. Each time he brought her to the edge of the paradise he'd promised, then retreated, exquisitely building a fire within her that raged hotter than any she'd ever experienced.

When she thought the need couldn't soar any higher, Zane lowered his head. His lips, encircling her taut nipple, caressed it with moist strokes of his tongue, sending wave after wave of pleasure through her. Her head tossed restlessly back and forth as the torment continued until she thought she'd scream. Finally she couldn't stand the aching pleasure any longer. Her eyes opened to meet his glittering eyes, burning a hot sapphire, and she knew his fingers had kindled the same heat of desire in her own. It was a desire she wanted satisfied— *Now!*

No inhibitions stopped her, as with hands as hungry as his had been she ripped his robe open. Eagerly she explored the muscled breadth of his chest, tangling her fingers in the curly blond hair, but the allure of what would come tempted her hands to move lower. As she touched him, stroked him, curled her fingers over the power that soon would be hers, his moan echoed her own fiery passion.

"Ashley, stop!" he gasped. "I can't take any more!"

But this order she didn't obey, wanting him to suffer the same delicious agony he'd stirred within her. With a moan of pleasure Zane rolled onto his back, letting her have her way. For a moment Ashley couldn't draw her gaze away from the wondrous desire her caresses had created in Zane, but looking wasn't enough. As her fingers curled around him again, Zane trembled.

Quickly his arms swept around her and he pulled her on top of him. Ashley slid into the most intimate embrace, and a racking shudder shook her, then another, answered by one from him. But even then he wouldn't let the pleasure end, as he rolled her onto her back to begin building the passion again.

Butcher had been an impatient lover, rushing to satisfy his need with little concern for her pleasure, so Ashley had no idea how passionately long loving could be. The howling winds, the crashing surf outside mirrored the power of their need for each other, as again and again Zane brought her to the peak of desire where the pulsating waves of satisfaction only served to make them want to feel that magic anew. With his hands, his mouth, his tongue, with the velvety thrusts she craved he gave her pleasure in a dozen ways—and as he'd promised, she loved every one of them.

The lashing rain had slowed to a gentle pelting and the candles were burning low when Ashley's eyes fluttered open. Still one, they'd fallen asleep on the sheepskins. She reached up to stroke his tousled blond hair and Zane stirred in her arms. The lazy smile of a well-satisfied man curled the corners of his mouth as he lifted his head from the warm pillow of her shoulder.

"That was some storm!"

"Storm?" she teased. "I didn't hear a thing."

He grinned that impish grin, making her smile. "I meant the one in here. Nature has no power to compete with you!"

"Hmm." She wriggled her hips suggestively beneath him. "Do I feel a bit of another storm blowing up again?"

"Keep doing that and you'll get one *hell* of a storm, I promise."

She moved again, wrapping her legs around him. "I always did enjoy a good storm."

He lowered his head to take her nipple into his mouth. Between gentle sucks, he murmured, "I knew we were destined for each other. We like the same things! One storm coming up."

The dawn was trying to break through the ceiling

of gray clouds when they again fell into an exhausted sleep.

Four hours later Ashley stood at the stove and glanced down at the frying pan. "A six-egg omelette!" she muttered. "I'd forgotten how much you jocks eat."

"Hey, stop complaining," Zane joked. "Can I help it if I'm hungry? I worked hard last night."

"Work!" she fussed, brandishing a spatula at him. "Is that what you call it?"

He came up behind her and his hands slid under her loose blouse to cup her breasts. Nibbling for a delightful moment on the back of her neck, he murmured, "You know I was only teasing. What I call last night was finding paradise. And I don't mean Hawaii. I mean being with you, being inside of you. That is as close to heaven as I'll find on this earth." He chuckled. "And I'm delighted you led me to that heaven so often. Do you suppose that means you're an angel?"

She laughed self-consciously. "I don't think angels are allowed to do what we did last night. They'd probably get kicked out of heaven. I think we shocked your fish." Blushing, she confessed, "I know I shocked myself."

Zane reached around her and turned off the stove. Taking her hand, he guided her back into the living room, sat down on the sofa with her, and gathered her into his embrace. "For someone who keeps professing she's older than I am, you're awfully innocent. Are you sure it isn't the other way around?" he teased. Then his smile faded. "Ashley, it's called loving. Nothing we did last night was wrong."

"I know, but . . ."

Strong fingers lifted her chin, forcing her to look at him. "Tell me the truth. There hasn't been any other man but Butcher, has there?"

Mutely she shook her head.

"It must have been a lonely time for you, but I'm glad. Maybe I'm old-fashioned, but I like the idea of teaching you the ways of love."

"Zane, don't forget I was married."

"Yes, and to rather a dull dog I'd say, if last night was a revelation for you. I'll bet he was an advocate of the ol' missionary position, wasn't he?"

Her eyes widened. "How—how did you know?" she whispered.

"Because I've known a lot of guys like Butcher. You thought he was egotistical, but from what you've told me, I think he was basically insecure. And insecure men have to be in control. I guess it makes them feel more powerful. I think the real beauty of making love is sharing the pleasure. If you do, what's returned is doubly sweet."

She smiled and spoke from her heart. "Last night was sweet, Zane, the sweetest night I've ever known. I want you to believe that. I guess I won't ask where you got all that experience."

"From Miss Jones, of course. Remember the glowing recommendation she gave me?"

Ashley laughed. "Well, I guess I can't be jealous of a figment of my imagination."

"You have no reason to be jealous of anyone, real or otherwise. I've never met a woman like you, and that's no line. As I said, Butcher was a damn fool to let anyone as special as you slip away."

Ashley tilted her head to one side and studied him. "You know, you may be right about Butcher. Maybe his egomaniac bluster was just a show to cover his insecurities as a man. I know he was not at

115

all pleased when I received several awards for my first journalism assignment, about a halfway house for battered women. He wanted all the attention centered on him."

Zane ran his hand through her dark hair. "If I'm getting too personal here, just tell me to shut up."

Ashley laughed. "I don't think you can get any more personal than last night."

"You've got a point. I did enjoy exploring every inch of your delectable body."

"I thought you Vikings ravished instead of exploring," she teased.

"You certainly played the part of the willing captive with a lot of zest. Let's see, where can we go from here? I could be a pirate and you a Spanish noblewoman I seize from your galleon. Or how about me as a Roman and you as one of the Sabines? I sort of like the idea of throwing you over my shoulder and taking off to some secluded cave where I could have my way with you."

"I thought that's what you did last night," Ashley joked. She started running her hand up his bare leg, reveling in the feel of the curly hair tickling her palm. "On the other hand, you might have a good idea there. I think you'd look cute in a toga, but I doubt the guys on the team would ever let you hear the end of it if you draped yourself in a sheet to chase after me."

"I could always quit and chase you full-time."

"What?" Ashley demanded, pretending shock. "Stop playing football. You'd be miserable."

"Maybe. But you're right," Zane admitted. "I can't quit now."

"And you keep telling me you're different from Butcher," she teased.

"Damn it, Ashley, I am!"

116

She leaned nearer, opening the robe so she could run her hands up his bare chest. "You are different." She winked, mimicking him. "You're a whole lot better lover!"

"That's me, Superstud. Just as Miss Jones promised. Guess I'll have to have them call you for recommendations from now on."

Ashley's teasing caresses froze at his words. A pain, twisting like the thrust of a knife, tore at her heart as she thought of him in the arms of another woman. Tears stung her eyes. It terrified her how much it hurt. How had she let him become so important to her?

"Hey, I was just kidding," Zane reassured her, gently gathering her into his arms. "There's only one woman I'm interested in, and I'm holding her right now."

She snuggled against his warmth, wanting to believe his words, but he was so attractive he probably had a dozen women chasing him. She tensed. What if he let himself get caught?

Zane felt her disquiet and began to drop featherlight kisses on her dark hair. Then his kisses descended to find her ear. "I thought I proved that over and over to you last night," he whispered. "Shall we have another demonstration, just to be sure?"

That brought back her smile. "No, you were most convincing."

When he felt her relax, he said, "I have a confession. There is something else I'm interested in besides you."

She twisted in his embrace to look at him. "And what's that? I thought I was the only thing occupying your mind."

"It's not my mind I'm worried about. It's my

stomach. Ashley, I'm starving. Do you suppose you could finish cooking that omelette?"

"Food!" She laughed, straightening up. "That's all you men think about."

"Unfair," he murmured, sliding his hand under her blouse to cup her breast again. "I didn't mention food once last night. I was hungry for something else then, and if I just had a little food for energy I might get hungry like that again."

She smiled, savoring the surge of warmth flowing through her at his touch. "I can't think of a better reason for feeding anyone. But first I'd better call Ray and tell him I'll be in late." Her fingers closed over his, trapping his hand against her heart. "To use your words, I'll tell him I'm 'working' at home this morning."

After breakfast Ashley smiled as she watched him stretch lazily, trying unsuccessfully to stifle a yawn. "What you need is a swim to pep you up!"

"What I need is a nap. You about wore me out last night."

"Me?" She laughed, rising. "You were the one with the wild ideas about sheepskins and candles." She grabbed his hand. "Come on. The rain's stopped."

But when she tugged he didn't budge. "Ah, have a heart, Ashley. I'm pooped. Besides, I can't go swimming. I don't have a suit."

"That argument won't work, lazybones. There're no neighbors to see us if we choose to go skinny-dipping, and since the cockatoos' cage is still covered and your fish can't talk, who's going to tell?"

Wriggling provocatively out of her blouse, she let it drop to the floor. A hot glint burned in his eyes as she stood before him, bare to the waist. "You're right. A swim might be just what I need to 'perk me up.' ''

With a sharp intake of breath, he watched her step out of her jeans. "Yes, indeed, I'm feeling a surge of that old energy already."

She smiled, enjoying the way he looked at her. "Good. Race you to the water."

She ran through the living room, but as she pushed open the French doors she froze, confronted by the damage the storm had done. Her normally sparkling clean beach was littered with debris. One of her palm trees had cracked at the base and was lying on the sand, which was cluttered with palm fronds stripped from the trees by the wind. There were even some coconuts tossed up by the high waves.

Zane came to stand beside her. "Holy cow, what a mess!"

"I agree. Sort of takes the edge off the desire to go swimming, doesn't it." Sadly she walked to the fallen palm. It had been one of her favorites. After a moment she sighed, kneeling to scoop out the soft core.

"What are you doing?" Zane asked.

"Trying to get some good out of this tragedy." She held her hands up for him to see. "Tonight we can have heart of palm salad. It's a real island delicacy, and a rare treat, because the only way you can get it is for a palm to be felled. I'll take this inside and be right back."

When she rejoined him, Zane pulled her gently into his embrace, not with passion but to comfort her. He rocked her as if she were a child. With a deep sigh he said, "I've got some more bad news. You'll have to eat that heart of palm salad by yourself."

She threw back her head and looked up at him. "What do you mean?"

"I didn't want to tell you and spoil our day, but the team is flying out tonight. Sunday's game is in Denver and the coach wants to get us there early so we can have a couple of days to adjust to the altitude." His embrace tightened. "Damn it, I can't even be here to help you clean up this mess."

She placed a kiss on the warm flesh of his shoulder. "You were here last night to help. That's when I really needed you. I understand. If the coach tells you to go, you gotta go."

"Those nights in Denver sure are going to be long and lonely." Suddenly his eyes gleamed. "I don't suppose the *News* will send you to the mainland to cover the game, will they?"

"No such luck. Besides," she teased, tweaking the hair on his chest, "what good would it do? Didn't you read my column? Your uncle has hired some ex-F.B.I. heat to make you guys behave. And Sammy told me one of his prime responsibilities is to make sure no women are allowed in the rooms to keep the players from getting the rest they need."

"Aha, so our illustrious trainer is your inside source!"

Ashley's hand flew to her mouth, as if trying too late to stop the words. "Zane, promise me you won't tell anyone, especially not your uncle. Sammy's a friend, and I don't want him to get into trouble."

A roguish grin touched his mouth and his hand swept down the length of her body. "I'm open to bribery. My silence could be arranged. Got any ideas?"

The rising surge of his desire, pressing against her, did indeed stimulate all sorts of interesting ideas, but before she could say anything she heard the telephone ringing.

"Don't answer it," he begged.

"What if it's Ray, telling me Monica wants me to go to Denver?"

"What a dilemma. Okay, you can answer the phone, but keep it short. I want my bribe!" Reluctantly he allowed her to escape from his embrace. Ashley ran into the house and was able to catch the phone on the fifth ring.

"Ashley, I'm glad I caught you," Ray said. "You're not going to believe what happened. The Kings just traded for Steve 'Touchdown' Broczinsky, the top quarterback last year in the CFL. There's a news conference in an hour. I want you to be there."

Zane came up behind her. With one arm around her waist, he snuggled her against him. One touch and there was no question he wanted her, wanted her very much, as he began to rub against the softness of her back. "Ashley, are you there? Did you hear me?" Ray demanded, but the delightful sensations Zane was arousing had stolen her voice.

She closed her eyes a second to regain some control over her emotions. "Yes, Ray," she answered. "I heard you, but I don't know . . ."

His voice dropped conspiratorially. "Are you with your source? Is that why you're hesitating?"

Zane's hand eased between her thighs to find the well of sweetness there, and it was all she could do not to moan at the wonderous ache of pleasure his touch evoked. "Yes, I'm with my source." Her hand covered the receiver as she whispered so only Zane could hear. "Yes, I'm with my source, my source of pleasure."

"Ashley, what's wrong? Your voice sounds so strange. Are you sure you're all right?" Ray asked.

Before she could stop him, Zane's caress became even more exciting as he eased into her, filling the aching void with the touch she craved.

"Ahhhhhh," she murmured, closing her eyes. "Yes, I'm just fine. In fact I feel wonderful. Everything is perfect right now just the way it is."

"Well, if you're sure." Ray sounded doubtful. "You'll be at the stadium in an hour, right?"

As the rhythm of Zane's thrusts increased in tempo Ashley murmured, "I've go to go, Ray. Something's come up that needs my undivided attention."

"Will you be at the interview?" he repeated.

A shiver of sheer delight rippled through her as she confessed, "Yes . . . I'm coming. Good-bye."

CHAPTER EIGHT

An hour later Ashley walked into the interview room at the stadium. A contented smile touched her lips, evidence of Zane's hurried but totally satisfactory lovemaking.

"What in the hell do you look so happy about?" snapped Razor Williams, the unexpectedly deposed quarterback. "I suppose you're here to feast on the carrion, like all the rest of these damn reporters."

She flipped open her notebook. "Would you like me to quote you?"

"Hell no!" he quickly insisted. "The last thing that Clyde Winston will tolerate is a troublemaker. He made it clear at the first meeting we'd better be team players, or else." He paused, considering his words. "Just say that I want the Kings to be a winning team, and if it takes Touchdown Broczinsky to do it, then I'm happy he's here."

From the way he sneered, Ashley knew that this was far from what he was really feeling. But losing the starting job was never pleasant, and she could hardly blame him, so she didn't try to trap him into making some damning statement. He had enough trouble without being given a hatchet job by a reporter.

When she'd finished taking down his quote, Razor tapped the page. "You can also add I'll do my best to beat out Touchdown for the starting job." His unpleasant, cocky grin widened. "Now, baby, since we've got that garbage out of the way, how about talking about the two of us making a pair? I've had my eye on you for quite a while. How about dinner tonight, and then we'll go out to Diamond Head for some stargazing?"

Razor tried to slip his arm around her waist, but she avoided him. "Sorry, but I don't like to mix business and pleasure."

"Too bad. But it's your loss, baby," Razor bragged, strutting off.

Ashley's fingers clenched around her pen. His arrogant attitude was so typical of the football players she'd known, and she hated it. At least Zane didn't act like that . . . or did he?

A frown creased Ashley's forehead as she remembered the way Zane had come slamming into her office the day her first column appeared. And what about last night? He had certainly allowed no protest. Of course, she hadn't resisted, but what would he have done if she had? Would he still have had his way, even if she'd said no? She trembled at the question, and quickly collected her thoughts.

She was being ridiculous. Zane had been both the best and the gentlest lover any woman could ask for, making sure the desire crackled as hot in her as it did in him before completing his conquest. Not the way Butcher used to do, hurrying, taking her whether she was ready or not. Still a tiny doubt about Zane lingered.

She was pulled out of her disturbing reverie when Clyde entered the room. Quickly she hurried toward him, planting herself in front of him. "Mr. Winston, tell me why did you make the trade for

124

Broczinsky when you already have Razor Williams and Micky Jones, two excellent quarterbacks—if your press releases are to be believed."

Clyde looked right through her as if she hadn't even spoken. Without breaking step, he walked around her to the podium.

With his camera in his hand, Jake moved to her side. "If looks could kill, Ash, you'd be dead. Obviously you've gotten under the great Mr. Winston's skin."

"It's not me, it's my columns. I write what other people only dare to think, and he doesn't like it."

As the microphone crackled to life, Jake squeezed her shoulder. "Glad to see you survived Hurricane David. We were worried about you."

"Believe it or not I enjoyed the storm, but you should see the beach in front of my house. It should be declared a disaster area. I even lost that beautiful royal palm by the driveway. It'll take days to clean up."

"Maybe Kakalina and I can help." Jake tossed the suggestion over his shoulder as he hurried toward the front of the room to take some pictures of the new quarterback the Kings had just acquired from the Canadian Football League.

As she jotted down the expected string of glowing superlatives regarding Broczinsky's record, she realized it might be boringly predictable, but at least she had an easy column to write for tomorrow's paper. That meant she had her evening free. Too bad Zane wouldn't be around to enjoy it with her.

Thinking of him brought a warm glow, but that didn't soften her style any as she typed the opening lines of her column: "If Ralph 'Razor' Williams and Micky Jones are as great as the Kings have been telling the fans, why bring in a high-bucks player like Touchdown Broczinsky? This is the question Clyde Winston refused to answer today at the Kings' press conference."

As she drove out of the city, Ashley could see the ugly scars left by Hurricane David, but knowing others were suffering didn't make it any easier to accept the damage done to her own property. She loved her home, and every tree and flower growing around it. As she walked around her house to see what needed to be done, it made her sad to see the white gardenias, now bruised and broken by the pelting rain, and the shreaded hibiscus still clinging bravely to their tattered branches. With a deep sigh of regret, she headed into the house to change into her jeans and get to work.

She worked for hours, stopping only to stretch her muscles, made sore by all the bending. The sun was starting to slide into the sea when she finally stopped. Ashley felt certain sleep would come easily after all the exercise, but it didn't. She tossed restlessly for what seemed an eternity before she finally gave up and went back out into the living room.

For long moments she stood staring at the twin sheepskins still lying in front of the fireplace before she realized what was bothering her. She missed Zane. Just thinking about him warmed her blood. She curled up on the lush wool to remember and dream of the night before. Trailing her fingers through the wool, all the stirrings of that night sprang back to life. She smiled, admitting to herself that his lovemaking really could become addictive, an addiction that could delight . . . or destroy.

Her smile faded. What if she lost Zane? Maybe last night satisfied his desire for her. Maybe he just wanted to defeat her because she'd said no, something she was certain few women did to him. Now that she'd tasted fully of loving, could she live without it? Or would she spend the rest of her life searching and failing to find someone with the power to arouse her to the exquisite heights of passion Zane had?

Her futile round of doubts was interrupted by the ringing telephone. Ashley grabbed the receiver with relief, glad of any excuse to stop the questions.

"Hi, captive, this is your Viking. I know it's the middle of the night there, but I just wanted to hear your voice and tell you how much I miss you."

"Zane! Are you calling from Denver?"

"Yes, love, and it's as cold as you say Green Bay was. I need you beside me in bed here to warm me up. Want me to tell you all the delicious ways I'd enjoy your body if you were here?"

"No," she protested with a laugh. "I'd have to fly there and bail you out of jail for making an obscene phone call. Your uncle never would forgive me if that happened."

"Thinking it over, you're right." He chuckled wickedly. "I'd much rather *show* you all the things I've planned. That would be a hell of a lot more fun for both of us."

Ashley hesitated before asking the question that was in her heart. "I thought maybe after last night and this morning, you'd be tired of me. Particularly when you found out I wasn't as experienced as you probably thought I was."

Zane's voice dropped to a husky rumble. "If I was there I'd prove over and over again how wrong you are. I don't think I could ever tire of holding you, Ashley, of listening to your sweet gasp when I touch you all the places that stir your senses. You intoxicate me. Every time I taste of you I just want to

127

drink more deeply. And as for your naiveté, if anything, it makes you more endearing."

"Zane, you're making me blush, and I'm too old for such nonsense."

"I'd really give you something to blush about if I was there," he teased. Suddenly his tone became serious. "Ashley, think of me tonight and know that I'm missing you and wanting you. Monday, when I can hold you again, kiss you again—make love to you again—seems like an eternity away."

After Ashley hung up the phone, she curled up again on the sheepskins. This time sleep came easily. As she slept she dreamed of blond conquering Vikings, of willing captives . . . of Monday.

The next morning she was rudely jarred awake by the shrill whine of a chain saw. She hastily threw on some clothes and hurried outside.

Kakalina came toward her with a smile. She patted her bulging middle and teased, "I'm in no shape to pick up branches and leaves, but at least I can supervise Jake's work with the chain saw. If I don't watch him he gets carried away with the pruning, and suddenly you have a lot of denuded trees." They watched him reduce the fallen royal palm to a pile of firewood. "Heard any Chopin lately?" Kakalina teased.

Ashley pretended not to hear her over the sound of the saw. After carrying the last stack of wood out to the back, Jake joined them.

"I don't know how to thank you for coming over here before work to help me clean this mess up," Ashley said. "I was afraid I'd have to rent one of those things and cut up the tree myself, and they really scare me." She laughed. "I think it's the sound more than anything else. How about breakfast? That's the least I can do after all your hard work."

"Sounds great!" Jake gave his wife an affectionate hug. "Kakalina isn't up to much cooking these mornings."

Forgetting the sheepskins in front of the fireplace and the candelabrum with its candle stubs, she led them into the house.

One look and Jake let out a low whistle. "No wonder you enjoyed the storm," he teased. "Kakalina, we'll have to remember this idea for when after the baby comes. If we order the sheepskins now, they should arrive right on time."

Ashley's blush rivaled a sunset. "Let me explain. Ah, we didn't . . . I mean—it isn't what you think," she stammered.

"What we think," Kakalina firmly interrupted, "is that it's time you started living and enjoying life again and we're glad. And Jake, if you say another word it'll be the sofa for you tonight."

"Threats, always threats," he joked. "But you know you'd never do it. I'm too irresistible."

Kakalina stood on tiptoe to give him a kiss. "All too true. You are irresistible to me. Must be all those freckles. But I think Ashley likes another type —say about six four, long blond hair, dark blue eyes a shade on the primitive side, shoulders as broad as Hercules'—need I go on?"

Jake's eyes sparkled with mischief. "Hey, that sounds like that new linebacker. What's his name? Ah, yes, Zane Bruxton. No wonder you weren't interested when Ralph the Razor put the make on you at the press conference." He frowned with concern. "But, Ashley, old friend, I would have thought you'd had enough of football players after Butcher. Why are you walking right back into the fire?"

He was absolutely right. Ashley wished she knew why that fire seemed so tempting, but she really didn't want to talk about it, so she merely shrugged. "No comment. What do you want for breakfast?"

The rest of the week seemed to drag by. The columns came easily, and working on the beach cleaning up the debris should have filled the rest of the hours, yet the hands of the clock seemed to crawl. But the nights were the worst, when her body ached with need, longing for the touch of someone several thousand miles away. Only Zane's nightly calls helped to give her some peace.

By Thursday morning she had cleaned up as much of the mess from Hurricane David as she could. With gentle fingers she lifted a lacerated bird of paradise bloom, realizing sadly that only time and Mother Nature could repair the rest.

She stretched to ease her sore muscles, watching the morning surf. She'd been working so hard to clear the sand she'd missed her daily swims. But she had done all she could now, so with a smile Ashley hurried back into the house to slip into one of her many swimsuits.

The sun felt warm on her back as she dived beneath the waves. How beautiful to be at one with nature! In the calmer swells of deep water she swam. Stroke followed stroke as the warm water slowly eased her sore muscles and washed away the tension. Finally totally relaxed, she succumbed to the velvety touch of the water moving over her flesh. It was a touch so reminiscent of Zane's caress that she shuddered.

She headed back to shore to take off her bikini top and toss it onto the sand. She wanted no barrier to keep her from experiencing completely, from remembering deliciously, the feeling of Zane's hands upon her. Then she dived into the surf once more.

One night of love and he had changed her life, made her more boldly sensual, more eager to sample every pleasure life offered. Now every sensation seemed new, as the warm waters of the Pacific caressed her bare skin.

The smile of pleasure was still on her lips when she walked into the *News* an hour later. "Ashley! Boy, am I glad you're here," Ray said, hurrying out of his office to meet her. "I tried to call you but you didn't answer. Where were you?"

"Out swimming. I enjoy swimming while I think. It usually stirs up some really interesting ideas." She smiled. "Today it was especially stimulating." She didn't add the stimulation came from thinking about Zane, not planning her next column.

Noticing her contented smile, he commented, "You look like the kitten who's found the cream pitcher, so you must have come up with one heck of an idea paddling around out there. Anyway, I'm glad you finally got here. I wasn't looking forward to telling Monica I didn't know where our ace columnist was."

"Why is Monica asking about me? Is she planning to send me more flowers, or did she decide to renege on the raise you promised."

"Neither. She wants to take you out to lunch." Ray gave her a thumbs up sign. "You've really made an impression on her, and that isn't easy. She's as hard-nosed as they come. Keep it up and you may end up with my job," he teased, obviously too secure to be really worried. He glanced at his watch. "The limo will pick you up at one. Monica enjoys making an entrance when the restaurant is at its busiest."

Ashley glanced down at her brightly colored skirt and cotton knit sweater. She was dressed more for a luau than lunch at some exclusive restaurant. "I wish I had time to go home and change."

"Well, you don't," Ray insisted, slipping back into his editor role. "I need your column early today, because they're going to shut the power off at four o'clock so they can install a new air conditioner. The paper has to be put to bed no later than three thirty, so get those pretty fingers of yours to the keyboard and start pounding."

Ashley stared at the empty screen for thirty minutes waiting for an idea to come, but her inspiration seemed to have gone out on strike. In exasperation she flipped off the word processor. Maybe she should just settle for one of those sports trivia columns. Opening *The Pro Football Guide*, she started thumbing through the pages. Or maybe there'd be some interesting tidbit about the team that had traded Broczinsky she could hang a story on. Scanning the list of coaches on his last team, one name caught her eye.

Eagerly she grabbed the telephone. Waiting for the Canadian connection to be made, she muttered to herself, "Butcher, you may have been a rat, but at least you introduced me to some great contacts."

She was calling the coach of the team that had just traded Broczinsky, whom she'd met when he'd been Butcher's coach with the Chiefs. As soon as he came on the line, she asked, "I'm curious about why you traded Broczinsky. His stats are impressive."

Her smile widened and her pencil flew faster and faster, and before she even hung up the phone she'd composed her column. After thanking him profusely and promising to send him a case of fresh Hawaiian pineapples, she turned on her word processor to write her opening sentences: "According to sources on the Kings' new megabuck quarterback's last team, Steve 'Touchdown' Broczinsky should instead be called Steve 'Troublemaker' Broczinsky. Mr. Winston, you may have bought more than you bargained for with this jock."

At ten minutes of one she dropped the completed column on Ray's desk. After a quick dash to the lounge to check on her hair and makeup, Ashley walked out of the building. Her timing was perfect. She stepped out onto the sidewalk just as a long, sleek, silver Cadillac limousine slid to a stop in front of her. She made a move to open the rear door, but the scowl from the uniformed chauffeur stopped her. Clearly, that was his job.

The chauffeur tipped his hat to her. "Ms. Bennet had a meeting with her accountant at the marina and has asked me to escort you to the yacht club, where she'll meet you for lunch." After settling into the driver's seat, he inquired, "Would you care for a glass of wine?"

Amused, and sure he wanted to show off one of the car's gadgets, she nodded. "That would be delightful."

"No doubt at the yacht club you shall have fish. I'm sure you would not wish to ruin your palate for that, so I believe white wine would be in order."

He turned back to the instrument panel and pressed several buttons. A silver tray slid out with a glass of perfectly chilled chablis on it. As she leaned back against the glove-soft white leather seat and took a sip of the delicious wine, she decided the life of the privileged had its advantages.

The marina was so beautiful with the forest of colorful sails bobbing on the water that Ashley's steps lagged. The chauffeur saw her slow down. "Ms. Bennett is waiting," he quickly reminded her. But he unbent enough to add, "And waiting is something she doesn't like to do. So I would suggest you hurry, miss, if you wish to enjoy your lunch with your hide intact."

Monica was seated at a small linen-covered table by the windows. With an imperious flick of her wrist she summoned the younger woman. Nervous butterflies fluttered in Ashley's stomach as she walked across the room. It felt more like she was having an audience with a queen than lunch with her boss.

The sunlight streaming through the windows and glinting off the multitude of Monica's diamonds almost blinded Ashley as she took the chair opposite her. "I've ordered shrimp scampi for us. It's the only dish the chef here can prepare decently," Monica informed her gesturing for the wine steward.

Ashley raised her eyebrows at the high-handed treatment, but didn't protest. "Shrimp scampi's fine. It's one of my favorite dishes."

To her surprise, Monica's glacial facade cracked a tiny bit, and she said confidingly, "I love it too, but I hope your boyfriend won't mind the garlic. Jonathan never would let me kiss him after I'd eaten scampi." She turned to the sommelier and ordered him to bring a bottle of their finest French champagne.

"Is Jonathan your husband?" Ashley asked after he'd bowed away.

"Was. I'm a widow. He was one of the largest real estate developers in the islands. Suffice to say he left me well provided for when he died five years ago."

Something in the quality of Monica's voice when

she mentioned her husband told Ashley she'd loved his money more than she had him, but she still murmured the expected "I know you must miss him."

"I have the *News* and my investments. They help fill the time." Luckily the champagne arrived before Ashley had to respond to this rather cold statement.

The older woman raised her glass to Ashley. "This is my celebration and you're responsible," she toasted her rather mysteriously, and downed the wine.

"Mind if I ask what I did before I drink to that?" Ashley asked with a laugh.

"The morning after your column ran on the acquisition of Broczinsky, my accountant came to me with a very lucrative offer from an unnamed source who wants to buy the *News*."

Somewhat confused, Ashley said, "I'm delighted you're going to turn a nice profit on your investment, but I still don't see how I—"

"I have no intention of selling, no matter how much I'm offered," scoffed Monica. "I don't need any more money. I do need the *News*. It suits my purposes perfectly."

Ashley waited until after the scampi was served and Monica's glass was refilled before trying to unravel the mystery. "I must be a little dense, but if you're not selling the *News*, what are you celebrating? And why am I responsible?"

"When this unexpected offer arrived, my accountant did a little checking. It seems the mysterious buyer was Clyde Winston."

Ashley's eyebrows rose in surprise. "Clyde Winston wanted to buy you out? I don't understand. Why would he want the *News*?"

For the first time Monica smiled, a curious mixture of delight and spite. "Because of you. He wanted to buy the *News* so he could shut you up." She saluted Ashley with her champagne glass. "Your columns are hitting him where it hurts most —right in his ego!" She took a drink of champagne. "What's your column on today?" she asked.

Ashley told her what she'd learned from Butcher's ex-coach, and Monica applauded. "Wonderful! Keep those hell-burners coming! Clyde deserves everything you can throw at him, and more." She snapped her fingers and raised her voice, "Waiter!"

Ashley studied Monica over the rim of her champagne glass as they waited for the waiter to hurry over. She'd heard the thirst for vengeance coloring every word Monica spoke. She'd apparently landed in the middle of something a lot more serious than a business rivalry. Unless her investigative instincts were very wrong, and she didn't think they were, it had to be something personal between Clyde and Monica to evoke that kind of passionate response from her boss. But before Ashley could ask another question the waiter arrived.

Without consulting her, Monica said, "We'll have raspberry sorbet for dessert, and tell the sommelier to bring another bottle of champagne. And inform him this time to make sure it's properly chilled. Tell him not to uncork it until I've tested the temperature." She emptied her glass with one gulp. "This was at least five degrees too warm!"

The waiter refilled her glass before leaving, and again Monica drank deeply, clearly determined to enjoy fully what she considered to be a victory over Clyde.

When she put the empty glass down, Ashley spoke. "You sound like you know the owner of the Kings very well."

"I ought to. I used to work for him."

Ashley probed gently, "While you were married?"

"Hardly! Jonathan would never have allowed such a thing. He was the original chauvinist!" Maybe it was the champagne speaking. Ashley sensed Monica wouldn't be this open if she were drinking coffee. "No, dear," Monica continued, "Clyde and I go back a long, long way. I was his executive assistant before either of us married." Her voice hardened. "And before dear Clyde managed to turn himself into the almighty macadamia nut king of Hawaii. In the days I knew him he was exporting pineapple, island crafts, that sort of trash."

Ashley hesitated, trying to understand the strange combination of anger and sadness she heard in Monica's voice when she spoke of Clyde.

"I take it you didn't part on good terms," she ventured carefully.

Suddenly, as if Monica realized how much of her soul she was letting Ashley glimpse, her glance became icy again. "I have an appointment this afternoon. I hope you don't mind going home in a taxi. Put it on your expense account." She pushed back her chair. "When the champagne comes take it home with you. You've earned it."

Without waiting for the dessert to arrive Monica rose and walked regally out of the yacht club, leaving a very confused Ashley behind.

CHAPTER NINE

On Sunday, Ashley paced nervously as game time approached. Would Zane play as well as he had the week before, or would he have another terrible game like the first? She twisted her hands as she crossed the living room for the tenth time. She'd never been this uptight for one of Butcher's games. What was the matter with her?

Suddenly she stopped dead in the middle of the room as the realization hit. She was nervous because she cared for Zane. He'd very quickly become an incredibly important part of her life. Maybe it was because he seemed open, willing to let her be part of his life, something Butcher never really did. Butcher liked to keep things in compartments. His buddies, his teammates, were just as important to him as she was. No, that wasn't right. Being honest with herself, she admitted they'd been more important.

Thinking back over what Zane had said about Butcher's insecurity, she saw her marriage more clearly. To Butcher, his wife was an ornament to be dangled on his arm at press functions, but when he really wanted to relax or have fun he called one of the guys from the team. Zane wasn't like that. Somehow she sensed if he ever gave his love it would be to someone he wanted to share his life with totally. The joys, the sorrows . . . everything. Somewhere in her heart she knew that's what attracted her to him. He didn't shut her out. Her face flamed as she remembered their night of love. He made her feel what he was feeling. Was that what was happening now? Was he as nervous about the game with the Denver Broncos, as she was?

She glanced at the clock. One hour to kickoff, and it felt like a flock of butterflies were doing a tap dance in her stomach. Sitting through the game feeling like that would be pure hell. Before she even realized she'd reached a decision, she found herself dialing Jake's number.

Kakalina answered. "I've got the popcorn and the cold beer," Ashley said without saying hello. "Why don't you bring Jake and Jake Jr. over to watch the game?"

"Nervous about how Zane will do, huh?"

"Kakalina, you Hawaiians of royal lineage have claimed many things, but never that you were psychic, so put your crystal ball away and get over here. Please." Ashley's voice grew low. "I really don't want to sit through this alone," she admitted.

Kakalina laughed knowingly. "We're on our way. I hope you've got plenty of beer. Jake's insufferable if the brew runs out before the final whistle," she confessed.

They walked in during the opening kickoff. The Kings won the toss and elected to receive. During the first series of downs Ashley saw why Clyde had paid top dollar for Broczinsky, as he lofted a pass sixty yards into the end zone to the wide receiver.

When the defensive team took the field and huddled, Kakalina sighed. "I sure can see why Zane inspired sheepskins and candles. I love the way his blond hair curls out from under his helmet. It's

139

really sexy. And I haven't even mentioned how great he looks in those skintight pants."

"Hey, I thought you loved freckled-faced red-heads," Jake complained.

Kakalina ran her hand over the baby soon to be and smiled, "I do, but I can see why Ashley might prefer another type." Noticing Ashley's uneasy frown, she heaved herself, with effort, out of the easy chair. "Come on, the popcorn's running low. Let's leave Jake to his game and head for the kitchen."

Once the door swung shut behind them she demanded, "Okay, friend, what's the matter? Why does watching Zane play bring a frown instead of a smile? Good heavens, child, he's one gorgeous hunk!"

Ashley stared at the linoleum, trying to sort out her feelings. "I know you and Jake went through some rough times before you married. Your family didn't approve. There were other pressures. You must have had doubts, a hundred questions to pester you. Knowing there were problems ahead, how in the world did you ever decide this was the man you wanted to spend the rest of your life with?"

"You're right, there were many problems," Kakalina admitted. "But we made it." She laughed, patting her bulging middle again. "In more ways than one!"

Ashley didn't join in the joke. "This is going to sound strange coming from someone as old as I am," she continued "but how did you know it was love? How did you know what you felt was real"—she swallowed—"and lasting?"

Kakalina's face sobered. She spoke simply, from her own experience. "He must feel it too, the need to be one, that what you feel for each other is your destiny. Then, for yourself, you'll know it's right when the love becomes more important than the doubts. It's that simple . . . it's that complicated."

Ashley smiled sadly. "All I see right now is the complicated part. There's nothing simple about Zane and me."

Kakalina laughed. "Well, if I can't solve your love life at least I can appease my husband. Where's the popcorn?"

By halftime most of the butterflies had settled. Zane was having a great game, and Ashley's smile was firmly back in place. Still the score was tied. After giving Jake an ice cold beer and refilling the popcorn bowl for the third time they settled down for the third quarter.

Somehow, when Zane was on the field the game slipped out of perspective. Ashley found her gaze riveted to him in the huddle. She had to admit Kakalina was right, he did look great from that angle! Then when play started she didn't notice the offensive action, only his reaction to it. Each time his shoulder pads crashed into one of the Broncos she felt the blow. Each time he sacked the quarterback for a loss, she felt the surge of exhilaration. It was as if they were one, even thousands of miles apart.

She was so wrapped up in her own emotional involvement with the game she hardly noticed Kakalina or Jake until Kakalina gave an angry shout of scorn at an erring referee.

Jake grinned. "Sorry about that. My island beauty here may look calm, cool, and collected, yet under that facade she's a volcano. She can't watch a game and not get involved. She's convinced the referees steal more games than the opponents win."

"Well, they do!" Kakalina insisted hotly. "Everyone knows that. Ashley, you should write a column on the refereeing in the NFL. It's a disgrace!"

"Only when it goes against the team you're rooting for," Jake teased.

"Oh be quiet!" Kakalina ordered, but she smiled, putting her hand against the small of her back to ease the burden.

Late in the fourth quarter, the Kings were trailing by six. With less than thirty seconds left Broczinsky lofted a "Hail Mary" pass toward the end zone. It seemed to float forever, but finally the Kings receiver, in the middle of four defenders, somehow miraculously came down with the ball to tie the score.

Kakalina leapt to her feet in excitement, but froze at once, a startled, wondrous look on her face. Jake's eyes were still riveted to the screen, but Ashley knew just what was happening. "Jake, it's time," she said.

"Shh, they're about to kick the extra point."

Ashley raised her voice. "Jake, it's *time!* Now!"

He turned, perplexed. "What do you . . . Oh my God!" he erupted, catching sight of his tottering wife.

"Ashley, call the police. Call the fire department. Call an ambulance."

Kakalina took a deep breath, trying to relax as the pain of the contraction ebbed. "Jake, you remember our training. This is our first baby. We've got lots of time." Noting her husband's unusual paleness, she suggested, "Ashley I think you'd better come with us."

One look at Jake and Ashley grabbed her purse.

"But you've got your column to write," Jake protested, frantically hunting through his pockets for his keys.

"I'll work on it at the hospital. Besides, some things are more important than deadlines. Ray will understand. And if he protests, I'd just remind him I had lunch with the boss Thursday." She winked. "He won't give me any trouble. Just let me grab a notebook."

"There isn't time!" Jake yelled. "You can get some paper at the hospital." He heard Kakalina gasp as another contraction began. "We've got to go!"

They hurried out of the house, Jake fuming. "Why do you have to live way to hell and gone out here? It'll take hours to get to the hospital."

It took them twenty minutes. As Jake carefully guided Kakalina inside Ashley said a silent prayer of thanks no traffic cop had seen them. Jake's speeding ticket would have rivaled the national debt.

They got Kakalina settled in the labor room and Ashley left Jake pacing and fuming while he waited for the doctor and went to call Ray.

"Look Ashley, baby or no baby, we've got to have your column," he sputtered, after hearing her explanation. "Monica will have my head and yours if you skip a day."

"Calm down. I didn't say I wasn't going to do it. I'll just write it here and you can send one of the office boys over to pick it up. Then all you'll have to do is have someone type it up on the word processor."

"All right," he grumbled, "I guess we can do it that way. But let me tell you, I wouldn't do this for just anyone."

Ashley laughed, knowing Ray's thinking. "Yeah, I know. You'd only do it for someone Monica invites out to lunch."

"Wish Jake good luck with the kid. And tell him I

want him in by nine tomorrow so he can cover the surfing competition out at the Bonsai Pipeline."

"You're all heart, Ray," Ashley teased. "I'll give him the message."

Ashley returned to the pacing Jake. "Thank God the doctor finally got here," he said fervently. "He's in with Kakalina now."

"Jake, it's going to be a long wait. Why don't you sit down and rest? You can't help Kakalina if you pace yourself into exhaustion."

She started toward the nurses' station, but he grabbed her arm. "Where are you going?" he demanded. "I want you here in case Kakalina asks for you."

Ashley laughed. "It's a good thing Kakalina is having this baby and not you. You're such a nervous wreck I don't think you'd make it. I'm just going to ask the nurse if she has some paper. Remember, you wouldn't let me get my notebook and I've got a column to write."

Jake dropped his hand. "Sorry, Ashley. I'm acting like an idiot."

"Don't worry about it. All expectant fathers do."

As she approached the nurses' station, the nurse on duty glanced up from her charts. "Hey, I know you. You're Ashley Buchannan," she observed with an eager smile. "Your columns are great. My husband raved about them, so I started reading them and now I'm really hooked." The nurse held out a prescription pad to her. "Can I have your autograph?"

"You know, this is the first time anyone's asked me that," Ashley admitted as she signed the pad. "If you want to read tomorrow's column," she said, handing it back, "I'll have to ask you a favor. I've got a friend in labor, and we were in such a hurry to get her here I didn't have time to grab my notebook. Do you suppose I could borrow some paper?"

The nurse searched through the things on the desk, and handed Ashley a stack of paper. "These patient admittance forms are all I can find. You could use the backs. Will they do?" she asked, a little embarrassed.

"They'll be perfect. Thank you."

"Care to give me a hint about what tomorrow's column's going to be on?"

Ashley smiled. "Let's just say I'm going to right a wrong. Thanks again for the paper."

When she returned to the waiting room Jake wasn't there. She decided they must have let him in to see Kakalina, and pulling a table over in front of her chair, Ashley got to work. "Isn't Nepotism a wonderful thing?" she wrote. "Without it the Kings might not have Zane Bruxton, who had an excellent game against the Denver Broncos." She went on to describe Zane's play. A happy smile touched her mouth as she wrote about the man who more and more filled her thoughts.

When Jake finally came out of the labor room, Ashley took one look at his ashen face and hurried to him. "What's wrong? Is it Kakalina? The baby? What's happened?"

"It's going to be a long night. The baby's breeched."

Ashley let out a long sigh of relief. "Jake, you really frightened me. A breech delivery is difficult, but usually not dangerous. I thought it was something terrible."

The waiting seemed interminable, but it was worth it. At four o'clock in the morning she stood by Jake and watched the nurse roll an incubator containing a little red-headed baby boy over to the window for them to see.

"Isn't that the most beautiful baby you've ever seen?" Jake grinned happily. "I hope Kakalina's parents don't mind that he doesn't have black hair," he added, his grin suddenly turning into a frown.

"One look and he'll steal their hearts, don't worry. Speaking of her parents, you'd better go call them. Even if it is four in the morning, I know they won't mind being awakened by this good news."

He hurried off, and her gaze returned to the tiny baby. Suddenly tears blurred her eyes and her arms ached with emptiness. Would she ever experience the joy of holding her child in her arms? Damn Butcher and his "wait until next year." Then with a determined sniffle, she pushed the angry thoughts away. She'd done enough crying over the past.

She looked at the sleeping child once more, her tears drying, and suddenly she saw another baby lying there, one with a halo of blond hair. She smiled. What would it be like to hold Zane's child in her arms?

Deliberately she stifled the desire. That was really rushing things! They'd only had one night of love and already she was thinking of having his baby. Was it a baby she wanted, or *Zane's* baby? The question disturbed her. She wondered if the yearning to hold his child signaled the first stirring of love, a love surrounded by so many problems she was afraid it could only end in heartbreak. Her heart had been broken once, and she never wanted to live through that kind of hell again. Be careful, guard your heart, a warning voice whispered. Yet even as the warning echoed in her mind, the memory of how Zane had looked rising from the whirlpool bath made it hard for her to hear.

When Jake rejoined her, his huge grin told her Kakalina's parents were delighted with the news they were now grandparents. "The nurse told me visiting hours don't start until ten," he explained. "Why don't you let me take you home so you can get some sleep?"

"What about you?"

"I'm too excited to sleep. Besides, I've got important stuff to do. I've got to go find some cigars. Then I'm going to buy the biggest bouquet of orchids in Hawaii for my wife."

Ashley let herself in to her house. She stood in front of her closet for a moment, and realized suddenly she was too keyed up to sleep, so she pulled out a swimsuit instead of her nightgown, hoping a long swim would help her unwind and let her get some rest.

On her way out of the room, she caught a glimpse of herself in the mirror. She made a face at her reflection, noting how faded the bikini was. No one was going to see her, she thought, shrugging, so it didn't matter if the suit was old.

The first rays of dawn were streaking the tropical sky in luscious shades of rose when she dived through a cresting wave and started swimming out into deeper water. She'd taken only a few strokes when something closed around her ankle like a vise.

With a startled shriek, she tried frantically to jerk her foot away, terrifying visions of great white sharks flashing through her mind. As she flailed about in the water, a strong arm suddenly slipped around her waist, pulling her back against the warmth of a man's body.

Ashley whipped her head around to meet Zane's laughing eyes. "You almost gave me heart failure! Didn't you see *Jaws?*"

147

"Sure, but don't worry, I'll protect you. I promise, if anyone devours you, it'll be me and not some shark."

Side by side they swam back to shore. Zane faced her as they stood up in the shallow water, his smile gone. "Ashley, where were you last night? I wanted to see you. I wanted to be with you. I tried calling as soon as the plane landed, but you weren't home. I tried all night and when I still didn't get an answer, I was afraid something had happened to you. I decided I'd better get out here and see if you were all right. Where were you?" he repeated.

Ashley looked at him, mischief sparkling in her gray eyes. "If you really want to know, I spent the night with another man."

"You did what!" Zane thundered. "Damn it! Who is it? I'll kill him!"

"Well, to be honest, actually there were two."

"Two!"

She nodded, delicately patting back a yawn. "It was an exhausting night. You see, the first man introduced me to this second guy. Then he had to leave so I stayed with the other fellow for a while. He was an adorable redhead," she teased, enjoying the jealous fire darkening his blue eyes.

His hands knotted into fists. "Ashley, how could you?"

The betrayal she saw in his eyes made her feel guilty. Needing to see his smile return, she confessed, "Zane, I'm teasing you. I did spend the night with two men, but it's not what you think. I invited Jake and Kakalina over to watch the game, and Kakalina went into labor, so I went with them to the hospital. She had trouble with the delivery. In fact their baby, the adorable redhead I mentioned, wasn't born until about four this morning."

Zane roughly yanked her into his arms. As he buried his face in her damp hair, he muttered, "God, I can't believe how much it hurt—thinking of you in another man's arms, thinking of him touching you, making love to you. You're going to pay for teasing me like that."

Ashley's hands stroked his body, slipping beneath the tight nylon of his briefs. As her caress aroused his immediate response, she murmured, "Maybe I could think of a way to apologize."

"I can think of a dozen ways and you're going to do every one of them, starting right now!" Zane challenged. Before she could protest, he undid her bikini top and tossed it into an oncoming wave.

"I'm not going to have any clothes left if you keep . . ." Her words faded into a pleasurable *ahhhh* as his mouth descended to capture her nipple, his tongue stroking the sensitive tip until her breast ached sweetly.

"We can't discriminate," he whispered, deserting one breast to tease the other with identical velvety rasps. His teeth, pulling gently, drew a moan from her, and she arched her back, needing more intimate contact with him.

His hips moving with hers sent delicious shivers up her spine. The thin nylon of their suits, allowing them to feel but not really to touch, prolonged the arousal, building tension, stimulating wonderfully warm sensations until her whole body throbbed with delicious need.

She sighed with regret when his mouth left her. His eyes burned hotly. "Weren't you the one who wanted to go skinny-dipping?" he reminded her. "How about now?" His hands slid in one long caress down the length of her body until he reached her bikini bottom. As he tugged it slowly down her

149

legs he urged, "Ashley, touch me. I want to feel your hands on me."

Not needing to be told twice, she stripped his trunks away. Tossing them casually into the surf, she snuggled against him with a satisfied sigh, knowing soon she'd be his again. Moments passed as they stood locked together, body rubbing body. His hard muscles against the soft lushness of her skin, the hair curling across his chest tickling her breasts, teasing them as he brushed his chest against her, the ancient rhythm ignited a desire that burned too hot to deny.

"Ashley, wrap your legs around me." The husky yearning in his voice transformed the order into a plea. "Let the sea be your bed. I wanted to take you on the sheepskins like the first time I made you mine, but I can't wait. I want you now! Right now!"

She eagerly complied, whispering, "I can't wait either."

His strong embrace cradled her as she wrapped herself around him, and as he'd told her to, she lay back, letting the ocean support her. Time after time he drove into her, and with each thrust the embrace of her legs tightened, pulling him deeper and deeper into her body until it felt like he was reaching into her soul.

Over and over, faster and faster—almost desperately, as if he could not get enough of her loving, Zane moved within her. The warm water seemed to seal them into a primeval world where sensation ruled, as together they soared to one shuddering climax after another.

Finally spent, he cradled her against his chest. Ashley let him lift her into his arms and carry her out of the water, not sure her legs would support her. Completely sated, her eyes closed, her head sank onto his chest, and she heard the beating of his heart as he carried her naked into the house.

"You see I am a man of my word," he murmured, as the door swung shut.

Slowly Ashley's eyes fluttered open. "I don't believe it," she gasped with a laugh. Muumuus were scattered all over the living room.

Zane bent his head to give her a lingering kiss. "I promised to buy you a new one when I ripped that other muumuu from your gorgeous body," he explained. "This is planning ahead. What man wouldn't want a dozen nights of R and R with you? I'm just providing the props. Now, where are those sheepskins?" he asked, setting her on her feet.

"Zane, you're insatiable."

His hands stroked her body as if to memorize every curve. "Ashley, I don't think I could ever get enough of loving you." He went to the sofa. "Now, let's get those sheepskins. I've fantasized about this for days. Now I want the real thing."

"But, Zane," she protested with a shaky laugh, "haven't you had enough? I don't think I can—"

The fiery glimmer in his eye stopped her words. In two strides he was in front of her. "Is that a challenge, my sweet captive? Do you think I can't make you want me again—and again, and again—as I want you? I burn for you, Ashley. You will feel that heat too, until the fire's so hot within you you'll beg to be taken."

He reached for her, and she came willingly. As he led her to the sheepskins tossed in front of the fireplace, she admitted, "One apology made, but as I recall I do owe you eleven more. How would you like me to make apology number two?"

His proud laugh told her the answer, and as he'd

warned he made her beg before giving himself to her for her pleasure.

The lesson in loving was sweet, but all too soon reality intruded. Neither had slept the night before, and they'd drifted off to sleep, exhausted, after she'd made apology number three. It was almost noon when the shrill ring of the telephone jarred them awake.

"Ashley, this is Ray," he greeted her groggy hello. "I know you were up all night with Jake and Jake Jr., but I still need your column. What time will you be in?"

"Slave driver," she muttered under her breath. "Ray, I haven't forgotten you or the *News*. I'll be in within the hour. And, yes, you'll have your precious column on your desk by five."

Zane, propped up on his elbow, watched her as she hung up the phone. "You could have told him two hours." He sighed. "But there's always tonight after the party," he added, brightening.

"What party?" Ashley yawned. "Right now the way I feel, there's nothing I want more than to turn in my column and go to bed."

"My idea exactly!" he chuckled, rising. "But we have to squeeze in a party before I can slip into your bed, pull you against me, and start—"

She held up her hand with a laugh. "Yes, I know, start my apology number four. Or your R and R scene number three. What's the next one to be?"

"I'll surprise you."

"Hmm, sounds interesting." She stretched to ease her tired back. "What party?" she asked.

Zane looked down at the carpet, avoiding her eyes. He scraped his toe through the nap. "My uncle's throwing a bash to celebrate the Kings first win. I've got to be there," he admitted.

"Well I don't! In case you haven't noticed, I'm not your uncle's favorite columnist. He'd probably take one look and throw me to the guard dogs! Chihuahuas I love, but I never have liked Dobermans. I think I'll pass."

"Ashley, it's important to me. I want you at my side when I walk in that door. I want to show the whole world you belong to me."

What a complex man! One minute the conquering Viking, carrying her off, making her do and feel things she'd never experienced before, and now he looked like a kid about to lose his favorite marble.

With a smile, Ashley went to him. As she ran her hands across his broad chest she murmured, "You seem big and strong enough to protect me. What time's the party?"

"At eight. Wear something sexy, okay?" His glance raked over her nude body. "Of course, the most expensive gown in the world couldn't improve what I see now." He shook his head. "Next time tell Ray you'll be there in two hours." He patted her bare bottom. "Okay?"

CHAPTER TEN

Ashley hesitated at the front door of Clyde Winston's mansion. "Are you sure this is a good idea?"

Zane gave her waist a reassuring squeeze. "Don't worry, Clyde won't bite you." He winked. "I'm the only one who does that."

"Yes, I remember." She laughed, realling the once-bitten-twice-shy episode on the beach.

She took a deep steadying breath. "Okay, let's go. Just remember, you promised to protect me if he decides to toss me to the dogs."

The instant they walked in Clyde erupted. Leveling a shaking finger at her he roared, "Get out!"

"Is that any way to treat one of your guests, Uncle Clyde?"

"Damn it, Zane, do you know who that woman is?"

His angry outburst drew a curious crowd. Noticing Razor and a couple of the other players drifting over to enjoy the altercation, Zane lowered his voice. "Yes, of course I know who she is. If you insist on discussing this, don't you think we should go someplace a little more private?" Zane suggested.

"You're right." Clyde's eyes narrowed to two furious slits. "Follow me, but keep your keys handy. You're not going to be here long."

He spun on his heel and stomped off, heading for the library.

The instant the heavy carved door swung shut Clyde exploded again. "You must be crazy to bring this woman here! You know how I feel about her damn columns! And if that's not bad enough, are you forgetting what she wrote about you? Furthermore, I told all the papers no reporters were allowed at this victory party!"

Zane refused to budge. "Ashley is not here as a reporter. She's here as my date and she's not leaving."

Clyde angrily tossed his head. "Date or not, I won't have Monica Bennett's paid assassin in my house!"

"Ashley isn't—"

"Zane, let me handle this," Ashley interrupted, speaking for the first time. "Mr. Winston, I am a columnist. I get paid for writing what I think. I don't call that being an assassin, and I resent you doing so."

"Don't try to fool me. I know Monica, and she likes nothing better than to stab me in the back. She's just using you to do it."

"No matter what you think, Mr. Winston, I was not hired to slander your football team."

She might as well not even have spoken. "It's just like Monica to hire someone like you," Clyde raged on. "She knew how I'd feel, having a woman invade my locker room."

"Sex has nothing to do with it. That's not the reason I got this assignment," Ashley protested. "When Monica decided at the last moment that she wanted a columnist covering the Kings, I was the logical choice. I'd been asking for a change from the life-style section. I also had a lot of knowledge

155

about football. And since I'd been married to a professional player, I had the contacts."

"I'd been wondering where you were getting all that inside dope," Clyde snapped, staring daggers at Zane. "Now I know. Great! Along with Monica, I'm being stabbed in the back by my own nephew!"

"Zane is not my source. He has never given me one story idea," Ashley insisted.

"I don't believe you! Is she repaying your tips in the bedroom? Is that why you're doing this to me, Zane?" Clyde demanded.

Zane's fist clenched. "Even if you are my uncle, one more innuendo like that and I swear, I'll deck you!"

Quickly Ashley stepped between the two men. "I don't want you quarreling over this. Mr. Winston, I repeat: Zane is not my source." His suspicious glare remained. "Think about it," she continued. "There is no way Zane could have known about that ex-F.B.I. guy you hired."

"Yeah," Zane added. "And I was out on the practice field with the defensive unit when Razor and Micky started mixing it up. I didn't even know about the fight until I read about it in Ashley's column the next day. If you don't believe me, ask Coach Mitchell."

Their assertions forced a grudging apology from Clyde. "I'm sorry I jumped to the wrong conclusion, Zane. But that doesn't change anything. This woman's been writing a lot of trash about my football team and I don't want her in my house!"

"I don't write trash," Ashley retorted, keeping her voice level only with great effort. "I write facts."

Clyde threw up his hands. "If you call that drivel you've been printing facts, then I'll—"

"Mr. Winston, before you make any rash statements you'll regret, I have one question for you," Ashley said briskly, interrupting his tirade. "If you can tell me one fact I had wrong or one story that wasn't true, I'll print a retraction and a personal apology tomorrow."

When Clyde remained silent she pressed her advantage. "I know my hard-hitting stories bruise your ego, but except for that, I honestly don't think you have any other legitimate complaint concerning them, do you?"

"Come on, Uncle, admit it. Ashley's right. Heck, even about me. In that first game I was terrible!"

There was a tiny twitch at the corner of Clyde's mouth almost as if he was fighting a smile. The smile won. With grudging respect in his eyes he confessed, "Young lady, it isn't often I have to admit I'm wrong, but I was wrong to attack you. Maybe I let my ego get in the way of my good judgment. Or maybe I was just being overprotective of my investment. I've sunk a lot of money in the Kings. But though I may not like what you write, I have to admit, you do get your facts straight."

"Thank you." Ashley nodded. "By the way, don't worry. There won't be a column written about our discussion tonight. It's strictly off the record."

"Good. I'd hate to give Monica the satisfaction of knowing I had to back down. She'd be laughing for a week!" Clyde muttered. "By the way, your column today was the first one I enjoyed." He patted his nephew on the back. "You deserved it."

"Deserved what?" he asked. He grinned at Ashley. "For some reason I didn't have time to read it."

"She really sang your praises, but I'll let her tell you about it. I'd better get back to my guests."

Clyde stopped at the door. "Needless to say you are welcome to stay Ms. Buchannan." He glanced back at his nephew. "Zane, I've got to admit you've got great taste. There aren't many women who can talk me into a corner. She's both beautiful and bright. You're a lucky man," he added in a strangely wistful voice.

Zane slipped his arm around Ashley's waist and nestled her beside him. "That's exactly what I've been telling her, but she's a little hard to convince," he remarked.

Clyde smiled sadly. "If you feel that way, then don't let such a woman get away," he advised mysteriously. "You may spend the rest of your life regretting the mistake."

The door closed behind him, and Ashley wanted to question Zane about his uncle's strange statement, but before she could Zane asked, "Did you write another column about me?"

Ashley allowed herself to be sidetracked. "I had to," she answered happily. "I couldn't let your great game go unnoticed. You can read it tonight if you want to see all the wonderful things I said about you."

He grinned with pleasure but shook his head. "Nope, tonight I have more important things to do than read about myself. Tonight I plan to think of some ways to thank you for what you did."

Ashley patted his chest. "Somehow I don't think you'll have much trouble."

He drew her more tightly against him. "We're all alone. The walls are thick. There's a sofa over there. I could start thanking you right now."

She smiled, shaking her head. "I'd rather talk."

Zane heaved an exaggerated sigh. "Bored with my lovemaking already. I guess I'll have to be more creative. I'll have to think of some new ways to love you to recapture your interest."

Ashley blushed. "Zane I don't think there are any ways you haven't tried already. We've done things that aren't even in *The Joy of Sex.*"

"Are you complaining? You're so damn desirable I want you every way I can have you."

She wound her arms around his neck. "I'm a big girl. I could always have said no." She kissed him softly on the mouth. "I love how you make love to me. I love how you make me feel. I love how you touch the wild part of my soul—a part I never even knew I had before."

"Hmm, I like the sound of those words." He kissed her slowly, deeply, yet with a gentleness that touched her heart.

Long delicious minutes later, he murmured, "Sure you want to talk? That sofa looks awfully lonely over there. I know it would like some company."

She smiled. "A lonely sofa is one of the saddest things in the world. Let's go make it feel wanted."

"That's not the only thing that's wanted," he whispered, taking her hand and leading her across the room.

He had just unbuttoned the first two buttons of her silk dress to slip his hand inside when someone knocked on the door.

"Damn!" he muttered under his breath.

"Maybe they'll go away," she whispered.

The knock came again, louder this time, and the butler's voice called through the door, "Mr. Bruxton, Ms. Buchannan, Mr. Winston requested I ask you to join him. He wishes to make a toast to the Kings and he wants everyone there."

"We'll be there in a second," Zane answered.

"Very good, Sir. I shall tell Mr. Winston you will join him presently."

159

Ashley started to button her dress, but Zane brushed her hand away. He opened the silk fabric, leaned nearer, and whispered against the softness of her breasts, "See you two later." Then he buttoned it for her.

"Zane, you're incorrigible!" Ashley laughed. "Come on, we'd better go before Clyde sends a search party after us."

After they finished the round of toasts to the Kings first victory, they took their refilled champagne glasses out onto the moonlit terrace. Below Clyde's mountaintop mansion sprawled the lights of Honolulu.

"I'd rather go back to the sofa, but we'd probably just be interrupted again, so we might as well talk. What did you want to talk about?"

"Your uncle and my boss. Didn't you notice how Clyde acted? There's something going on between them and I've ended up in the middle. Have you any idea why they each explode at the mention of the other's name?" Ashley asked. "I'd really like to know. It might keep me out of trouble."

Zane was silent a moment as he stared down at the twinkling lights below. He glanced around to make sure they were alone. "Sure you want to hear this?" he asked. "It's not a pretty story."

"Somehow I didn't expect it would be. There's too much anger, too much hostility between them for that. Monica said they went back a long way," Ashley prompted.

Zane nodded. "Twenty years, to be exact. The only reason I know the truth is that I overheard my parents talking about it when we came over here for Beatrice's funeral."

"Beatrice?"

"She was Clyde's wife. She died several years

ago. Anyway, Dad commented that Clyde didn't seem terribly broken up by Beatrice's death. Mom very calmly asked why he should be, when he'd never loved her. Then she went on to tell Dad about Clyde, Beatrice, and Monica. I don't know why she hadn't told him the truth about her brother before. Maybe she kept the secret to protect Clyde."

"Monica said she used to work for Clyde, as his executive assistant."

"She was a whole lot more than that. She was also his lover," Zane explained. "From what Mom said I gathered they really were in love. But there was something Uncle Clyde loved more than Monica, and that was money. Apparently Monica expected they'd marry eventually, but when Clyde stood in front of the preacher to say 'I do,' it was to Beatrice, not your boss."

"You don't have to spell it out. Beatrice was wealthy and Monica wasn't," Ashley observed with a frown.

"To be precise, Beatrice owned a mountain on Maui and on that mountain just happened to be thousands of macadamia nut trees."

Ashley let out a low whistle. "No wonder Monica wants a piece of his hide!" After a pause she said, "You'd think after twenty years the lust for vengeance would fade, unless . . ."

"Unless what?"

"Unless they're still in love and don't know it. I sensed Monica hadn't loved her husband and you said Clyde never loved Beatrice. Maybe that explains why there's still so much anger between them. Anger is a form of passion, after all."

"Not the kind I enjoy." He raised his eyebrows. "You know what kind of passion I like, and in case you've forgotten, I plan to give you a refresher

161

course tonight." But it was plain she hadn't heard him.

He waved a hand in front of her eyes. "Ashley, you aren't listening to me. I'm trying to tell you all the wonderfully erotic things I'm going to do to your body tonight and you're staring off into space."

"I was just thinking about Monica and Clyde. I wonder if we can get them back together."

"Women!" Zane mocked her. "You're all born matchmakers! If my uncle wants Monica, he could pick up the phone and call her. I want you thinking about me tonight, not about two people who had an affair twenty years ago."

As Ashley started to answer, Coach Mitchell pushed open the terrace door and shouted, "Zane, get in here. They're going to show some highlights of the Bronco game. I think you'll enjoy the show. You were outstanding, as Ms. Buchannan noted in her column today."

"I'll get us one more glass of champagne, then let's split," Zane suggested, after the lights came back on. "That red dress is sexy as sin, but I'm anxious to get you out of it, if you know what I mean."

But he got waylaid at the bar by the coach, and when Razor saw Ashley was alone he joined her on the sofa. "I figured with Zane gone it's a good time for me to make my move," he said confidingly.

"The only move of yours I'm interested in is the one that gets you away from me," Ashley retorted.

Razor looked across the room at Zane. "What do you see in that guy anyway? He's just a green kid. You're old enough to enjoy a real man. And I," he bragged, "am man enough for any woman! Why don't you call me sometime, and I'll prove it!"

Ashley disliked his arrogance almost as much as his persistence. "I don't mean to be rude, but you don't seem to be getting my message. I am not interested in seeing you, dating you, or even talking to you. Right now the only man I am interested in is Zane, so why don't you go hit on somebody else? Maybe they'll be dumb enough or desperate enough to fall for your line."

"Oh, I get it," Razor observed with a smug smile. "You're one of those."

"One of what?" Ashley asked with distrust.

"One of those women who enjoy robbing the cradle," Razor sneered. "Of course, I realize it's kind of kinky. Is that how you get your kicks, initiating young men to the ways of sex? Or do you do it because it makes you feel younger?"

His words were like a spear driven into her body. She wanted to yell at him that he was wrong, wanted to tell him she wasn't robbing the cradle, and that if anyone was being initiated it was she, not Zane. But tears choked her.

When she didn't speak, Razor stood up, looming over her. "When you get tired of playing with little boys, call me. I'll make your day," he taunted.

Zane caught sight of Razor standing in front of Ashley, and abruptly broke off his conversation with the coach. "Ashley, what's wrong?" he demanded as he reached her.

"Nothing," she lied, refusing to raise her eyes for fear he'd see her tears. But Zane sat down beside her. Lifting her chin, he observed, "That's what I thought. You're crying. What in the hell did he say to you?"

She swallowed. "Forget it, I don't want to talk about it. It—it isn't important."

"If it made you cry, it is important. Tell me, Ashley. Don't keep secrets from me."

It was on the tip of her tongue, yet she couldn't force the truth out. Every minute she spent with Zane, he became a more and more important part of her life. She couldn't bear the thought that she'd lose him if he discovered just how much older she really was. She knew she didn't look thirty-three, and guessed he probably didn't think there was six years between them. How could she risk telling him? She couldn't. So she lied—or at least, she didn't tell him the whole truth. "Razor made a pass at me, and when I rebuffed him he didn't exactly take it like a gentleman," she explained. "He said some pretty ugly things about our relationship. It upset me, that's all."

"What things? What did he say?" Zane insisted.

"What would be the point of telling you, you'd just get mad. Let it go, Zane, okay?" She squeezed his hand. "Tonight I want to see you happy, not angry."

At first she thought he was going to push harder, but he shrugged. "Well, you know what makes me happiest of all, so let's go!"

They stood on the sweeping drive in front of Clyde's sprawling home, holding hands and waiting for the parking valet to bring Zane's van. "I don't want to offend you, but somehow that blue van of yours just doesn't look right sitting in front of a mansion," Ashley mused as the driver pulled to a stop. "You should have a Ferrari or a Jag, something dashing."

"If Uncle Clyde ever wanted to give me one I wouldn't turn it down. But as for me, I've got better things to do with my money than waste it on a flashy sports car. Between my van and my motorcycle I get were I need to go."

"What better things?" she asked, climbing into the van beside him.

"You should know," he teased. "Better things like muumuus and coffee ice cream. Plus I've got a few other reasons I need to save my bucks."

As they wound down the mountain, Ashley fell silent, wishing with all her heart she could forget Razor's taunts, but finding she couldn't.

Zane glanced at her out of the corner of his eye. "Why so quiet? Are you still upset about what that damn Razor said? I wish you'd tell me exactly what it was."

"No, it isn't that. I was just thinking about the concert you missed last Friday," she lied, trying to distract him. "You would have loved it. It was Wagner."

"Great!" He laughed. "They only play the macho stuff when I'm out of town. Maybe I'll be luckier next time."

To her relief Zane dropped the questions, and the rest of the way to her house he devoted himself to their shared love of music. "I've never asked you, do you prefer Ravel to Rachmaninoff?" he inquired. "I hope so, because I sure do. I like his fire."

The instant Zane stepped into the living room, Kaipo screeched and dived at him. "What the hell!" he yelled, throwing his hands up to ward off the cockatoo, but Kaipo still managed to yank out a few strands of his blond hair, before flying triumphantly back to the open cage.

"Oh, Zane, I'm so sorry," Ashley apologized, unable to stifle a giggle at her bird's antics. "I didn't want to lock the cage until he was done."

165

"Done with what, scalping me?" he demanded, rubbing his head.

She grabbed his hand. "Come, I'll show you. When I found Kaipo shredding my newspaper this morning before I even got a chance to look at it, I suspected something was up. Now I'm sure."

Kaipo was bouncing around on the bottom of the large rattan cage, squawking happily as he worked, but his mate, Kanani, sat motionless on her perch. Ashley reached in and gently stroked her feathers, murmuring, "It's going to be all right."

"What's that crazy bird doing?" Zane pointed to the busy Kaipo.

"Can't you tell? He's making a nest. That's why he wanted your hair. Unless I'm very mistaken I'm about to become godmother to a baby cockatoo." She locked the cage door and started pulling down the night cover. "Let's give the proud parents a little privacy."

"You mean, let's give us a little privacy. I don't want to be dive-bombed by that damn bird just when I'm ravishing your delectable body."

Ashley smiled, but ignored his comment. "Thinking of babies reminds me of something. Do you want to come to the hospital with me tomorrow to visit Kakalina and Jake Jr.?" she asked.

"Nope, I'm not wild about squally brats. Not that is, unless they're mine." A soft gleam lit his eyes. "Come to think of it, I wouldn't mind holding a beautiful baby daughter with hair the color of midnight and eyes the shadowy gray of the mist." He stroked a caress across her stomach. "How about starting on that little project tonight?"

"Zane!" Ashley protested with a shaky laugh. "Don't be silly. You know I have a lot of reservations about our relationship as it is. I'm certainly not ready to have your baby."

"Okay. I'm not going to push you. I'll give you time. For now, how about just having me?"

"Now that's a possibility," she agreed, glad for any reason to stop talking of children—their children. She smiled. "Monica gave me another bottle of champagne." She glanced across the room. "And would you believe our good luck? There's another lonely sofa sitting right over there."

"Great!" He rubbed his hands eagerly together. "Just what we need for another night of R and R. When I'm near you I'm always in the mood to pillage."

"I sincerely hope it's just when you're around me," Ashley commented, suddenly needing assurance.

Zane looked almost hurt. "How can you ask that? I've told you how I feel about you. I feel like I've been searching a lifetime for you, for the one person who touches my soul, my heart, my desire. Before I met you I always thought all that talk about destiny was a lot of romantic hogwash. But out of all the seats in that concert hall, the fact I chanced to have the one next to you almost makes me believe. Come to think about it, maybe I do believe in it." He cupped her face in his warm hands and gently kissed her. "The longer I'm with you the more I think we're destined to be together. Forever."

There were tears in Ashley's eyes when Zane finished kissing her. "Hey, I didn't mean to make you cry," he said, concerned.

"Sometimes people cry when they're happy," Ashley explained, wrapping her arms around his waist to hug him.

"Now that I've made you happy, I seem to remember your saying something at the party about wanting to make me happy," Zane reminded her with a lusty gleam in his eyes. "I've got the perfect idea. Why don't you go put on one of those muumuus I bought you, while I pop the cork?" He stroked a fingertip across her breasts. "And be naked for me underneath. We Vikings don't have much patience with underwear."

Ashley blushed. "Zane, I've never—"

He laid two fingers against her lips, stilling her protest. "Please do it for me. When I slip my hands beneath that muumuu I want to feel nothing but the warmth of you. I want to be able to touch you, to feel how much you want me. I want to know you want me as much as I want you. Please," he repeated, giving her that irresistible half smile.

"I can't believe the things you make me do," she protested with a laugh.

Zane chuckled. "Wait until you see what I've got in mind for tonight."

Ashley reached for one of the muumuus, a shudder of pleasure running through her. Remembering her wild fantasies and how they became so wonderfully real that night, she trembled with desire. Zane wasn't even touching her, yet at the thought of him, her pulse quickened and a warm throbbing started where she most needed his touch to cool the fire already burning within her. She stripped and slipped the cotton muumuu over her head.

When she returned to the living room she found Zane reclining like some sultan on the sofa with a champagne glass in his hand, nude. Zane opened his arms wide. "Come pleasure me, wench. This Viking has need of your love, to say nothing of your body."

Pretending she had no choice but to do his bidding, Ashley gazed demurely down at the carpet. "If it is your wish, I shall."

"You'll do anything I wish?"

Her eyes met his. She didn't retreat or blush at the fiery intensity of the desire she saw there. "Yes, anything," she whispered.

Maybe she was desperate to lose herself in Zane's lovemaking so she could forget Razor's jeers. Maybe she wanted more assurance he was telling the truth when he said he found her desirable. Maybe she just wanted him so much, that need burned away all her inhibitions. Whatever the reason, she took the initiative for the first time. She took the champagne glass from his hand and smiled. "Tonight you don't need wine. I want to be the one to intoxicate you."

Zane grinned. "I'm all yours. Intoxicate me."

She did. It was her mouth that captured his. It was her tongue that plunged eagerly into his mouth the instant his lips parted. It was her hands that roamed over him, stroking, arousing, making him writhe with where she touched him. Again and again she caressed him, igniting his desire until his breath came in short gasps.

With a moan, Zane tried to slide his hands under her muumuu but she wouldn't let him. Keeping the fabric between him and what he sought, she teased him, continuing, with her hands, her lips, her tongue to build his need into such a raging inferno he couldn't stand it any more.

Finally, desperate to possess her, the light cotton ripped under his frantic hands. The desire burned so hot he gave her no preliminary caress, but parted her thighs and with one conquering thrust took what she so willingly offered. As before, he couldn't seem to get enough of her, and over and over they moved together, hips meeting hips, both covered with a sheen of sweat. And still he prolonged the exquisite delight, not wanting it to end. In response to this wild frenzy she'd stirred within him, Ashley trembled violently—not from fear, but from the sweetest ecstasy she'd ever known, as finally they found paradise at the same magical moment.

When their breathing had returned to normal Zane raised his head. "Ashley, I can't believe what you did to me. I swear to you I didn't mean to rip another muumuu from your body, but you drove me crazy, making me wait like that." He sighed with deep contentment. "Tonight I feel like I was the one who was ravished."

"Are you complaining?" Ashley asked, half afraid her boldness might have displeased him.

"Are you kidding! Beautiful lady, you can have your way with me any time you wish!"

Then the laughter fled from his eyes as he twined his fingers through her dark hair. Guiding her lips to his, he kissed her softly, a kiss of gratitude, not of desire.

When they parted, he confessed, "You're the most unusual woman I've ever known. Part wanton, part innocent. One minute you blush when I ask you to come to me naked, the next you do things to me that drive away my sanity."

She rubbed her breasts teasingly against his chest, and smiled when she felt the flutter of his response deep within her body.

"What part do you like best? The innocent or the wanton. I want to please you."

"Oh, you're going to do that several ways tonight," he challenged, and the flutter grew until it filled her completely. "To answer your question, the innocence is undeniably part of your appeal.

But tonight I want the wanton, and I want her right now."

"The champagne's getting warm again," she teased.

"Who cares! Now shut up. It's your turn to be ravished."

"Mmm, I can't think of anything I'd like better."

CHAPTER ELEVEN

Ashley flipped a macadamia nut pancake over in the skillet and turned to Zane. "Are you sure you don't want to go to the hospital with me this afternoon? Jake Jr.'s so adorable, I know he'd steal your heart."

Zane came up behind her and wrapped his arms around her waist. "He can't," he confessed, drawing her back against him. "It's already been stolen." He dropped a light kiss against her dark hair. "Handle it with care, will you? It's the only one I have."

"That's one of the sweetest things anyone has ever said to me," Ashley said sincerely, turning in his arms to give him a kiss.

"Hey, watch the pancakes," he said. "They're going to burn. After what you did to me last night, I need energy."

"After what I did to you?" she asked with raised eyebrows. "What about what you did to me?"

He chuckled. "I didn't hear any objections."

"No, it was wonderful," she admitted, blushing. "I didn't know making love could give me such exquisite pleasure. You are one fantastic lover, Zane Bruxton!"

"It helps to have a partner who really gets into the spirit of things. Are those pancakes ready yet? I'm starving!" He waggled his eyebrows. "And for the first time I'm hungry for something other than you."

As they were eating, she asked again, "Are you sure you don't want to go to the hospital with me?" she asked persuasively. "I'd like you to meet Jake and Kakalina. They're good friends of mine. He's the one who helped me cut up that fallen palm tree." Ashley wanted him with her as long as possible.

Zane dug his fork into his third stack of pancakes. "I wondered about that. I'm glad the guy who helped you is safely married. I had visions of you batting those gorgeous eyes of yours to get help from some single guy with a chain saw. I don't want any competition."

The truth came from her heart. "You don't have any competition. I don't think any man would have a chance compared to you."

"Ah, such flattery." Zane winked roguishly. "Too bad I can't demonstrate how really incomparable I can be, but the day's booked solid. This morning we review the game films, and for once it's going to be a pleasure to sit there and watch Coach Mitchell run and rerun the key plays. Let me tell you, there's nothing worse than seeing yourself miss a tackle for the tenth time."

On her way back to the stove she patted his broad shoulder. "You had a great game! You have the right to gloat a little."

"I thought you hated football players, with their mega-egos."

She spooned more batter into the skillet. "Only if they get obnoxious about it, like Butcher."

Zane poured coconut syrup on his pancakes. "Guess I can stop worrying then. I've found a

173

unique way to control my own mega-ego when I feel it starting to bloat."

Ashley frowned at the bad memories as she muttered, "Butcher never did. What's your secret?"

"I'll show you sometime," he answered enigmatically. "But not today. I don't have time."

Intrigued, she started to ask for more details, but he continued running down his schedule. "Then after the films and practice I've got some business to settle."

Her back was to him so she didn't see the grim set of his mouth. It would have worried her if she had. Zane really looked like he was spoiling for a fight.

When she walked into the newsroom an hour later, Ray was waiting for her. He approached her and walked all the way around her as if on a tour of inspection.

"What's wrong?" she asked, surprised at his odd behavior. "Is my slip showing?"

"I'm just making sure my star columnist is still in one piece."

Still confused, Ashley inquired, "Why wouldn't I be? Did you hear I was in an accident or something?"

"No, but I did hear you got into a public brawl with Clyde Winston last night. You've got more nerve than I do, Ashley. He's one powerful man to tangle with."

"How did you hear about that?"

"You're not the only one with inside sources. Remember, I covered the sports desk for a lot of years. I've still got a few of those contacts left," he reminded her with a smug smile.

"What's this about Ashley getting into a fight with Clyde?" Monica demanded, coming up from behind to join them.

Remembering her pledge to Clyde, and knowing what big ears reporters have, Ashley said, "I suppose you do have a right to hear the whole story, since it concerns the *News*. But could we talk about it somewhere a little more private? I don't think Mr. Winston would enjoy having the story of our altercation spread all over town."

"Sure. We can talk in my office," Ray offered.

"No, if this concerns Clyde Winston I want to savor the details in comfort. *My* office," Monica insisted, turning to go to the elevators. On her way she snapped her fingers at Dave Jenkins, who was engrossed in reading a file. He looked up. "Tell Elvira to bring coffee to my office," she ordered. Ignoring his scowl of displeasure at being asked to perform such a menial chore, she proceeded on her regal way.

Typical of Monica, when she had bought the *News* the existing owner's office wasn't grand enough for her, so she had had a new one constructed on the roof of the building. From this lofty penthouse suite she lorded over her hirelings. Ashley had heard about its opulence from other reporters privileged to gain admission, but this was the first time she'd actually been invited to visit the inner sanctum.

Ashley could hardly believe her eyes. It was like stepping into an oriental museum. Her footsteps as she followed Monica through the cavernous waiting room into the office were cushioned by a series of priceless Persian rugs. As Monica headed for the massive slab of green malachite mounted on ornate brass legs that served as her desk, Ashley let her eyes wander about the room, drinking in the breathtaking beauty.

Antique painting on silk first caught her eye, but her gaze was soon captured by the bronze statue of

Vishnu. Three feet high and sitting on a block of marble, it stood to one side of Monica's desk. On the other side, to balance, was a gold-plated eighteenth-century Indian deity. Ashley had seen its twin in the Metropolitan Museum the last time she'd visited New York.

She sighed. All this magnificence made the temple rubbings her parents had brought her from Bangkok seem a little like poor-man's art. Still, she cherished them, even if they weren't gold-plated.

Monica didn't even glance at the beauty surrounding her as she waved Ray and Ashley to the two embroidered silk chairs in front of her desk. Ashley smiled, noticing for the first time that Monica's desk was mounted on a dais. No doubt Monica felt it gave her a psychological advantage, but Ashley refused to feel intimidated. Calmly she crossed her legs.

"Now tell me about your fight with Clyde," Monica ordered. "I want every last detail."

"As you may know Mr. Winston threw a party at his home last night to celebrate the Kings first win," Ashley explained. "Well, the moment I walked into his living room he yelled at me to get out."

"In front of all of his guests?" Monica asked, obviously surprised.

Ashley nodded. "Yes, he didn't seem to care who heard him."

Monica beamed with catty pleasure. "Clyde was always so pompous, preaching about the importance of proper etiquette. For him to forget his manners means you're really kicking him where it hurts. How delightful! Go on. What happened next?"

When Ashley reached the part where Clyde had

to back down, Monica clapped her hands. "Ray, give this lady a raise."

"But I just—" Ray tried to protest, but faltered under Monica's icy glare.

"Don't tell me how to spend my money! Just do it!" she snapped.

"Yes, Monica," he mumbled.

At that point Elvira, in a black maid's uniform, arrived with coffee on a silver tray. The break helped ease the tension crackling through the room.

Ashley took a sip of the delicious brew, frowning. Something Clyde had said when they'd argued had stayed with her, nagging slightly, and she wanted to get rid of the tiny doubt. "One of the reasons Clyde was so furious at me was because he believed the only reason I was given this assignment was that I was a woman." She looked directly at Monica. "He felt you knew he'd hate having a woman invade his locker room, so you gave the column to me simply to spite him, and not because I had the qualifications to do the job."

Monica smiled coldly. "Clyde always was a male chauvinist."

Ashley didn't like the slight note of evasiveness in Monica's answer. She began to press for a more complete explanation, but decided against it. Monica must merely mean Clyde didn't think a woman could handle the job, and was angered when she could.

"Ashley, I'm impressed with you," Monica admitted. "There's only been one other woman who got the best of Clyde Winston, and that's me."

Ashley chose her words carefully. "Mr. Winston seems to be on your mind a lot lately." She hesitated, wondering if she was going to get her head chopped off for asking, but she went on. "You said the two of you went back a long way. Is it a business rivalry, or are you still angry with him over something that happened when you first knew each other, even after all these years? If I'm out of line—"

"Yes you certainly are!" Monica snapped angrily. "You're way out of line! What I think of Clyde Winston is none of your business. The only thing I want from you is good writing," she insisted, obviously intent on killing the subject for good. "What is your column about today?"

Ashley took a long sip of her coffee, studying Monica. Monica's words had been ice cold, but for just an instant, when Ashley mentioned that Clyde seemed to be in her thoughts a lot, there had been no ice at all in her eyes. Ashley realized this was such a touchy subject, she'd better not push Monica any further about her feelings for Zane's uncle, if she valued her job—and she did. Setting the china cup in its saucer, she answered, "I thought I'd do something on the Kings first victory."

"You did that yesterday, when you wrote about that Bruxton guy," Monica observed with a frown of displeasure.

But Ashley refused to let Monica intimidate her. "When a team has an exceptional game, don't you think that's as legitimate a story as when they have an awful game?" she retorted.

Unexpectedly Ray came to her support. "She's got a point, Monica."

Monica tapped her long scarlet nails against the malachite desktop. "Writing nice sweet stories doesn't sell newspapers. Check the circulation figures. Controversy, inside dirt, hell-burning scandals—that's the type of stories our readers want."

178

"You mean you want stories that continue to bruise Mr. Winston's ego?" Ashley asked, bravely meeting Monica's glare.

"I repeat, columns that are real hell-burners sell newspapers," she insisted. "Sappy sentimentality doesn't! I don't expect to have to mention this to you again." With a wave of her hand, she dismissed them. "We all have work to do. You may go."

In the elevator, Ray turned anxiously to Ashley. "Take my advice and don't butt heads with Monica. You can't win. If you oppose her, I guarantee she'll chew you up and spit you out. I've seen her do it more than once."

"Thanks for the warning. I'll think about it," Ashley promised. "It just makes me angry when someone tries to tell me how to do my job, that's all."

"Just take the raise and keep your mouth shut, and everything will work out."

When Ashley got back to her desk, she filed the notes she'd made on the Kings victory. She had to admit to herself that Monica had a point. Most subscribers would rather read an account of a good fistfight than platitudes honoring a good game. Still it bothered her a little to always have to play the heavy. On the other hand, that's what they were paying her for.

She chewed on the end of her little finger several moments, then, reaching for the phone, she dialed the Kings training facility and waited with crossed fingers while it rang. With luck, Razor might be bold enough or mad enough to give her a suitably negative quote about Broczinsky's performance against the Broncos, which she could use to head-line her next column.

He came on the line and she identified herself. "Hey, doll face, I knew it was only a matter of time

179

before you called me," he boasted. "What's it to be, your place or mine?"

"I can't believe your lack of originality. Talk to Zane. Maybe he'll give you some better lines," she retorted.

"I've already talked to him, and I'll be damned if I'll do it again. The man's a raving maniac," Razor whined.

"What are you talking about? What did he do?"

"None of your damn business. Besides he's a nothing. Let's talk about us."

"There is no us. There's never going to be an us," Ashley insisted firmly. "Right now I'm working. This is not a social call." She crossed her fingers again. "I'd like to get some quotes from you for my column, assessing Broczinsky's performance in Sunday's game."

Her luck was out. Razor wasn't stupid enough to be trapped into making some damning comment that could boomerang and bring the coach's wrath down on his head.

"I thought Touchdown's performance was incredible," he answered blandly. "That Hail Mary pass rivaled Roger Staubach at his best. But if you need a column idea, I've got a humdinger!" he offered, obviously trying to score points with her.

"What is it?" Ashley asked cautiously.

"How does this headline grab you: 'Wide Receiver Decks Doctor'?"

"Sounds like it might be interesting, if it's correct."

"Oh, it's legit all right. I was there. Here's the inside dope."

She wrote frantically as he told her how one of the Kings wide receivers had reacted violently, throwing a fist in the doctor's face when the doctor informed him he'd flunked the physical and was off the team because of bone chips in his shoulder. Razor went on to relate that the player claimed he'd had surgery in the off-season and was fine, and that the Kings only wanted to avoid paying him his admittedly large salary.

After handing her this scoop, he tried again. "Okay, you owe me one. How about dinner? Hell, you're good-looking enough I'd even spring for that new snotty French restaurant out by the Chinaman's Hat."

"What a charming way to ask a person for a date," Ashley commented sarcastically. She wrinkled her nose in distaste at what she had to say next. "But I do want to thank you for the column idea." Before he could make another pass, she hurriedly said good-bye and hung up the receiver without waiting for any reply.

Not really trusting Razor or his wild story, she called Sammy for confirmation. "Did anyone lose two teeth this afternoon?" she asked guardedly.

"It's okay, I can talk," he reassured her. "And yes we had quite a donnybrook down here." He filled in the details Razor had omitted. "I'll bet Razor didn't admit he also almost got into a brawl today himself," Sammy added.

"No, he didn't say anything about that. What happened?" Ashley asked, pulling her pad toward her again.

"Unfortunately I don't know the whole story. You see, I needed to get some tape from the training room. When I went in Zane Bruxton had Razor backed up against the lockers, and the language flying would have turned the moon blue. I don't blame Razor for backing off. Usually Bruxton's a pretty cool guy, but not this afternoon. Something

181

sure must have set him off, because he was out for blood."

"I wonder what it was?" Ashley murmured, blushing. "Well, I'd better run and get this column to Ray. What do you want this time, cigars or Scotch?"

"Neither," Sammy grumbled. "The doctor's put me on this strict diet. No booze. No smokes. It's hell!"

"Well, Sammy, you still have women," Ashley teased. "See you soon."

She was just doing the final edit on her column when the phone rang. At the sound of Zane's voice her smile warmed the whole room. "What did you do to poor Razor?" she asked after he'd said hello.

"I'll tell you the whole story tonight, but believe me, after last night he deserved everything he got. That's not why I'm calling, though. You've been cooking for me a lot lately. How about if I return the favor tonight?"

"Are you any good?" she joked.

"Let's say I can broil a steak without burning it. Please say yes," he begged. "My fish told me they miss you. How about it?"

Ashley laughed. "I know all about those fish of yours. They're nosy. Remember how they watched every move we made during the hurricane? You can't fool me. They don't miss me. What they really miss is the X-rated show!"

"They're not the only ones," Zane chuckled. "We'll have to see what we can do to entertain them tonight. I'll pick you up at six, okay?"

"Sure, I'll take advantage of any opportunity not to have to cook."

"Great!" She smiled happily at his enthusiasm. "Where will you be?" he asked.

"My column's almost done. Have you heard about the great bone chip controversy?"

"Yeah, I heard about it. I don't know who I feel sorriest for."

"I know what you mean!" Ashley spoke from her heart, remembering Butcher's reaction to being told he'd never play again. With an effort she forced herself back to the present, a very delightful present, as thoughts of dinner and Zane filled her mind. "After I give my column to Ray I want to go by the hospital and see Kakalina and Jake Jr."

"You can't fool me." Zane laughed. "You just want an excuse to buy a stuffed toy."

Ashley's eyes widened in disbelief. "How did you—"

"How did I know you were planning to buy a stuffed toy for Jake Jr.?" Zane finished her sentence. "I know because I know you. There's a lot of the playful child in you Ashley, a child you've tried to deny for too long."

Silently she agreed with him. Butcher, even though he was older, had always thought of his immediate gratification first, and the consequences usually not at all. From the moment they were married, she was the one who had to cope with the piles of bills, the angry bar owners when Butcher had gone on one of his wild binges, and a hundred other details that forced her to grow up in a hurry, because her husband wouldn't. Somewhere in the marriage the child had died within her. With Zane she felt free to play. That was one more gift he was giving her.

"Okay, I confess. I adore stuffed animals. Anyway, to answer your question I should be home by six." She paused, wishing for the dozenth time her home wasn't so far out of Honolulu. "Are you sure you want to drive all the way out there? I could simply meet you at your apartment. Wouldn't that be easier?"

"No way, fair maiden. I guess I'm an old-fashioned guy, but I pick up my dates. They don't deliver themselves to me."

"Oh really?" she challenged, cooing sexily. "I thought I'd been delivering myself to you fairly frequently lately."

"You have, and I have no complaints about what you've delivered!" Zane agreed with a husky laugh of longing. "But I'll still be at your house at six."

Secretly pleased, Ashley gave in. "Okay, you win."

"I know, I always win. It's part of my irresistible charm," Zane answered.

"That remark sounds suspiciously like something Razor would say," she teased.

"Oh, hell, I guess I'll have to change my line." His voice grated with an anger she didn't understand. "If there's one person in this world I don't want to sound like, it's that creep Razor Williams!"

She heard his fury as he said the name, but before she could ask another question about their confrontation, Zane went on. "Sorry, but I've got to run. And in case you get the wrong idea, don't think I don't enjoy talking to you. Your sexy voice is enough to make tonight seem light-years away. It's just that I've got a lot to do before six. I want tonight to be special."

"Zane, don't you know you make every night special?" she confessed, a hot blush searing her cheeks.

"I aim to please, ma'am. That's my motto," he said cockily, obviously delighted.

"Well, you certainly manage to do that!" Ashley agreed as all sorts of warm impulses started firing

184

through her at the thought of the night to come. "I have no complaints, even if you do rip my muumuus and toss my bikinis into the waves."

His voice grew soft. "I'm glad you feel that way. You should always be surrounded by happiness." There was a pause. "I'll see you tonight at six. Wear something sexy. Bye, love," he added huskily.

Ashley typed the last few lines of copy into the word processor and printed it out. When she dropped it on Ray's desk she stated, "It's all hell-burner and no sappy sentimentality. Hope you're satisfied."

He scanned the first few lines. "I am, and Monica will be too. You did us both a favor. If you'd turned in another flattering article she'd probably come down on both our backs."

"Is it okay if I knock off early today? I want to visit Kakalina and Jake Jr."

"Sure, and tell her congratulations from me."

Her tour through the gift shop at the hospital was fun. Ashley had the delightful problem of trying to decide between the cutest stuffed bear dressed in a baseball uniform and a pink rabbit clutching a whole bunch of carrots. She'd just about decided on the teddy bear when she spotted something even more irresistible—a soft and cuddly purple dragon. There were two of them, and for a wild moment she was tempted to buy one for herself, but she resisted. Still, she felt a twinge of regret as she presented the dragon to Kakalina.

They chatted a few minutes about Jake Jr., her parents' joy when they saw him for the first time, and her plans for after she went home. "You've got a funny look in your eyes I've never seen before," Kakalina observed. "You seem half ecstatic, half sad. What's wrong?"

Ashley sighed. "I didn't know it was so obvious. Well, do you want the good or the bad news first?"

"The good. I assume Zane is putting that sparkle in your eye."

Ashley nodded. "Yes, he's so wonderful, so understanding"—she lowered her eyes, blushing—"so passionate." She cleared her throat to cover her embarrassment at the admission. "Every hour I spend with him is more special than the last."

"It sounds to me like you're falling in love with him, and since the man's obviously interested in you, what's the problem?" her friend asked. "You should be on cloud nine, and all I get is a frown."

"After last night I guess I'm just facing a problem I've been trying to ignore."

"What happened last night? I thought Jake said you were going to a party at Clyde Winston's house. That should have been fun."

"Part of it was, but I also got cornered by one of the players. He accused me of robbing the cradle, being with Zane."

Kakalina indignantly tossed back her waist-length black hair. "Tell him to go take a flying leap off Diamond Head! From what I've seen of Zane, he looks like a grown man to me."

Ashley rose and went to stare out the window. "It isn't just that. What he said made me look at everything else that's wrong. You know what the trouble is. We've talked about it before. It's all the damn doubts! I thought I was in love with Butcher. I thought what we had would last forever, but it didn't. Except for the philandering, all the problems that blasted apart my first marriage could come up in this relationship with Zane. What if he's traded? I don't think I could bear to leave Hawaii again. What if he's injured, and can't play any longer? Could he cope with it any better than Butcher? And there's a dozen other possibilities that could ruin everything." Hot tears filled her eyes. "Then toss in the age difference and you can see that I've gotten myself into a real mess!" she whispered.

"Why don't you tell him how old you are?" Kakalina suggested. "That way, if it's going to be a problem you'll find out before you get in any deeper."

"I can't," Ashley admitted. "I'm terrified of losing him!"

Kakalina's voice was stern. "Ashley, have you recently looked at yourself in the mirror. You're a gorgeous woman with a great figure. Until you told me how old you were I honestly thought you were well on the sunny side of thirty, so stop worrying!"

"I wish I could," Ashley whispered sadly. She drew a shaky breath and tried to shrug away the bad thoughts. Turning from the window, she forced a smile. "When do they bring Jake Jr. in for his feeding? I can't wait to see him. Do you think he'll like that purple dragon I bought?" she asked.

Kakalina tried to give another round of advice, but when Ashley didn't respond, she let the conversation return to babies, bottles, and diapers. Ashley left the hospital with her gray eyes still clouded with sadness and uncertainty.

CHAPTER TWELVE

Ashley walked into the house to the wildest screeching. Convinced her two cockatoos were trying to kill each other, she rushed to the cage, laughing in relief at the sight that greeted her.

"So you're so proud of yourself you want the whole world to know about your accomplishment, is that it, Kaipo?" she asked, watching the male bird doing his squawking victory dance. Proudly sitting in the nest he'd built carefully guarding one pale pink egg, was Kanani.

"What's going on in there?" Zane called through the door. "It sounds like World War Three."

"No, it's just Kaipo celebrating. He's going to be a father."

Zane came up behind her to see the egg. "Lucky bird!" he whispered, wrapping his arms around her waist. Ashley winced, but didn't say anything. "But that squawking is really getting to me," he continued. "How can I seduce you with my smooth line if we can't hear each other? Think of some way to shut him up."

"If all you're handing me is a line, then I'm not sure I want to," Ashley retorted.

"The truth is never a line," Zane insisted, raising his voice so she could hear him over the proud bird. "And the truth is I want this evening to be extra special. If that noise keeps up you're going to get a headache, and you know what that means. No fun and games."

"Just what sort of games do you have in mind? I may indeed feel a headache coming on," Ashley teased, leaning back to revel in the feel of the muscled hardness of his chest.

"Oh, fun games. Like pin the tail on the donkey, post office, stuff like that," he joked.

"Sounds innocent enough. I guess I'm safe. I'll shut the bird up, I don't want a headache. I haven't played pin the tail on the donkey in years."

"How are you going to do that? He sounds like he plans to go on bragging all night."

"You just have to be firm," she explained, opening the cage door. Instantly Kaipo hopped up onto his perch. Quickly, before he could let out another screech, she closed her fingers gently over his beak. "That's enough noise! No more!" Then she smiled, telling the bird, "I'm proud of you."

When she let go, Kaipo returned to Kanani's side, silently. "I don't believe it," Zane commented. "One word from you and the dumb bird shuts up. You really must have a special rapport with animals."

Ashley turned around. Patting his chest, she winked. "I do. That's why I get along so well with you."

"I don't know if I like being called an animal," he protested, but he laughed. "Maybe you're right. You do seem to bring out the animal in me." He drew her tighter into his embrace, a deep growl rumbling in his throat. "And I'd better warn you, this lion plans to prowl several times tonight."

"Is that before or after pin the tail on the donkey?" Ashley joked.

189

"Why don't you wait? It can be a surprise," he murmured as his hands began roaming over her back. "In fact, I've planned a lot of surprises for you tonight."

She stood on tiptoe to softly kiss his mouth. "I can't wait for those surprises to begin, so if you'll let go I'll go get ready."

Zane sighed deeply. "The thought of letting you go even for an instant isn't very appealing, but I guess I'll make the sacrifice."

"Pour yourself a glass of wine. I won't be long," Ashley promised, heading for the bedroom.

The day had been hot and sultry, without the usual sea breezes. Her clothes felt sticky as she slipped out of her skirt and blouse, tossing them into the clothes basket. Quickly she hurried into the bathroom and turned on the tap, sending a blast of warm water into the shower. Usually she lingered, savoring the feel of the water cascading over her body, but tonight she was in such a rush to rejoin Zane and start their evening she finished her bath with lightning speed.

Wrapping a fluffy towel around her damp hair, Ashley walked back into her bedroom. Intent on deciding what she wanted to wear, she didn't notice Zane lounging on the bed.

"I see you're ready," he observed, his gaze raking over her naked body.

"Zane!" Ashley gasped, feeling very foolish that although he'd seen her naked many times she still had an urge to cover herself. "What are you doing here?"

He smiled with all the innocence of an impish child as he held out her wineglass toward her. "I brought you your wine."

She didn't know whether to laugh or throw a

pillow at him. Finally the absurdity of the whole thing restored her sense of humor. "Thank you for the wine. Now if you'll please leave I'll get dressed." She smiled, taking the glass from him.

"Nope," he said, crossing his arms behind his head. "I've undressed you enough times. Now I want to watch you get dressed."

She could feel the blush stealing over her whole body. "But I've never . . . I mean, Butcher didn't . . ."

"Oh, I get it." Zane chuckled. "The ol' dress in the bathroom scenario. I said it before and I repeat, Butcher was one dull dog." His gaze roamed possessively over her. "Please, Ashley, don't say no. I want to see you make yourself ready for me."

Her embarrassment almost made her refuse, but somehow she knew she wouldn't. Ashley felt the heat rise within her as she looked at him. "You're the most sensuous man I've ever known," she admitted.

There was no teasing in his eyes as he confessed, "Only with you. You inflame my desire like no other woman I've ever held in my arms."

She put her hands on her hips, forgetting she was stark naked. "And just how many others have there been?" she demanded.

"Enough to teach me how to give you pleasure, pleasure in lots of different ways." He plumped up the pillow. "You'd better get dressed, or I'm afraid I'll lose control and show you a few of those ways right now."

"The things you make me do!" Ashley muttered, putting her wine on the nightstand and going to the chest of drawers. She bent over to open her underwear drawer without stopping to think.

"Now that's what I call an interesting view!" Zane

191

chuckled. Ashley straightened up instantly, panties dangling in one hand and a bra in the other. "Nope, not tonight," he insisted.

She looked at him, confused. "What do you mean, not tonight?"

"You won't need those tonight, so just toss them back in that drawer."

"But I've never gone out without—"

"Tonight's the night for a lot of firsts, Ashley." He gave her that pleading look she couldn't resist. "Please put them back. I like the idea of knowing you're open to me whenever I want you, that I can touch you, feel you completely, any time . . . anywhere."

With her blood pounding at the thoughts his words stirred, she dropped the two garments back into the drawer. Why did he tempt her to do such wild and crazy things? Then she knew, she knew she wanted exactly what he did. She wanted nothing between her and his touch. Just the thought of his hands caressing her bare flesh drowned out any need for modesty.

Her gaze boldly met his. "Then you do the same."

"My, what a lusty wench you've become, Ashley my love."

Her heart tumbled at the word *love*, but she put a rein on the surge of joy. He'd never said "I love you." The "my love" was probably just affectionate. She mustn't hope for more than there was, she must protect herself.

"You've made me into one. I hope it pleases you."

Zane sat up. "Oh, it does. Believe me, it does!"

With eyes as sparkling as his had been when they gazed at her naked body, she watched him kick aside first his pants then his briefs. It was all she could do not to rush across the room and throw herself onto the bed with him. And there was no concealing the fact he wanted her as much as she wanted him. But he made no move toward her.

His voice was husky with longing. "Ashley, get dressed. Tonight is too special to rush."

With a smile of understanding, she went to the closet and pulled out a hot pink sundress with a plunging neckline and no back. She turned to find he'd dressed, and held it up for him to see. "This is my new sundress. I'll wear it for you tonight if you promise not to rip it or throw it into the ocean."

"You may have to stop me forcibly, but I promise I'll try."

She shook her head as her gaze wandered across the massive expanse of his shoulders. "I'd have as much chance trying to forcibly make you do anything as an ant would an elephant. You could make me do anything you want."

"I guess I could. But I'd never make you do anything you didn't want to do, you know that." Then the gleam returned to his eyes. "I'm just glad you have such varied tastes!"

At that, she threw a bottle of perfume at him, which he deftly caught. "Ah, just what we need. Perfume to scent the night and arouse the senses," he murmured, crossing the room to her.

Ashley felt she'd explode if she got any more aroused, but she didn't protest. "Where shall we put it first?" he asked, pulling out the stopper. He sprinkled some on his hands, then freeing her hair from the towel, he stroked the perfume through the long locks. "Mustn't forget behind the ears. That's one of my favorite places to nibble," he said, putting a few drops behind each one. "Now for this luscious body of yours." He tilted the bottle and let the perfume trickle between her breasts.

"That's enough!" she protested.

"No it's not," he murmured. He tilted the bottle again and she gasped as the cold perfume flowed over her stomach and lower. "But now it's enough." He sighed with satisfaction, putting the stopper back in the bottle.

He reached for the sundress. "Shall I help you? Veiled mysteries can sometimes be as enticing as nudity. They hint at what will be."

Ashley swallowed, battered by a dozen different impulses. She wanted to entice him. She wanted to seduce him right then and there, while her body burned so hot. Yet she also wanted to prolong the pleasure, as was obviously his intent. She's never known anyone like Zane. One moment, driven by frenzy, he tore the clothes from her body. And now, although he wanted her, he was willing to wait. She smiled. She knew that waiting would be sweet.

"Since I want nothing more than to entice you, help me slip into this dress."

His fingers trembled as he buttoned the tiny buttons at the back. "Do me a favor," he muttered as he worked. "From now on, buy dresses with zippers. Buttons drive me crazy!"

"Only if you're in a rush," she teased.

"With you I can't feel any other way," Zane countered. "Let's get out of here before I forget all the surprises I've planned and start some spontaneous improvising."

When they were settled in the van, Zane reached behind the seat. "Surprise number one," he offered lifting the fragrant lei of plumeria and orchid blossoms from its hiding place. He draped it around her

194

neck, kissing her gently on the mouth. "Aloha, Ashley."

Tears misted her eyes and the words almost stuck in her throat, but she had to know. "In Hawaiian that can mean hello *or* good-bye. Which is it to be?"

He'd started the van, but hearing the uncertainty beneath her words, he turned the key, stilling the rattling motor. Zane looked almost as hurt as she felt. "How can you ask that?" he demanded. "You know how I feel about you!"

Ashley felt guilty she'd hurt him after the endearing way he'd started the evening. "I'm sorry. I shouldn't have said that," she admitted. "It's just, in case you haven't noticed, I've got an inferiority complex as wide as the Waimea Canyon. Butcher professed to want me—right up until the day he packed and moved out."

"Ashley, tonight of all nights, forget Butcher. I want all your thoughts, all your passion, reserved for me. Is that so much to ask?"

She cradled the fragrant blossoms of the lei against her cheek, reveling in the softness of the petals caressing her face. "No," she whispered, "that's not too much to ask. It's what I want too."

"Great, two minds on the same wavelength! Hold on to your seat belt lady, we're off for the adventure of our lifetime," Zane promised, turning the key to start the van again.

Ashley glanced sharply at him as they neared his apartment. They'd been chatting about the events of the day, but the closer they came to his home the more excited he became. Zane obviously had something up his sleeve, and based on some of his past surprises, Ashley had no idea what to expect as he pulled into the parking lot and stopped the van.

He lived in a high rise, one of the many dotting

the area around Waikiki. They joined an elderly lady in the elevator. Zane slipped his arm around Ashley's waist, nestling her against him, and leaned over to whisper in her ear, "I'm dying to kiss you, but I don't want to shock Mrs. Brown. She feeds my fish when I'm out of town for the games."

He punched five for Mrs. Brown's floor, and eighteen for his. "Evening, Mrs. Brown," he greeted her. "How's Sylvester?"

The lady frowned. "He's doing poorly, I'm afraid. Still off his feed." The lines around her eyes crinkled mischievously. "I might have to tempt him with one of your fish. Bet he'd eat that," she teased. Her appraising glance swept over Ashley, "First time I've seen you sporting a young lady on your arm. You might introduce us."

After Zane made the introductions, Mrs. Brown advised, "You've got a good man here. Any time I have a spot of trouble in my apartment, like a jammed garbage disposal, why he's right there to fix it. Aren't many young men around who'd bother with an old woman."

Zane shifted his weight from one foot to the other, embarrassed. "Heck, you know the only reason I let you pester me is because I can't resist your cherry pie."

"Nonsense!" Mrs. Brown scoffed. "You do it because you're a nice young man and you care. Take my advice, young lady, and hang on to him."

Ashley smiled. "I'll try."

Zane chuckled as the door slid closed at the fifth floor. "Alone at last, and thirteen floors to enjoy it!" The elevator started silently upward, and he gently pushed her back against the wall, snuggling against her. "You're trapped. Now what are you going to do?" He rubbed his chest against her,

196

gently bruising the flowers of her lei. As the heady scent rose around them, adding special magic to the moment, Ashley sighed with pleasure, sliding her arms up around his neck.

"I suppose I don't have any choice. I guess I'll just have to kiss you."

The hard surface behind her, which kept her from sinking even an inch away from him, made every sensation even more intense as his kiss claimed her. She could feel every ripple of muscle as her breasts were crushed against his chest. She could feel his heartbeat flutter, then surge, as her lips parted to let him drink his fill of her. Finally to her delight she could feel through her dress the power of his desire grow, pressing eagerly against her with a thrilling hardness.

Zane deserted her mouth to start trailing kisses down into the warm hollow of her throat, his hand slipping under her dress. With a gasp, Ashley felt his touch find her.

All too soon the door of the elevator opened, and reluctantly Zane let her go. As they started out he grinned. "Tonight's going to be fun!"

"It already has been," she retorted with a grin of her own.

"Lady, believe me, it's only going to get better!" Zane promised with a confidence that added new fire to her already hot blood.

When they arrived at his door, he ordered, "Ashley close your eyes."

"Why? So you can pounce on me again?" She laughed.

"Oh, I'm going to do plenty of that tonight," he assured her, grinning wickedly. "But not now. I just don't want you to see until I have all the lights on."

"I guess I'll trust you. Usually all you want to do is turn the lights off," she teased, closing her eyes.

He left her for a moment, returning to take her hand. As he led her into the apartment he murmured, "Surprise number two is coming up. I hope you like it. Okay, open your eyes, love."

Ashley blinked, hardly believing what she was seeing. His whole living room was full of bobbing helium-filled balloons. On each one in gay letters was printed *Happy Birthday.*

She laughed, "Zane I don't believe it. How did you know I love balloons? It makes me happy just to look at them. There's just one problem. It isn't my birthday."

"Yes, it is," he insisted. "Check the calendar. Today's your thirty-third-and-a-half birthday. In exactly six months you'll be thirty-four gorgeous years old."

She turned to look at him, almost afraid to see the expression in his eyes. "You know," she whispered.

"Ashley, I've known from the beginning."

"But how? No one here but Kakalina knows how old I am."

He took her hand again and led her to the sofa, brushing aside the dancing balloons. "When that first column came out I wanted to know who in the hell was this Ashley Buchannan of the acid pen," he explained as he sat and cuddled her against his shoulder. "So I did some checking. When I found out you were the ex-wife of the infamous Butcher Buchannan, I called a friend of mine who used to play for the Packers. Remember Bulldog O'Riley?"

She smiled. "Sure I do. They were expecting triplets, and Emily went into labor at the party the owner threw for the players in the off-season. Talk about a wild scene! But it turned out all right. They had three of the most adorable little girls you've ever seen."

"Yeah, he told me, and he also told me about your thirtieth birthday party that he and Emily attended. He said Butcher was a fool to let a St. Patrick's Day baby get away. He said every Irishman knows they bring good luck. Well, six months from today is March seventeenth!"

"This is a very sweet surprise, but why did you decide to . . ."

His arm tightened around her, interrupting her question. "You ought to know. It was because of last night. I knew something that scum Razor Williams said upset you. When you wouldn't tell me what happened I decided to shake it out of him."

She pulled out of his arms to look at him. "Sammy told me he'd interrupted your fight. You didn't really hurt him, did you? I don't want you arrested for assault and battery. That would be typical of the type of trick Razor would pull."

"No, I didn't lay a finger on him." She could feel the anger in him as he growled, "Not that he didn't deserve it for dumping all that robbing-the-cradle garbage on you!"

"How did you get the truth out of him?"

Zane looked grim. "Let's just say sometimes it helps to be big, brawny, and mad as hell. He took one look at me and knew he'd better come clean. Ashley, I realized how hurt you were by what he said. And when you hurt, I hurt. So I came up with the idea of throwing you a birthday party, to let you know I know the truth and I don't give a damn!" He hesitated, "Ashley, why didn't you tell me?"

"I was afraid to," she whispered, refusing to meet his gaze.

His voice was full of hurt. "Do you trust me that

little? Haven't I made my feelings clear to you over and over again?"

"Zane, don't you understand? I was afraid I'd lose you if you knew. That's why I didn't tell you, not because I didn't trust you. I assumed that while you knew I was older than you, you thought it was only a couple of years, not six. I was afraid that would scare you off."

"It would take a hell of a lot more than that!" He took her face between his hands, kissing her gently on the mouth. "I've told you, you're the first woman to touch every part of my soul. You make me feel complete, as no one else ever has. Your age has nothing to do with those feelings you stir within me."

"You say that now. But in another ten years, when I'm over the hill . . . then what?"

"I'll just go over the hill with you. That's another one of my fantasies. I've always wanted to make love in a valley."

For once his teasing didn't bring a smile. "Zane, I wish I could believe that. This relationship already has so many potential booby traps, it scares me. My age is just one of them. What if you're traded? What if—"

He stopped her questions with a kiss. When he drew back from her enticing lips, he murmured, "My mother always used to say, 'Don't borrow trouble.' That's what you're doing, and I won't allow it," he insisted firmly. "Tonight I don't want any doubts clouding your happiness." He slipped his hand under the pink fabric to touch the softness of her breast. "Tonight I want you to feel, not think."

She sighed. Waves of pleasure rippled through her at the warmth of his touch. "You make that very easy to do. Maybe too easy."

"I haven't heard any objections before," he challenged.

"No," she admitted with a shy smile. "How can I object when I adore how you make me feel. One caress and you make me all soft, warm and sexy and ready for love."

"Prove it," he murmured, bending forward and easing the fabric aside until he could take her nipple into his mouth. Round and round, the velvety rasps of his tongue encircled it until the aching in her breast became almost unbearable.

When he lifted his head a happy smile lit his face. "Yep, I guess you were telling the truth. But I don't know about the soft part. Right then your nipple felt plenty hard and hungry to me."

"Zane, I wish you wouldn't say things like that to me. You make me blush."

He pretended to pout. "But that's one of my favorite things to do. I love doing things to you to make you blush. It means you're experiencing things for the first time, and I enjoy being the man to teach you those new things."

"You've certainly done enough of that," Ashley admitted, winding her arms around his neck. "And I've enjoyed everything you've taught me, so go right ahead, keep on making me blush. I don't mind at all."

"What a challenge," Zane laughed. "As I said, tonight's going to be a hell of a lot of fun! And all that fun's going to take energy, so I'd better feed you." He removed her clinging arms. "I hate to do this, but when you touch me, food isn't exactly the thing that comes to mind. Come with me to the kitchen so you can watch Chef Bruxton in action."

Battling their way through the sea of colorful balloons they finally made it into his dining room.

"Zane, I thought you were kidding," she said, giggling, when she saw the huge pin the tail on the donkey game hanging on the wall.

"This is a birthday party, isn't it? And at a birthday party what do you do? You play games. Trust me. I got a lot of games in mind for tonight! But first we eat, then we frolic."

She turned to go to the kitchen and saw for the first time the huge aquarium he'd built on top of what, no doubt, had been intended to be a bar. "Oh, Zane, that's incredible!"

"Like it?" he asked proudly, joining her in front of the crystal tank.

"I thought the only aquarium you had was the one you brought to my house. I had no idea you had anything like this."

"Well, I couldn't exactly move this giant thing. I just had to hope it'd be okay. The smaller one is in my bedroom."

"I've never seen such colorful fish before. I had an aquarium when I was a child, but all I had in it were guppies and goldfish."

"This is a saltwater aquarium. I caught every one of those beauties myself."

"How?"

"All it takes is some scuba gear, a coral reef, a small net, and a huge amount of patience. Here, let me introduce you."

He pointed to a bright yellow fish, striped black and white. "That's Bozo, the clownfish. The orange and white striped one hiding behind that piece of coral is Squirrely, the barred squirrelfish. The one with all the spines is Porky, the porcupine fish. You have to be careful of him. His spines are tipped with poison. The striped one over there with the soaring dorsal fin has an Hawaiian name. He's called

Kihikihi Laulau. And the bright yellow one with the spot on her tail I call Sneaky Lady. The idea is, if a predator attacks, with luck it'll go for the tail, thinking it's the eye, and maybe she'll escape. Now over by that black rock is . . ."

On and on he went, introducing her to each of the two dozen varieties he'd captured. When he finally got to Herman, the starfish, she admitted, "You know, I keep forgetting you studied oceanography. Most of the football players I knew, including Butcher, majored in phys. ed. Which, no doubt, was the only thing they could pass."

He tapped his chest. "That's me, a man of varied interests." He winked. "I'll show you a few more later tonight, but right now what I'm interested in is food. I hope steak, baked potatoes, salad, and champagne will be all right."

"Sounds wonderful. Want me to mix the salad?"

Zane made the dinner extra festive in honor of her half birthday. There were balloons tied to her chair, and even a party hat he insisted she wear. When the last piece of steak had disappeared, she started to gather up the dirty dishes but he stopped her.

"We're not done yet, birthday girl. We haven't had the birthday cake yet."

A few minutes later he came out of the kitchen proudly carrying a rather unusual-looking dessert, and stuck in the top was one lit candle.

"What's that?" Ashley asked, eyeing the strange concoction. "I don't mean to be rude after that wonderful dinner, but that doesn't look like any birthday cake I've ever seen."

"I guess I should rephrase that. We're not having birthday cake. We're having birthday pie. It's one of my mother's specialties—mud pie!" He beamed happily. "I had to call her this afternoon on the mainland to get the recipe."

"Uh, I hate to be difficult, but mud pie doesn't exactly sound appetizing."

"O ye of little faith! Don't condemn until you taste it." He scooped up a spoonful and held it toward her lips. The thought that he was pulling a prank crossed her mind, but still she opened her mouth for him.

Her tongue curled around the luscious mixture and she sighed happily. "What was that?" she asked, savoring the last wonderful drop. "It was fantastic! It almost makes turning thirty-three-and-a-half worthwhile."

Smiling, he watched her dig her spoon into his treat for a second serving. "I knew you'd love it. It's my favorite too. All you need is crushed chocolate cookies for the crust, a half gallon of frozen coffee ice cream for the middle, chocolate syrup for the topping, and one candle for a very special lady to make it perfect."

"Aren't you going to join me?" she asked, taking another spoonful.

"Are you kidding?" He laughed, joining her in the coffee ice cream–chocolate bacchanal.

Minutes later Ashley looked at the destruction they'd wrought and laughed. "One mud pie blown to smithereens. I swear, knowing you has destroyed all my control."

"Do you see me complaining?" he asked with a chuckle. "I love it when you lose control!"

"I was talking about my diet regime. Do you realize how many more miles I will have to swim to get rid of this delicious indulgence?"

"There are other ways of getting exercise."

Ashley waved her spoon at him. "I know all about

204

your ideas concerning exercise. They're all X-rated."

"I'm hurt. I truly am." Zane tried, but failed, to look virtuous. "Here I was thinking of the innocent exercise of playing pin the tail on the donkey, and you accuse me of having lecherous designs on your body."

"You aren't really serious about doing that, are you?"

"Sure. Why else would I have bought the game? But first you have to open your half-birthday present," he said, handing her a small gaily wrapped box.

She ripped open the paper to find the skimpiest bikini she'd ever seen.

"See," he said, grinning, "I told you I'd replace the one I tossed into the sea."

She laughed. "If I wear this the shore patrol will probably bust me for indecent exposure."

He winked. "I'd bail you out. Now, come on. It's time to play pin the tail on the donkey. You're going to love it!" He laughed lightheartedly. "I haven't done this in years."

But she refused to budge. Zane came around the table to her. "Ashley, there's a lot of child in you, a child who's been deprived." He grinned. "And you're making progress. Look, you're even wearing that silly hat. Why not play the game?"

She looked up into his incredibly blue eyes. "If it will make you happy, I'll play any game."

He laughed with all the power of a conquering Viking. "I'll remember that!" he said, holding out his hand. "Come, I've got everything ready, even the blindfold."

"You know, you're crazy," Ashley insisted, but she put her hand in his.

"Of course I am. It's part of my charm."

The flannel felt soft and pleasant as he fit it over her eyes, blocking her sight. Her fingers fumbled but she finally grasped the sharp pin and paper tail he gave her to hold. His strong hands spun her around until she had no idea which way she was facing. Stumbling forward, she started out. "If you go that way, you'll crash into my fish tank," Zane advised. She turned and tried again. "If you go *that* way, you won't find the donkey, but you'll probably pop a lot of balloons," he warned, laughing softly.

She tried yet another direction and bumped into a very solid, a very massive, a very warm object. As his arms swept around her, she asked, "What about the poor donkey?"

He took the pin and paper tail from her hand and dropped it on the table. "I had to stop you. I didn't want to bring the SPCA down on our heads. Where's your compassion? Think of the cruelty, sticking sharp pins in some poor donkey's derriere! Ashley, how could you?" He drew her tighter against him.

She wrapped her arms about him, the blindness seeming to heighten all of her other senses. The feel of his massive chest, the play of his muscles against her softness, the scent of the crushed plumeria blossoms of her lei; everything seemed sweeter, better, more sensual.

Before she even realized she'd spoken the words in her heart escaped. "You know what game I want to play, and it has nothing to do with tailless donkeys or paper hats."

"Yes, I know, because it's what I want too." With one sweep of his arms he picked her up and started for the bedroom.

She began to take off her blindfold, but he

206

stopped her. "No. Tonight I want you to feel. If you can see, you might think."

"Zane, this is ridiculous! I want to see you. I love the way your blue eyes fire with hunger. I love the way you take advantage of my . . . *Ahhh.*"

Her protest faded to a murmur of pleasure as he lifted her dress and his questing fingers found what they sought. Only then did he rip the blindfold from her eyes so she could see the desire she'd stirred in him. Her hands reached for his belt. "I'm tired of thinking," she pleaded. "Make me feel!"

CHAPTER THIRTEEN

As if hating the thought of being apart from her even for a second, Zane knelt on the bed to lay Ashley back against the pillows, following her down into the lush softness of the mattress without ever letting her out of his arms.

The fire raged within her as she wound her arms around his powerful neck and pulled his mouth down to plunder hers. Her lips parted eagerly, yet he refused to take all she offered, instead brushing light kisses against her lips and then deserting her mouth for her ear. Even through the barrier of their clothes she could tell how powerfully his desire raged, yet he didn't hurry. He blew words of love in her ear, drawing a moan from her as his tongue plunged into the sensitive interior.

She moved her hips suggestively against him, whispering huskily, "Zane, you're driving me crazy. I want you. Make love to me. *Please.*"

He lifted his head to look at her, his blue eyes flaming, and shook his head. "Oh, I promise I will make love to you tonight, over and over. But not now, not yet. I want to show you how much I want you. I want you to burn with the same need."

She swallowed. "I'm already burning," she admitted shyly.

He smiled. "You're not hot enough, my love, not

hot enough. But you will be," he promised, easing the straps of her sundress down her arms, leaving her bare to the waist except for the fragrant lei.

As she took off his shirt, his hands cupped her breasts almost reverently. "You have the most beautiful body I've ever seen."

Pushing his unbuttoned shirt aside, Ashley ran her hands over his chest, tangling her fingers in his thick curly blond hair, exploring every muscle. "You have the most beautiful body I've ever seen," she said.

A spark of jealousy flared in his eyes. "And tell me, Ashley, just how many have you seen? I thought you said your only lover had been Butcher."

"So I lied. I've seen hundreds of male bodies," Ashley answered with complete truthfulness.

Zane's hands came down on her shoulders, pushing her deeper into the mattress. "Hundreds!" he demanded in a voice sharpened by anger.

"Sure. Haven't you ever heard of a beach? Oahu has dozens of them, and they're all full of sexy men!" The teasing note faded from her voice. "But none as sexy as you," she admitted.

Zane collasped against her, burying his face against her neck. "Ashley, tease me like that again and I won't be responsible for my actions. I want you so much the thought of you even looking at another man hurts!"

"I'm only human. I can't promise I won't look if a gorgeous hunk struts by, but"—she paused as she ran her hand down his side, slipping it between their two bodies to caress the place already hard and throbbing with need for her—"I do promise I won't touch."

"You'd damn well better not!" Zane insisted, his voice raspy with desire. "The only man I want you to touch is me." He closed his eyes. "Touch me, Ashley. Love me as I love you."

Her fingers trembled as she pulled down the zipper of his slacks to fulfill his wish. She'd forgotten she'd made him take off his briefs, and froze at the shock of finding him naked beneath her questing fingers. At once, the warmth of what she'd found urged her on.

She began stroking him, until with a moan Zane grabbed her hand, making her stop. "Ashley, my God, what you do to me," he rasped. "We've got to slow down, or the loving will be over before I can satisfy you." Zane swallowed, and with obvious reluctance, eased away from her. He stood, his pants dropping around his ankles, and he kicked them away, staying for a moment to look down at her.

Butcher had always insisted they make love in the dark, so sight had never played a part in her arousal. Now, with no darkness to hide the source of her pleasure, Ashley let her eyes roam over Zane, caressing him with her gaze. Blond hair streaked by the Hawaiian sun; that incredibly sensual brow hinting at the savage, the primitive within his soul; blue eyes now hot with his need for her; the lean cheeks, the mouth so capable of giving her exquisite pleasure; somehow as she looked at him, she knew his face would remain forever etched in her mind.

Zane made a move to join her on the bed, but she held up her hand. "No, I want to look at you," she murmured, gazing on his chest as if wanting to memorize every ripple of muscle, every strand of blond curling hair. Then, because she had no power to stop herself, her eyes traveled lower.

"Like what you see?" he asked softly.

"Mmm, I sure do. If you come here I'll show you how much."

Ashley sat up, reaching behind her to unbutton her dress, but Zane stopped her. "No. I want to take you as you are." He pushed her gently back against the pillows, kneeling beside her. Her heart pounded as he reached for the hem of her sundress. As he slowly eased it up her thighs, the brush of his hand sent shivers of delight directly to the place he most wanted to find. When it was folded above her waist, his hand reached to touch what his eyes couldn't desert. As his fingers found her moist and ready—oh, so ready for him, his control snapped.

Somehow making love still partially clothed seemed wickedly sinful. Like the Viking fantasies that had fired her desire, it ignited the wanton part of her soul. At first it had been he who drove her to a frenzy of passion. Tonight she drove him, offering everything, denying nothing, until finally they found that magical place were nothing but sensation existed.

As he collapsed weakly into her arms, he kissed her softly in gratitude. "I was supposed to make this night special for you, and you're the one who made it special for me," he confessed.

Her arms tightened around him. "If you're happy and satisfied, believe me, so am I."

Their passion had been so wild both were exhausted, and without another word they drifted off to sleep. It was the middle of the night before he roused her by rubbing the flowers of the lei she was still wearing against her cheeks, her mouth, her closed eyelids.

"Mmm, that feels good," she murmured sleepily.

"I know something that feels better," he teased, propping himself up on one elbow, a wicked gleam sparkling in his blue eyes. "I've got an idea. Why don't you roll over on your stomach?"

Startled by the suggestion, her eyes flew open. "Zane no! I can't! You . . . can't! We—we just can't."

He laughed at her embarrassed confusion. "My, my. So my innocent love has some decidedly naughty thoughts inside that beautiful head of hers. Shame on you!" he teased. "All I wanted to do was unbutton your dress."

She'd blushed before, but nothing could compare to this. Ashley rolled over and buried her face in the pillow so he wouldn't see.

Zane took his time unbuttoning her sundress, as if savoring each inch of flesh he bared, easing it away from her body and tossing it to the floor. Before she knew what he intended to do, he leaned over, kissed her on her bare bottom, and gave her a hard pat.

"Okay, you're as indecently clothed—or as unclothed, I should say, as I am. You can turn over again."

She did, and he smiled, gently touching the flowers, which were the only thing she wore. "I do love a woman who knows how to wear a lei." He nestled her against him under the sheet, murmuring, "Tired? Do you want to go back to sleep?"

"Do you?"

"What do you think?" He laughed.

"I think we think the same way," Ashley answered, raising herself up to kiss his mouth.

Even though Zane had talked about fun and games—all the pouncing and prowling he planned to do—through the remaining hours of the night his lovemaking was gentle, joyously prolonged, thoroughly loving; as if through the adoration of her body he hoped to prove to her how sincere he was when he said the six years between them meant

212

less than nothing to him. By morning Ashley could almost believe him.

Over the next weeks as the Kings moved out of the preseason into the regular schedule, Ashley was happier than she'd ever been. Her hard-hitting columns continued to delight Monica; the Friday night concerts with Zane at her side were marvelous; the Kings continued to win and Zane to be outstanding. But that wasn't what was putting the radiant smile on her face. Zane was—Zane and the nights of love he gave her. The only time the smile faded was when the doubts, those doubts that stubbornly refused to leave her, sneaked in to steal a bit of her happiness.

It was Monday morning after the Kings had won again, when the phone on her desk rang. The blank screen of her word processor stared back at her, and she grabbed the receiver eagerly, hoping it was Sammy. It wasn't.

Ashley frowned at the words that greeted her. "Hey, pretty lady, guess who this is?"

"I have no idea," she answered, trying to put as much ice in her voice as she could.

"This is Touchdown Broczinsky, or as you renamed me, 'Troublesome' Broczinsky. Bet you thought you'd have to be the one to call me, didn't you?"

"I really hadn't given it much thought."

Obviously unused to this uninterested attitude from the usually adoring press, Broczinsky snapped, "Hell, lady, I'm good copy. Don't you know that?"

Ashley smiled as a sweet memory returned. "Yes, I do. In fact, I've already done a column on you."

"Yeah, I know! And let me tell you . . ." Realizing anger wasn't the wisest tactic, he let the harshness fade from his voice. "Yeah, well you know how nicknames are. Some are earned, most are just jokes. 'Troublesome' was one of the latter. But hell, that's ancient history. What I want to know is why you haven't devoted another column to me. Damn, I've saved this franchise single-handedly! If it weren't for me they'd still be in the cellar, not at the top of the division. But do I see my stats in your column? No. Do I even see my name in your column? No! Look, baby doll, what is it? Do you want free tickets for your friends? It's done. Do you want an exclusive interview with the great Broczinsky? It's done. Are you mad because I haven't put the move on you, like Razor Williams? Hell, we can even fix that. Are you getting my message, baby doll?"

"I certainly am Troublesome. And I have a very simple answer. Don't call me, I'll call you."

As his shouted, obscene remark about her parentage burned down the line, Ashley very delicately hung up the receiver, smiling, and started typing: "What type of man makes a pass at a reporter just so he can see his name in the headlines? Today this reporter found out."

Thirty minutes later, after she'd delivered the finished column to Ray and returned to her desk, the phone rang again. "Great!" she muttered. "Just what I need. This time it's probably Razor Williams with his usual macho line." The phone jangled for the fourth time. "Yeah, I'll bet it's him. It's been at least three days since he's called," she muttered in disgust. The phone rang again, and again, before curiosity got the best of her.

"Thank God, it's you," she said when she heard Zane's voice. "You wouldn't believe the phone call I got a little while ago from your great quarterback, Broczinsky."

"Oh yes I would. He came charging back into the locker room after he talked to you. And I'll tell you this, things he said about the woman I wish was in my arms right now were uh— Well, let's just say they weren't complimentary."

"You see what I mean about all football players?" she asked, fuming. "That man's ego could float a battleship!"

Zane sounded hurt. "I thought I'd convinced you I had my ego under control."

"Zane, I'm sorry. But I can't stand that type of macho egotistical line. Hey," she went on, "you never told me how you keep your ego under control, and I admit you deserve to have one after the great games you've been playing."

"Give me five minutes," he said mysteriously. "If I can fix it, I'll call you back."

"Fix what?" she demanded, but Zane had already hung up the phone.

"That man is just one surprise after another," she muttered. Remembering his surprise of the night before, when he'd sprinkled fresh gardenia petals over her nude body before joining her in bed, she smiled. Come to think of it, surprises were kind of nice. At least his surprises!

Ashley glanced at her watch. Four minutes and thirty seconds. Four minutes and forty-five seconds. Four minutes . . . A few seconds before the five minutes were up the phone rang. "You just made it," she joked.

"It's all set. Is your column done?"

"Yes, and wait until you hear what Broczinsky has to say about me tomorrow!"

She could see his massive shoulders shrug as he

215

muttered, "Who cares? Be out front in twenty minutes. I'll pick you up. I hope you're wearing slacks," he added to her befuddlement.

"I am, but why—"

"Great! Just be there, okay, love?"

"Sure, but why do you want me to—" The phone went dead before she could finish the question.

Eighteen minutes later she reached the lobby. Just as she was wondering if she should go outside to wait for Zane, she heard the whine of a high-powered motorcycle. Her first thought was, He wouldn't! But at once, she realized he would.

Going outside she found Zane idling at the curb. She took one look at his bike and shook her head. "You've got to be kidding. I'm not getting on the back of that thing! I'm too old to play Hell's Angels!"

He cut the motor, put down the kickstand, and dismounted. "Why not?" He held out a shiny black thing that looked like a space helmet to her. "I even bought you your own helmet." Before she could say anything, he went on. "As the ad says, 'Try it, you're going to like it.' Have you ever ridden on the back of one of these? It's a real experience, especially with someone else on board." He closed his eyes. "Picture this. We hit a bump. You're crushed against my back." He grinned, with his eyes still closed. "Imagine what that would feel like. And then there's the wind. Remember the night of the hurricane? Well, on my bike the wind wouldn't be outside, it'd be—"

"Okay, I get the picture." She laughed. "Balloons, mud pie, pin the tail on the donkey, seduction scenes where all I'm wearing is a lei—what's next?"

He climbed back on the cycle and moved the

powerful machine back and forth between his legs. "Climb up behind me and you'll see."

She sighed, jamming the helmet onto her head. "Zane Bruxton, you may be the death of me yet."

"No, Ashley Buchannan, if you weren't so stubborn you'd see I'm your life," he retorted, revving the motor to prove it. "Hang on, here we go."

Ashley had never ridden on a motorcycle in her life, and for the first couple of miles all she could do was hang on to Zane and pray. But when nothing awful happened she began to relax. With the wind whipping past them at speeds she didn't want to think about, it was impossible to talk. With every bump, with every extra rev of the motor she experienced sensations very alien to her usual world. Finally she let herself go with the pulsations throbbing between her legs, resting her head against Zane's back and letting the real world slip away until only feeling remained. When he finally killed the motor, she lifted her head and was astonished to find herself in the middle of what was obviously a university campus.

Even before he got off the motorcycle, someone hailed him. "Zane, I've been looking for you. Don't you know Jamison is desperate for—"

"Dr. Maitland, I'm just going over to meet with him. In the meantime I'd like you to meet Ashley Buchannan."

"*The* Ashley Buchannan?" The rangy professor straightened to his full six foot six inches. "I don't admit this to many people, but I'm a sports addict. And your column is the best. I love the way you cut through all that PR bull and just give us the facts."

"Thank you. It's nice to know somebody reads what I write."

"Not somebody, everybody!" Dr. Maitland said

warmly. "Now I've got to be off. My computer is waiting. Say hello to Oscar for me."

"Who's Oscar?" Ashley asked as they watched him lope off.

"It's a surprise," Zane answered. "Now let's go find Dr. Jamison."

As they walked through the sprawling complex, Ashley said, "This is going to sound like a stupid question for someone who was raised in Hawaii, but where are we? I know this isn't the university."

"It's the oceanographic institute. I hope to study here."

They found Dr. Jamison leaning against the rail of a huge tank, watching a hammerhead shark swim around in slow circles.

Ashley shuddered. "Ever since I saw *Jaws* I can't stand looking at those things."

"Nonsense!" Dr. Jamison shoved his glasses back on his nose. "Sharks are magnificent animals. They should be admired, not feared. Why, do you know more people die from bee stings each year than shark attacks?"

"No, I didn't know that," she admitted.

The professor turned to Zane. "When can I have your data? You're holding up my research."

"You'll have it next week," he promised. "Is everything arranged?"

For the first time a smile cracked his stern demeanor. "Indeed it is, thanks to my most efficient secretary." He reached into his pocket and tossed something to Zane. "There are the keys. Oscar is yours for the afternoon."

"I'll send your secretary some flowers as a thank-you present."

Dr. Jamison leveled a finger at Ashley. "Remember, young lady, what I said about sharks. When you see them today, look at their beauty and their sublime grace as they move through the water, not their teeth."

Ashley smiled. "I promise."

She linked her arm with Zane's as they started off. "Where are we going to see sharks today? Are you taking me to Sea Life Park?"

"Nope, we're going to get a lot closer than that. But I'm not going to tell you how, so don't bother to ask."

Ashley pinched his arm, "Brother, are you being mysterious today! But I didn't become an ace reporter through lack of persistence, so I'll try again. What data do you have that Dr. Jamison needs?"

Rounding the corner of a building, they could see the ocean spread out before them. Zane sighed. "There's something about the first glimpse of the ocean that always stirs my senses." He looked down at her and winked. "It also stirs my Viking blood."

Ashley clutched at the neck of her blouse. "Now I know I'm in trouble," she teased. "I just bought this a week ago."

"I'll try to control myself, but I make no promises."

She squeezed his arm playfully. "I guess I'll take my chances. I don't think even you are brazen enough to throw me to the ground, rip off my clothes, and have your way with me with all these people around."

Zane sighed with pretended frustration. "I guess my R and R will just have to wait until we find a more private place. I bet Oscar can find one."

"Oscar, Oscar, Oscar," she muttered in disgust. "When am I going to meet this mysterious friend of yours?"

"When we get to where he lives," Zane answered evasively, obviously intent on keeping it a surprise.

"Okay Mr. Unhelpful, I'll try the other question. What are you working on for Dr. Jamison?"

"That I can answer. It's an extension of some work I did on plate tectonics at USC."

When Ashley sighed, her frustration was real. "Well, you answered the question and I don't know any more than before. What's plate— Whatever you said?"

"It's pretty complicated but I'll try to explain. As you probably know, the earth's crust is not static. It's riding on a series of plates. I'm trying to help Dr. Jamison find out how, why, and when they're going to move," Zane explained.

"That's kind of a strange hobby," she said, laughing, "but I guess if it turns you on, why not?"

Zane started to say something but changed his mind. They'd arrived at a small boat house. Unlocking the gate with the keys Mr. Jamison had given him, he guided Ashley through. "Take hold of my hand and close your eyes."

"Oh, no, not again. Last time it was balloons! Now what?"

"I thought you were anxious to meet Oscar."

"Okay, okay, I give up. The suspense is killing me," she confessed, closing her eyes.

He took her hand and led her onto the jetty.

"Oscar, this is Ashley. Ashley, meet Oscar."

Ashley opened her eyes and looked at the small white cylindrical craft which was moored inside the small building and asked, "Okay, I see it. Now tell me what I'm seeing."

"It's Oscar the minisub, and it's ours for the entire afternoon."

"We can't both fit into that thing!"

"Well, I admit it's going to be crowded," Zane said, leaning over to open the hatch. "I'm afraid you'll have to hold the picnic basket on your lap."

She hugged him. "Zane, you're the most wonderful man!"

"I wondered when you were going to notice." He waggled his eyebrows at her. "I was afraid you'd accuse me of using this as a sneaky trick just to get you alone on some deserted beach so I could practice a little R and R on your delectable body," he said, winking. "Of course, that's exactly what I'm doing. But if you won't tell, neither will I."

"Do you think we can trust Oscar to keep his mouth shut?" she joked.

"Ah, never fear, Zane is here—with a plan." He leaned over to whisper in her ear. "When he's not looking we'll toss your blouse over his headlight. That way I can ravish your body any way I want to, and he'll never know."

She patted him on the back. "A stroke of genius. Your willing captive awaits. Let's go."

He helped her through the hatch. "Watch where you step. The picnic basket is there on the floor. I don't want you to turn the potato salad into mush."

He hadn't been kidding about the tight fit. After he'd struggled to fit his massive frame through a hatch designed to accommodate normal-size people, they could barely move. But Ashley didn't complain. She enjoyed touching him.

Zane started flipping switches, explaining what was happening. "Usually these subs have to be launched from a ship, but the water's so deep here we can submerge without worrying about the waves. Hang on, you're in for the ride of a lifetime."

"I thought I had that last night."

He chuckled at the compliment without replying,

221

turning on the headlight as they started to submerge.

For the next minutes as they cruised along the reef, Ashley spoke not a word, but her *oohs* and *ahhs* told Zane how beautiful she was finding his world of crystalline azure water, coral, and colorful darting fish.

"Well, now you know my secret," he said. "You can see how this magnificence would control anyone's ego."

"It does make you feel pretty small and insignificant, doesn't it?" she agreed.

He was about to say something else when she gasped, "Oh, Zane, look!" Ashley pointed in excitement at the elegant stingray gliding by outside the porthole. "He doesn't even seem to notice us. You'd think he'd be scared."

"With a tail like his he can afford to ignore anything. He knows no one will come near."

An hour later he asked, "Have you seen enough?"

"I don't think I could ever see enough of this beauty!" She leaned over and kissed him on the cheek. "Even if this was just a trick to lure me to some deserted beach, I thank you. I'll never forget today."

"I'll never forget any day I spend with you," he countered with a loving smile. "Now, how about that picnic? I'm getting hungry."

"Where is this deserted beach? In Hawaii it's almost impossible to find one."

He turned the minisub away from the reef and headed out into the open sea. "I discovered this place by accident when I was checking some faulting of the ocean floor near Molokai. It's a tiny little lagoon with a break in the guarding reef just big

222

enough to sneak the sub through. You won't even have to get your feet wet wading ashore. The sand is so clean I can moor the sub right at the shoreline.''

Ashley was looking out the side porthole. "How would you like to run into that on a dark night?" Zane asked, tapping her on the arm.

Ashley shuddered as she looked at the twenty-foot striped tiger shark swimming slowly in front of them. Yet even gripped with a tremor of fear, knowing it was one of the few Hawaiian sharks dangerous to humans, she had to admit Dr. Jamison was right. It was a magnificent animal.

It was tricky, maneuvering through the reef off Molokai, but the result was worth the effort. Zane beached the minisub and opened the hatch for her to see their private piece of paradise. Glistening white sand, golden shower trees in full bloom; there was even flowering jasmine vining through the palm trees to greet them.

Zane helped her out of the minisub, and reached back in for the picnic basket. Dr. Jamison's secretary had thought of everything. A whole bucket of fried chicken, potato salad, flaky biscuits, and a bottle of champagne iced down in its own little cooler. There were even crystal wineglasses. The only thing missing that would have made it absolutely perfect was some coffee ice cream.

With a snap of his wrists Zane spread out the bright red and white checkered tablecloth, as Ashley gathered some sprays of fragrant white ginger she spotted growing under the palm trees to decorate their picnic setting. He handed her a glass of champagne and clinked his glass with hers. "To you.''

"That's not a very original toast," she teased.

"It's hard to be creative on an empty stomach.

223

But believe me, after we've eaten I'll be plenty creative, and you'll enjoy every creative idea I think of. Now hand me that chicken. I'm starving!"

When the chicken was reduced to a pile of bones, Zane moved the picnic things aside and stretched out on the tablecloth, locking his arms behind his head. "It almost feels like we're alone on a deserted island with nothing to do but eat, sleep, and make love on the sand."

"That probably sounds more romantic than it would be. I bet you'd be bored in a week."

Zane turned his head to look at her. "If you were the woman I was making love to, I could never be bored." He closed his eyes. "I think I'll take a nap."

"I think I won't let you," Ashley threatened.

"How do you propose to keep me awake? Let's see . . . to do that I guess you'd have to . . . stimulate me somehow."

"Well, let's see how creative I can be." She slid over next to him. "First I think I'll unbutton your shirt. That way maybe the sea breeze caressing your bare skin might stimulate you."

As her fingers worked, Zane asked, "Just the sea breeze? Is that the only thing that's going to be caressing my skin? I don't think that would be enough to keep me awake."

"You don't?" Ashley pretended to be surprised as his shirt fell open. "Guess I'll have to think of something else. Ahh, the perfect thing," she said, grabbing a sprig of the white ginger blossoms. She trailed the blossoms over his chest and some of the petals crushed, releasing a heady scent.

"Sorry, that's not working, my eyelids are starting to droop," he commented, slowly closing his eyes.

He faked the deep rhythmic breathing of sleep. "I

224

know just the way to stimulate you," Ashley said, glancing around.

"I wondered when you were going to figure it out," Zane mumbled. "Go ahead, stimulate me. I'm waiting."

With impish delight Ashley scooped up a handful of ice from the cooler. The unsuspecting Zane let out a wild yelp as she started rubbing the ice against his chest. His eyes flew open and he made a quick grab for her hands.

"You see, I knew I could wake you up," Ashley said, laughing.

"That's not exactly what I had in mind," he muttered, throwing the ice away.

"Then there's only one thing left to try. Lay back and close your eyes."

He looked profoundly doubtful. "The last time I closed my eyes you pounced on me with ice cubes. What are you going to do this time, pelt me with chicken bones?"

"Go on, lay back. You've given me enough surprises for this afternoon. Let me give you one."

"Oh, well." Zane chuckled, lying back down on the tablecloth and closing his eyes. "If you try anything too wild, I guess I'm big enough to fight you off." He heard Ashley rise. "Where are you going?" he demanded. "You can't surprise me if you aren't here."

"I'll be right back. There's something I have to do."

"Better hurry. I'm feeling sleepy again."

"Don't worry," she assured him, "this will certainly wake you up."

Quickly she went over to the minisub, took off her blouse, draped it over the headlight, and stripped off the rest of her clothes. Her bare feet made no sound as she returned to Zane. Kneeling beside him she began to rub her breasts lightly and teasingly against his chest.

He sighed deeply at the touch. "For a bright lady it sure took you long enough to get it right," he murmured as his arms came up to pull her against him. He opened his eyes and saw she was completely naked. "Your surprises are getting better and better!" He grinned. "And you're right, seeing you like this does stimulate me enough to make me forget all about that nap."

"I'm glad, because I've got better things to do than listen to you snore."

"What things? Give me a hint."

She took his face between her hands. "Oh, things like this," she murmured, bending to kiss him.

The Hawaiian sun, burning bright, warmed her bare back, but it couldn't compete with the warmth Zane's touch sent spreading through her. As always his lips, his tongue, the words blown in her ear built a passion within her too hot to ignore, as his hands found the secret places that gave her the most pleasure.

Eagerly her hands went to the waistband of his slacks, but he stopped her. "Not yet, love. What I'm feeling is too fantastic to rush." He pushed her gently onto her back. "Now it's your turn to close your eyes."

"Only if when I open them you'll be nude too. I'd hate for you to have to explain to Dr. Jamison that your pants were ripped because you were attacked by a sex-crazed reporter."

"That's one deal I'm sure not going to turn down. In fact, why don't you wait a minute before you close those beautiful eyes of yours? There's an image I want you to remember."

Quickly he shed his clothes. As he stood before her, splendidly naked, splendidly aroused, he whispered, "Think of me like this when you cannot see."

As she looked at him Ashley trembled, wanting him so badly she didn't know if she could wait. "Hurry. If I have to wait much longer the fire's going to flame so hot I'll get first degree burns."

"If you want me to hurry, then close your eyes."

Ashley obeyed, carrying the image of him standing before her with her into the darkness. She felt him sink to the tablecloth beside her and she opened her arms to receive him, but he didn't come. Gasping, she felt the sting of an ice cube between her breasts.

"Zane!" she protested. "Stop it."

"Sorry, love, but no. Relax, just feel," he whispered, using the ice cube to caress her nipples.

The sun beating down coupled with the heat within her made her flesh burn, heightening the contrast of the ice. The pleasurable torture was so exquisite she moaned, as she felt her nipples harden at the touch. He moved the ice lower, tracing over her stomach, some of the drops trickling into the place that burned the hottest. Ashley writhed beneath the touch, and still he didn't stop. Moving the ice over the soft inner part of her thighs, Zane sucked in his breath as her legs parted, offering him the most intimate caress. When she felt the ice touch her she shuddered alone in her pleasure.

CHAPTER FOURTEEN

During the days that followed, Ashley was happier than she'd ever been in her life. Not even the wild exhilaration of being pursued by Butcher could match the deep heart-filling satisfaction she found with Zane. Whether it was listening to music together after dinner, walking on the beach in the moonlight, or making love, each moment seemed more special than the last. Not wanting the magic to end, she pushed the lingering doubts about the future away, and let herself float through each day, knowing it would end in Zane's arms.

Ashley walked in to work one Wednesday morning to find Ray waiting for her. "I just got off the phone with Monica, and let me tell you she is really flying high. The circulation figures for last week have just been released and there's been another five percent increase. And as everyone knows we owe that five percent directly to your column. It's the talk of Honolulu."

Ashley glowed with pleasure. "I just hope Monica appreciates the effort. It's not easy coming up with five columns a week. Especially when she doesn't want any on the laudatory side—which I still contend is unfair, considering how well the Kings are playing."

"Take my advice, don't bring that up again.

Monica can be a real tiger if crossed. And as for appreciating your effort, she appreciates it enough to want to take you out to lunch again," Ray informed her. "The limo will be here at noon."

"Are you coming with us? After all, you are my editor. Part of my success is due to you."

"No, I can't." He scowled. "She invited me, but I've got to spend the day getting figures together for a budget meeting."

Ashley patted his arm sympathetically. "Better you than me. Math was never my best subject."

"Will you be able to get your column to me before you leave?" Ray asked.

"I don't know. It depends whether or not I can get to my source. There's only three weeks left before the trading deadline, and I thought I'd do a piece on who might go and who might be coming. That type of column always seems to hook the readers." She frowned. "I just feel sorry for the players' families. Of all the things I disliked about being married to Butcher, moving all over the country and never being able to put down roots was the worst."

Ray had no patience with tales of marital woe. "Well, you're settled now, so forget it. As for me I'd better settle down with my calculator." He turned to go. "Let me know when your column is done."

Ashley was lucky enough to catch Sammy when he was free to talk. After filling her in on all the trade rumors flying around the locker room, he added, "And there's one more tidbit. You remember Bubba Pirr, the linebacker who went down in that first preseason game?"

"Sure, his injury is what gave Zane the chance to show how good he really is." Ashley smiled.

"I just got the doctor's report. Bubba's knee is

229

healing faster than expected. He should be back in a week or two, but between you and me, coach Mitchell is so pleased with the way Zane is playing, I don't know if Bubba will get his starting job back or not."

"Thanks, Sammy. Even if Monica doesn't want me to say anything positive, that's one item that's going to get printed!"

Ashley had to rush but she managed to get the column on Ray's desk just before noon. The limousine was waiting at the curb when she got outside. The chauffeur doffed his cap and helped her into the back seat of the Cadillac, where Monica was waiting.

The older woman glanced at her diamond-encrusted wristwatch in disapproval. Before she could say anything Ashley hurried to apologize. "I'm so sorry that I was a few minutes late. Ray wanted my column in by noon, so I had to finish it."

As the huge car glided away from the curb, Monica's frown eased. "I suppose I can understand that. Just be sure you don't make a habit of keeping me waiting. Nothing tries my patience more."

"I won't," Ashley promised fervently, not wanting to be the recipient of Monica's wrath.

"What is your column for tomorrow about?"

They began disussing it, and Ashley didn't pay any attention to where they were going. Her eyes widened in delight when the limousine glided to a stop under a striped canopy and she saw the raised gold letters. Chez Anton was the most exclusive French restaurant in the islands, and so expensive she'd never even considered going there. Thank goodness Monica was picking up the tab. Lunch here would probably cost her a week's wages.

Monica was greeted like a favored customer. Chef Anton himself rushed out of the kitchen to bow over her jeweled hand. "Madame Bennett, you grow more beautiful with each passing day," he gushed, seating them at the prime table, where they could best see and be seen.

His towering white hat bobbing excitedly, he exclaimed, "For you, Madame Bennett, nothing but the best. A bottle of my finest French champagne, of course. Then to start, I suggest my special prawn soup, a heart of palm salad, followed by my *spécialité*, fresh salmon baked in pastry." He pressed his thumb and first two fingers to his lips. "And *finalement*, to crown a meal fit for a queen, the *pièce de résistance*, my famous macadamia nut souffle."

Monica glared at him. "You can take your *pièce de résistance* and ship it back to France. How dare you forget! I won't eat macadamia nut anything!" she snapped. The chef looked like he was about to cry.

Monica softened just a bit. "The menu you suggested will be fine, Anton, but see that we're served papaya sorbet for dessert. Is that understood?"

When he'd scurried off, Ashley couldn't resist asking, "Are you allergic to macadamia nuts, or are you allergic to the fact they're the way Clyde Winston made his fortune?"

Monica chose to ignore Ashley's question. "I assume Ray mentioned the rise in the circulation figures," she said, giving her a freezing glance.

Ashley nodded, letting the question drop. "I'm glad you are pleased."

"Pleased?" Monica gasped. "I'm more than pleased, I'm ecstatic!"

Through the delicious meal they discussed the impact her columns were having. As Ashley scooped up the last luscious bite of the salmon, she inquired, "Have there been any more attempts to buy the *News*? I thought maybe that's why you'd asked me out to lunch again."

"No. Clyde seems content to let his public relations department handle the situation. They've been bombarding the *News* almost daily with complaints about your columns. I don't like it." Monica insisted, downing her remaining champagne in one gulp.

"They can complain all they want to," Ashley observed, confused by Monica's vehemence. "It doesn't change anything. The Kings public relations department isn't powerful enough to hurt you or the *News,* is it?"

"Of course not!" Monica insisted with a wave of her hand, as if the Kings' PR staff were no more important than gnats. "Besides, that's not my point. I don't like the way Clyde has raised himself above the fight."

"I thought we were reporting on the Kings, not fighting them," Ashley protested.

Monica didn't even seem to hear her. "I don't even know if Clyde is even reading your columns anymore, and that is something I don't like," she complained.

Not yet having a very clear idea what was really bothering Monica, Ashley ventured, "So I may have lost one reader. From the circulation figures you just gave me, I've picked up hundreds of others."

Monica scowled at her. "Has that champagne addled your brain? If Clyde is not reading your column, then he isn't being affected by it, and that I won't tolerate."

"What do you expect me to do?" Ashley asked in confusion as the waiter arrived with the papaya sorbet. "I can't exactly tie him up and force him to read it."

Monica grabbed her silver spoon. "No, but you can make it so damn hot he'll have to read it in order to defend his team," she insisted, waving it at her.

"Monica, you're asking for the impossible," Ashley complained. "I've been making it as hot as I can. After all, I can only write about things that happen."

"No, you're wrong. You can *make* things happen. Now, in your next column I want you to discuss the savage quarterback controversy that's tearing the Kings apart," Monica ordered.

Ashley shook her head in disbelief. "But there *is* no quarterback controversy," she protested. "I can't even get a decent quote out of Razor Williams. Believe me, I've tried."

"Damn it, use what little brain God gave you. If there isn't a controversy, then you have to invent one," Monica explained, as if she were speaking to a two-year-old. "It'll be great copy!"

"Not if it isn't true. There's enough going on with that team to fill a dozen columns. I won't invent something just because you want to smear Clyde Winston," Ashley insisted bravely.

"Have you forgotten to whom you are speaking?" Monica raged. "The only reason you have this choice assignment is because I ordered it. If I say destroy Clyde Winston, I expect you to do it."

Ashley was just as adamant. "I will report the news as it happens. That's my job. But I will not distort the facts, even for you."

Monica snapped her fingers and instantly a waiter appeared. Rising, she tossed a hundred-dollar bill onto the table. "Call this young woman a cab," she ordered. He rushed off to do her bidding. "You're a fool, Ashley," she snapped.

233

"You're probably right, but at least I'm an honest fool," Ashley retorted, refusing to back down.

"So you like honesty," Monica jeered. "Well here's a bit more for you. Clyde was right. Naming you columnist for the Kings had nothing whatsoever to do with your so-called ability, contacts, or knowledge of football. The only reason I insisted Ray give you this job was that I knew it would bug the hell out of Clyde to have a woman anywhere near his precious team."

Ashley felt her throat close with tears as she watched Monica march out of the restaurant. Had she lost the best job she'd ever had over a matter of principle? The question pounded over and over in her head as she climbed into the taxi and headed back to the *News*. Catching sight of the mirrored building, she dried her eyes. Her chin lifted. Whatever happened, she hadn't been wrong. If she had lost her integrity she would have lost one of her most valuable possessions, and that was more important than any job.

The newsroom fell silent when she walked in, and the empty carton sitting on her desk told her all she needed to know. She was supposed to pack up her belongings and get out. As she stood there, transfixed, Dave came over to her. "Ray wants to see you in his office. Ashley, we've never been close friends, but I want you to know I'm sorry as hell about this. It's a lousy world. But with the great following you've built with your column I don't think you'll have any trouble finding another job."

She smiled weakly. "Thank you, Dave. I hope you're right. I've sort of gotten used to eating."

Ray was pacing around his office as she pushed open the door. "Ashley, you have no more brains than a dodo bird, and you know what happened to them. I *told* you not to lock horns with Monica. I warned you you'd get gored if you did. Well, you've been gored."

"I take it Monica wants me fired," she observed, trying to keep her voice from quavering.

"Fired? Hell, she'd boil you in oil if she could. Yes, you're fired."

"It's what I expected," Ashley admitted sadly. "Did she tell you why?"

"No, and frankly after hearing the fury in her voice I wasn't about to ask. What happened?" Ray asked, interested in spite of himself. "Did you tell her you wanted to write another favorable column on the Kings?"

"Oh, it's a lot worse than that. She wanted me to throw dirt on the team. When I tried to protest, she told me if necessary I was to invent stories to smear them."

"The damn idiot!" Ray barked. "Did she ever stop to think that might get the *News* sued for libel? I'll tell you the truth, Ashley. Monica is one of the brightest people I've ever known, but when it comes to the subject of Clyde Winston she becomes absolutely demented. Take this nonsense about firing you. I told her she was crazy to let her star columnist go. I threw the circulation increases at her." He spread his hands helplessly. "Nothing worked. Ashley, I tried to save your job. I want you to believe that."

"I know you did, and I thank you. I knew the risk I was taking when I refused to write the kind of stories she wanted." She looked directly into his eyes. "Was I wrong? What would you have done in my place?"

"I hope I would have had the courage to do exactly what you did. But," he answered honestly,

"I've got a wife and three kids to feed. I just don't know."

"Well, all I've got are two cockatoos and one hatching egg. There's one good thing to be said for birdseed, it's cheap." She hesitated. "I hate to ask you, but would you write me a letter of recommendation?"

"Sure," Ray agreed. "That's the least I can do. But don't be surprised if I type it on my typewriter at home. If Monica found out I was helping you, the next head to fall under her ax would be mine." He held out his hand. "Good luck. I really mean that."

As she turned to the door, he asked, "Is there anyone you'd like to call on my phone? The one on your desk isn't very private."

Her thoughts instantly flew to Zane. "It's sweet of you to offer. Yes, there is someone I want to tell I've just joined the great horde of the unemployed."

Ray left, pulling the door silently closed behind him, as Ashley lifted the receiver. It took over ten minutes to get Zane. "Sorry love, Sammy had to haul me out of the showers. Is something wrong?"

"That's the understatement of the year. I'm upset, unhappy, and unemployed."

"We must have a bad connection. I thought I heard you say something about being unemployed."

"It's not a bad connection," Ashley assured him. "Monica fired me this afternoon."

"That's crazy! Why would she do something like that?" Zane demanded, as if he thought his hearing was playing tricks on him. "You're the best columnist in Honolulu."

"Zane, I'll explain everything to you tonight. Right now I'm too depressed to talk about it, and I've still got to clean out my desk. That's not a

236

particularly fun thing to do with everyone watching."

"I know you promised to fix me poached shrimp and *opakapaka* tonight, but don't worry about dinner. I'll take care of it."

"Whatever you say," she said wearily. "I'm too tired to argue. See you later. In the meantime, maybe you can think of some way to cheer me up. Right now I'm pretty blue," she admitted, as fresh tears prickled behind her eyelids.

"I'll do my best. I can hear the pain in your voice. I just wish I could be there right now to hold you, and maybe take part of that pain away."

"You know what happens every time you take me in your arms. I don't think Ray would approve of such displays of lust in his office," she managed to joke. "See you in a couple of hours."

Hours later the setting sun, starting its plunge into the sea, was streaking the sky gorgeous shades of pink and orange as her car rolled to a stop on the sand. But Ashley, exhausted, noticed none of the tropical beauty.

Fresh tears, this time tears of joy, came to her eyes as she pushed open the front door and saw Zane sitting on the sofa surrounded by a whole zoo of stuffed animals. Perched right in the middle of his lap was a cuddly stuffed purple dragon, the twin of the one she'd given Jake Jr.

"Oh Zane!" It was all she could manage, as waves of happiness and sorrow engulfed her.

He rose and brought the dragon across the living room to her. Handing it to her, he gestured to the sofa. "You sounded so down, I decided to call in some reinforcements to help cheer you up."

"How did you ever know I loved this little fellow?" she sked, rubbing her cheek against the plush fur of the dragon. An embarrassed blush warmed her face. "In fact, it took every ounce of willpower I possessed not to buy it for myself."

"Elementary, my dear Watson." He grinned. "I called Kakalina. I figured whatever stuffed toy you picked out for Jake Jr. was one you liked yourself."

Ashley wrapped her arms around him. "Thank you, Zane." Looking up into his eyes, she let him see how much he'd pleased her. "I know when I'm down just looking at my purple dragon and all the other animals you've given me will make me feel better."

"That was the idea, love," he murmured, happy that his surprise had brought back her smile. He grabbed her hand. "Bring your new friend along. I have another surprise," he said, leading her to the bird cage.

"Oh, Zane, Kanani had her baby! Isn't it adorable?" she exclaimed, watching the tiny cockatoo hopping around.

"I don't think my fish would think so," he joked. "Now come on, the champagne's on ice, the steaks are on the grill, the salad's tossed, the coffee ice cream's in the freezer, Chopin's on the tape recorder, and the moon is rising. How about a picnic on the beach while you tell me about Monica's sudden bout of insanity?"

He had already spread a blanket out on the sand. Beside it was a silver ice bucket holding a bottle of champagne. Hugging the purple dragon, Ashley told Zane what had happened over lunch.

He poured them both a glass of the sparkling wine. "You're right, when it comes to Uncle Clyde, the woman's just not rational," he said, shaking his head.

"Oh, that wasn't the only reason I was fired. Sure,

she wanted to smear Clyde, but she was also angry because I refused to do what she ordered. She's not used to people saying no to her."

"Well, forget her and forget her lousy newspaper. There are others on the island." He touched his glass to hers. "Here's to a new and better job. With your credentials I'm sure you won't have any trouble landing one."

"That's what Dave said. I wish I were as confident as you two."

Zane scraped the last bite of coffee ice cream from his dish and pushed it aside. He lay back on the blanket opening his arms wide. "Bring your little friend and come over here. Tonight I think you both could use some TLC."

Ashley settled against his chest with his heart beating strongly beneath her ear, and he held her close—not with passion but with caring. Gently, with soft strokes of his hands and murmured words, he began to ease the tension from her body. Instinctively realizing that what she needed that night was comforting, not passionate sex, he never allowed his caresses to arouse, just to soothe. After the wild emotions of the day it didn't take much for sleep to claim her. Ashley didn't even stir when Zane picked her up and carried her and the purple dragon she still held to bed.

The next week was one of the best, and the worst, of her life. Dave and Zane's prediction about how easy it would be to get another job proved overly optimistic. She trudged from newspaper to newspaper, from interview to interview. Everyone was impressed with her credentials, complimented her on the writing in her columns, and politely told her they had no openings. That was the worst.

The best were the nights spent with Zane. Thursday night they sipped mai tais, sailing their catamaran off of Waikiki. Friday night they held hands through Beethoven's Fifth. Saturday night they drove up into the Koolau Mountains and made love under the stars. Sunday night, after the Kings beat the Chargers, she massaged his sore muscles and more, as they showered together. Monday night they swam naked and loved till dawn.

Tuesday morning she wanted nothing in the world more than to sleep late, but Zane roused her at eight with a tray of coffee, scrambled eggs, and bacon.

"How can you be so cruel?" She groaned, as he yanked open the blinds. "Keep me up all night, then roust me out at dawn."

"It's not dawn. It's eight o'clock, and you've got a job interview to get to in less than two hours."

"What good will it do?" she mumbled, struggling to sit up. "I don't think I'm ever going to find another job. Yesterday I got so desperate I went to Sea Life Park to see if I could get some promotional work. Even the porpoises turned me down. I don't understand it. I know I've never won a Pulitzer prize, but damn it, I'm a good reporter. Why won't anyone hire me?"

"I don't know, love. Maybe today will be your lucky day," Zane said soothingly, pouring her a cup of coffee. "I know you told me, but I forgot. What newspaper are you talking to today?"

Ashley wrinkled her nose at the thought. "It's a small weekly up on the North Shore. If I get the job, it'll probably be covering all the exciting events at the local grocery store. Brother, talk about a comedown!"

"I know what I'll do. If this job doesn't work out,

240

I'll run out and buy you a stuffed unicorn after practice. That'll turn your luck around for sure."

"If you keep adding to my menagerie of stuffed animals I'm going to have to move to a bigger house," she teased, pleased he cared so much.

An hour and a half later, Ashley smoothed down the skirt of her apricot linen suit, made sure every hair was tucked neatly into her chignon, took a deep breath, and knocked on the door of the editor's office. The man glanced up over his half glasses and motioned her to a battered chair in front of his desk. When she was seated, she handed him her portfolio, with clippings of some of her columns and Ray's letter of recommendation.

The man didn't take it. "I'm going to make this short and sweet. There's no job for you here. My secretary shouldn't have wasted my time or yours by scheduling this interview." He nodded at the door. "Good day."

"But if you'll only—"

"Good day!" He repeated, more firmly this time.

His secretary looked at her sympathetically as she left the office. "That didn't take long," she observed. "I assume you didn't get the job?"

"No, and it's weird, he wouldn't even let me show him my work," Ashley complained.

His secretary glanced at the closed door, lowering her voice. "It's not so weird when you know the reason. Do you have time for a cup of coffee?"

"Sure." Ashley shrugged. "I have nothing else to do."

"You leave first. Go next door to the doughnut shop. I'll be there in a few minutes," she whispered conspiratorially.

As Ashley walked back out into the harsh sunlight, she wondered what the editor's secretary

241

meant. After the moment it took for her eyes to adjust to the dim light of the doughnut shop, she headed for a secluded booth. She ordered two cups of coffee and a couple of raspberry jelly doughnuts and tried to relax, rubbing the back of her neck where her muscles were knotted with frustration.

The secretary glanced nervously around to make sure no one was within hearing range and slipped into the seat opposite Ashley. Neither spoke until after the waiter had put their coffee and doughnuts on the table and left.

The gray-haired woman held out her hand. "I guess I should introduce myself. I'm Alma Adams."

Ashley shook hands. "Hi Alma, I'm Ashl—"

"Oh, I know who you are. I'll bet everyone in Honolulu knows who you are. You're quite a local celebrity."

Ashley looked doubtful. "Maybe, but it's sure not helping me get a job."

"I know. That's what's so unfair," Alma fussed, biting a huge chunk out of her doughnut. "You're a great writer. I really miss your columns, and so does everyone else I've talked to. In fact, several of my friends have canceled their *News* subscriptions, now that you're gone."

Ashley, consumed with her own troubles, hardly listened. "I don't understand it," she said, "I've had a dozen interviews and no one will hire me. I can't figure out what I'm doing wrong."

Alma lowered her voice. "It's not what you're doing. It's what you did."

"What's that supposed to mean?" Ashley asked, licking the sugar from her lips.

"What you did was enrage Monica Bennett. I could lose my job for telling you this, but I heard George—he's the editor who threw you out of his office a minute ago—talking to another editor on a paper about the size of ours. To put it bluntly, the owner of the *News* has put the word out that she'll destroy any paper that hires you. Unfortunately, she's too rich and powerful to ignore."

A wave of nausea swept through Ashley. "Well, at least that explains the cold shoulders I've been receiving. You realize this means I'll probably never get another journalism assignment on Oahu. I might as well give up and start thinking up jingles touting the joys of pineapple juice. That's probably the only kind of writing job I can get from now on."

"You could try making peace with that Ms. Bennett," Alma suggested.

"She doesn't make peace. She makes war. And right now I'm the enemy." Ashley opened her purse and put some money on the table to pay for their orders. "Thank you for telling me the truth."

She finally got a hold of Zane after practice. "I've finally found out what's going on," she told him. "Monica's out to sabotage me, and I don't think even your magical unicorn can do anything about that. I'll be lucky if I can get a job picking pineapples. She'd probably have the fields bombed first."

"Have a little faith. I'm sure everything will work out," Zane said encouragingly, trying to bolster her sagging spirits.

"How? How is it going to work out?" Ashley demanded. There seemed to be no hope with Monica up against her.

He hesitated, obviously searching for some words of assurance. "I don't know," he finally had to admit.

CHAPTER FIFTEEN

Even as depressed as Ashley was, she laughed when she pulled up to the house and saw the surprise Zane had arranged. Pushing his head through the French doors as if watching for her arrival was the largest stuffed unicorn she'd ever seen, complete with a gold horn and a purple mane.

She got out of the car and went up the veranda steps, slipping her arm around its neck and carrying it into the house. Zane was just coming out of the kitchen with a bottle of chilled champagne.

He grinned at her. Placing the bottle on the table, he observed, "I see you've met Jezebel, the Mythological Unicorn."

"Do you really think Jezebel the Mythological Unicorn has more power than Monica the Evil Witch?" Ashley asked, looking down into the unicorn's bright blue eyes. "She looks sort of helpless to me."

"I guarantee it!" Zane reassured her. From the mischievous twitch at the corner of his mouth, Ashley knew he was up to something. "Well, that's not exactly right," he continued. "I can only guarantee it if I have your cooperation. You see, according to an old Viking legend, the unicorn only receives its power if two people make love under a full moon while they're being guarded by a purple dragon."

Ashley raised one eyebrow skeptically. "An old Viking legend, huh? Sounds like a sneaky way your ancestors invented to get under some poor unsuspecting maiden's skirt so they could lust to their fill."

Zane pulled his hurt-innocent act. "Here I was prepared to sacrifice my body to bring you good luck, and you cast aspersions on the noble intentions of my Viking ancestors."

"Sacrifice your body!" Ashley teased. "And I thought you enjoyed making love to me."

"Now wherever did you get that silly idea?" Zane joked. "You couldn't seduce me if you tried," he challenged.

"Want to bet?" she asked, putting the unicorn aside.

Zane's eyes sparkled with mischief. "Have your way with me, use every womanly wile in your arsenal. But I warn you, it'll only harden my willpower."

"I have no intention of hardening your willpower, but I do intend to harden something else entirely." She glanced around the room. "Now, if I'm going to seduce you I need to set the stage. First the music." She winked at him over her shoulder. "I know how 'Scheherazade' affects you," she said, flipping on the stereo.

The sensual music flooded the room. "That's not playing fair," Zane complained. "You know I start to hyperventilate when I hear anything by Rimsky-Korsakov."

"I have no intention of playing fair." Ashley smiled. "You started this. And I never back away from a challenge. Now the lights," she murmured, dimming them romantically. Slowly, swaying to the music as if she were doing the dance of the seven veils, she began to remove her clothes one piece at

245

a time. She danced provocatively, slipping her arms out of her apricot linen jacket and tossing it onto the sofa. Her hands went to the buttons of her blouse, and one after one she unbuttoned them. Ashley shrugged the blouse away from her bare shoulders. The next undone button allowed it to drop lower, but she kept it around her, shielding her lacy bra.

Zane's gaze burned hot as he watched her dancing, baring herself for him, but he made no move toward her. Ashley quickly whipped off her blouse and threw it at him. For a moment Zane buried his face in the fabric, drinking in the mix of her perfume and the scent that belonged only to her. He let it fall from his hands.

"My willpower's weakening, but I'm fighting to be strong," he murmured.

Ashley smiled. "Fight all you want. You'll sacrifice your body for me yet."

Turning her back to him, she let the music flow through her, her body moving in sensual rhythm to every note. Her hands went to the waistband of her skirt, and it fell away. She wriggled enticingly out of her panties, without lifting her slip. Then, turning to face him, she let her bra fall to the floor.

Zane's breathing was ragged, but still he didn't move to take her in his arms, wanting to prolong the delight. Ashley's dance brought her to stand in front of him. "Now it's your turn," she whispered, reaching for his shirt.

It soon joined her jacket on the sofa. Linking her arms behind his head she began to sway against him in time to the music, brushing her breasts, her hips, in enticing rhythm against his body until she felt his arousal.

Zane shut his eyes, fighting for control, as she

stood on tiptoe to capture his mouth with hers. The rasp of her tongue, forcing its way between his closed lips, finally made him crack.

Almost roughly, he pulled her hard against him. Then bending her far back in his arms he began to ravish her mouth, her throat, her breasts, with hungry kisses. Desperate to touch, to possess her, he yanked down her slip, and kicked his own clothes aside until he was as splendidly naked as she. The passion she'd ignited burned too hot to wait even long enough to go to the bedroom, and they sank down on the carpet together, frantic to become one.

Later, much later, she stirred in his arms. Kissing him gently on the shoulder, she murmured, "I guess we let 'Scheherazade' carry us away. As I recall, according to the legend, we were supposed to do this under the full moon with a purple dragon guarding us. I wonder if making love on a carpet will work to give Jezebel the power she needs to defeat Monica the Evil Witch. Maybe it will if we pretend this is a magic carpet."

"I don't know," he said dubiously. "Viking legends are tricky things. We'd better not take any chances." He grinned, effortlessly scooping her up in his arms. Grabbing a blanket and the little purple dragon, he headed outside to find the full moon.

The next morning Zane looked across the breakfast table and asked, "What interviews do you have today?"

"None, but it doesn't matter," Ashley muttered, staring down into her orange juice. "I wouldn't get a job anyway, not the way my luck's been running."

"Ah, but that was before last night," Zane reminded her with a smile. "Remember, we made sure the unicorn was fully energized."

"Energized!" Ashley laughed. "Considering how many times we made love last night she ought to be in an absolute frenzy!"

"We had to be sure, didn't we?" He chuckled opening the newspaper. "Do you want to see the want ads?"

Ashley sighed. "Not today. I can't stand any more rejection. I think I'll go rent an Ingrid Bergman movie. It might be a good idea just to lose myself in *Casablanca.*"

He curled his fingers around hers and gave them a reassuring squeeze. "I hate to see you this down. How about if I pick up a pizza after practice? At least then you wouldn't have to worry about dinner."

"That would be nice, but knowing the way you inhale food, you'd better pick up two," she teased, managing a half smile.

Humphrey Bogart had just looked up to see his old flame Ingrid Bergman enter the smoky bar when the telephone rang. With a frustrated sigh Ashley clicked off the VCR.

Her fingers tightened angrily around the receiver as she recognized Clyde Winston's voice. "Ms. Buchannan, I want—" he began, but she interrupted him.

"Look, Mr. Winston," she snapped, "I'm in enough trouble right now. I don't need you harassing me as well. Or did you call to express your pleasure over my dismissal?"

"I don't believe asking you to have lunch with me should be called harassment," Clyde countered.

She held the receiver away from her ear and stared at it a moment in utter confusion. "Excuse

248

me," she said, holding it to her ear again. "I don't think I heard you correctly, Mr. Winston."

"I would like you to have lunch with me today," Clyde repeated.

"I thought that's what you said. I just couldn't believe it," Ashley admitted, perplexed. An idea glimmered. "Did Zane put you up to this?"

"No, I haven't talked to my nephew for over a week. He never seems to be at his apartment these days," Clyde observed. "But we've wandered from the point. Can you have lunch today, or are you busy?"

"Yes, I'm busy. I'm busy being unemployed!" Ashley muttered to herself. "Mr. Winston," she answered, "you're not exactly a fan of mine, so why the sudden invitation?"

"I have a business deal I wish to discuss with you. I would be happy to send my car for you."

Intrigued in spite of herself, Ashley agreed, "What have I got to lose? But I warn you, I am in no mood for tricks. If all you want to do is gloat over my present misfortune, I'm liable to sock you."

"My, such a forceful lady. But don't worry. I intend to gloat—in fact, to gloat a lot—but not at your expense, I assure you," Clyde insisted even more mysteriously. "My limousine could be at your door in an hour. Would that be convenient?"

"Yes, I can be ready by then."

"I need to issue orders to my chef. Would you prefer lobster in shrimp sauce, beef Wellington, or duck à l'orange?"

Remembering Monica's high-handed way of ordering for her, Ashley was surprised and pleased by Clyde's consideration. "The lobster sounds marvelous."

"Good, I'll see you in about an hour. Oh, by the

way, I do not want you to mention this meeting to anyone. Is that understood?" Clyde insisted, reverting to his usual assertive manner.

"Yes, of course," Ashley reassured him.

An hour later Ashley walked out of her front door and stood blinking at the silver limousine. For a split second she thought it was Monica's, but the chauffeur who climbed out and tipped his hat to her was a man she'd never seen before.

He held open the rear door. "Mr. Winston is waiting, miss."

Inside, Clyde's limousine could have been the twin of Monica's. Ashley smiled, realizing how very much alike the two of them were—right down to the type of chauffeur they hired, she learned before they'd driven a mile.

They had just turned on to the main highway when Clyde's chauffeur spoke through the intercom. "Mr. Winston's chef informed me you were having lobster for lunch. Might I offer you a glass of white wine to wet the palate."

"Yes, that would be nice," she agreed, knowing he wanted to press buttons and show off his fancy chariot.

No sooner had she spoken than a teak panal in front of her opened, and out slid a glass of white wine in a cut crystal glass. As she sipped the delicious French wine, she glanced around the back seat, noting for the first time that there was one difference between the two cars. Monica always had one perfect yellow rose in a silver holder on the wall by her seat. Clyde had no fresh flowers in his limousine.

Clyde, dapper as always in his navy blazer and gray slacks, was waiting for Ashley in his office high atop the landmark buildings of the Honolulu business district.

"I hope you don't mind if we dine in my office," he said as he greeted her. "In a restaurant, there are dozens of ears to overhear. I want our conversation to remain strictly private until we spring our surprise on an unsuspecting Honolulu."

Ashley stared at him, having trouble believing the change in him now that she was no longer working for Monica. "Let me assure you whatever is said here will go no farther. To be honest, I find it difficult to believe you want to work with me on any project, after all the abuse I've taken from you. But I will listen to what you have to say. I don't have a choice. As you probably know, I've been fired from the *News*. I'm out of work, and apparently Monica Bennett is determined to see that that is a permanent condition."

"Yes, I know. Although I am not in the news business, so to speak, my sources are as impeccable as any Monica can boast. Would you care for champagne?" he asked, going to the paneled bar.

Ashley straightened her shoulders. "No, what I'd care for is the truth! What is going on here?"

Clyde seemed mildly amused. "Ah, the impetuousness of youth. It seems so long ago." Then his smile faded. "I wish I had been less impetuous and more intuitive twenty years ago when I . . ." he admitted, letting her see into his heart a little. "Oh, well, I'm sure there are things in everyone's past they regret, but can't correct. Now, on to the current situation. What I have in mind is . . ."

To Ashley's frustration, his explanation was interrupted by the arrival of a waiter pushing a heated food cart. With a murmured "With your permission, sir," he started serving their elegant lunch.

After Ashley had sampled the wondrous lobster in shrimp sauce, she looked across the table at Clyde with narrowed eyes. "This sudden interest on your part in my well-being doesn't have anything to do with my relationship with your nephew, does it?"

Clyde met her questioning gaze squarely. "Ashley, I have no children. Zane is as close to a son as I'll ever have. But this luncheon meeting is business, and not familial business."

"Okay, then why am I here?"

Clyde looked distinctly uneasy as he admitted, "You know I disliked most of your columns. On the other hand they were accurate, and although I hate to admit it, well written enough to capture the interest of most of the readers in Honolulu." He snapped his fingers, reminding her again of Monica. "Please bring me those latest figures," he ordered a hovering secretary.

The folder arrived with dessert. He dipped into his macadamia nut soufflé and commented, "It's all there in that folder. The figures are clear. Your column's been gone just a week, and already circulation has dropped ten percent. Since nothing else has changed, that has to be because your column has disappeared. Monica was a fool to let you go. I won't be so stupid."

He snapped his fingers again and the steward appeared with a tabloid-size magazine. "This is what I want," Clyde insisted, handing her a copy of the *Dallas Cowboys Official Weekly.*

Ashley flipped through the magazine devoted entirely to the Dallas Cowboys. It was chock-full of action pictures of the team, reviews of their latest game, and in-depth interviews with the players, coaches, and trainers. It even had a feature on the cheerleaders. She glanced up at Clyde. "What does this have to do with me?"

He smiled. "How would you like to be editor in chief and contributing writer to the Kings official weekly? With all the attention you've received, I'd even be willing to call it *Ashley Buchannan's Football Weekly* if you'd like."

Ashley stared at him in disbelief at the magnitude of what he was offering. "Are you kidding?" she whispered, afraid she might be dreaming.

"Certainly not!" Clyde insisted. "You'd have complete control to hire the staff and set the format. Of course, I'd like to see the mock-up before we go to press, but I trust you to handle all the details. And it goes without saying that your salary will be equal to your responsibilities."

Ashley had been burned once and had no intention of letting it happen again. "Mr. Winston, before I agree to anything, there's one thing I have to know. Are you offering me this job just to get back at Monica, because if you are—"

"Young lady, I do not let my personal feelings interfere with my business decisions. I will admit the thought that *Kings Weekly* might further reduce the *News* circulation by competing with its sports section is not a displeasing possibility, but that is not the reason I'm offering you this job." He reached over and tapped the magazine. "A project like this is bound to generate interest in the Kings, and more interest means more ticket sales. It's as simple as that. Since I want to get this magazine on the stands as soon as possible, I must have your answer today. I only regret I did not think of this sooner."

There was no doubt in Ashley's mind as she held out her hand. "Shake hands with your new editor."

He did, sealing the deal. "You won't be sorry you gave me this opportunity," Ashley promised.

Clyde smiled slyly. "If by chance you wished to raid the *News* staff, I'll guarantee their salaries will be higher working for me." His smile widened. "Naturally, that will infuriate Monica, but after all, business is business. How soon do you think you can put the first issue to bed?"

"If you don't mind if I copy the format of the magazine you showed me, I think we can have the first issue out in under two weeks. Later we can personalize it to reflect the special spirit of the Kings."

Clyde pushed back his chair, indicating the interview was over. "Do whatever you have to do. As I said, I'll leave the details up to you. One last thing—I'm having a suite of offices prepared in this building for you and your staff, but until the redecorating is done, I'm afraid you will have to work out of your home. Will that be a problem?"

Ashley shook her head. "After the opportunity you handed me I'd be willing to work in a tree house if I had to."

"The chauffeur is waiting downstairs. He'll take you home."

As the sleek Cadillac turned north, the chauffeur commented, "Don't think me presumptuous, but I can tell by your smile that the interview with Mr. Winston went well. Is there anyone you wish to call with the news?"

Ashley had never made a phone call from a car and it sounded kind of fun. "Sure, but where—" Before she even finished the question another teak panel slid open and the telephone appeared. She dialed the Kings training facility, but Zane was out on the practice field and couldn't be reached. Stifling her disappointment at not immediately being able to tell him her great news, she dialed another number. When Jake answered, she asked, "How would you like to earn more money and have more time off to spend with Kakalina and Jake Jr.?"

Jake laughed. "Who died and made you Santa Claus?" he demanded.

"Clyde Winston, who else?" Ashley laughed. "Now here's the deal."

She explained what Clyde wanted to do. "Tell ol' Clyde you've just signed up the best photographer in Hawaii," Jake said. "I'll turn in my resignation today. And just between you and me, I won't be sorry to see the last of the *News*. After what happened to you, everyone here is really running scared."

As she hung up the phone, the shadow of a frown crossed her face. She knew Zane would be pleased for her, but could the job be a mixed blessing? It tied her even more firmly to the islands than she already was. The lurking possibility of a trade was a specter that just wouldn't go away. And Zane wouldn't even discuss it, as if it could never happen. Finally Ashley gave herself a hard mental shake. She should be flying high with excitement, and instead she was letting nagging doubts spoil what ought to be a day of ecstatic happiness. She turned her thoughts to the evening, when she could share the good news with Zane.

After the limousine dropped her off, Ashley called and left a message for Zane to forget about the pizzas. Then she dashed out again, jumped into her car, and headed for the grocery store. She'd been so depressed and frustrated about not being able to find a job she hadn't cooked a decent meal in a week. Tonight would be different, she thought,

255

and began concocting a delectable menu in her head.

She was just putting the shrimp stuffed with crab under the broiler when Zane walked in.

"Well, well, well. This sure isn't what I expected to find," he confessed, seeing her happy smile when she came to greet him. "Here I was all prepared to spend the evening trying to cheer you up, and you look absolutely radiant. Did something happen? Or do you always get this glow watching Bogart movies?"

Ashley went to give him a hug of welcome. "Actually, I never got to finish watching *Casablanca*." Her gray eyes glittered with mischief. "Right in the middle of one of the biggest scenes, a man called to invite me out to lunch."

She enjoyed seeing the jealous spark flare in Zane's eyes. "Do you mean another man made you look this happy?"

"Yes, he was absolutely charming. Handsome—wealthy too. Just about everything a woman could want, and he wanted me. It was wonderful!" Ashley teased. "Oops, I've got to go check the shrimp."

She turned and headed for the kitchen, but Zane grabbed the ties of her apron, preventing her from getting away. "Let the damn shrimp burn. I want to know who you had lunch with. I want his name!" he demanded.

She looked provocatively at him. "Jealous?"

"Damn right I am. The thought of you with another man makes me see red!" Zane admitted harshly.

"Even if the other man was your uncle?" Ashley joked.

"Clyde?"

"Uh-huh, and if you'll be a good boy and let go of

my apron strings so I can go save the shrimp, I'll tell you all about it."

Over dinner Ashley filled him in on the details of her meeting with his uncle. Zane said when she was finished, "What an incredible deal!" clapping his hands. "Maybe you should send Monica a basket of flowers for firing you."

"She'd probably throw them into the incinerator. Especially after she finds out I lured Jake away."

Zane took her hand. "Let's not talk about her. I have an idea. Why don't we celebrate with brandy in the living room?"

"You go on and get comfortable," Ashley urged, giving his hand a squeeze. "I've got a bottle, but it's really buried in the back of the cupboard. It'll take me a couple of minutes to find it."

When she walked through the kitchen doorway into the living room a few minutes later, Zane said, "Stop right there."

"Why?" she asked, perplexed at his request. "What's wrong?"

"Nothing's wrong. In fact everything's perfect." He grinned broadly. "I just had a revelation—or rather I had it earlier this evening and it just happened again right now."

"If you can't make sense cold sober, I think brandy will just make things worse," she teased. "Oh, well, I guess we'll risk it." She crossed the room, poured them each a snifter, and settled beside him on the sofa. "What was this great revelation?"

Zane took the snifter out of her hands and set it on the coffee table beside his. Gathering her hands in his, he confessed, "I realized tonight when I saw you coming out of the kitchen to greet me that

257

you're what I want to come home to for the rest of my life."

It felt to Ashley like her heart had leapt into her throat. "Ashley, marry me," Zane said. "Let that fantasy become real."

The words her heart had longed to hear, the words her mind feared to hear—he'd spoken them at last. "Zane, I'm just . . ."

"What's wrong, Ashley? I love you. I want to marry you. And although you've never said it, I think you love me. Why are you hesitating? Just say yes."

"Zane I do love you, but . . ."

He squeezed her hands. "If we have love, that solves all the buts."

Reluctantly Ashley pulled her hands from his. "It's not that simple, and you know it. I've tried to talk to you about this and you just won't listen." A pain twisted in her heart as she saw the hurt in his eyes, but she didn't stop. "I'm six years older than you are."

"I've told you over and over, that doesn't matter."

"Yes, but what if it does make a difference—five or ten years from now. I've had one man walk out on me. I never want to endure that kind of pain again. And there's another problem. You know how I feel about my home, and now with this great new job I couldn't bear to leave Hawaii. Yet at any moment you may be traded."

"I'm not going to be traded," he insisted firmly.

Ashley twisted her hands together. "You don't know that. And what if you get hurt and can't play? I watched that destroy one man I loved. I couldn't bear to see that happen to you."

"Ashley, none of this is important. Just marry me. Everything will be fine, I promise."

"How can you say that?" she demanded, tears coming to her eyes. "I had one marriage break up, and I thought it would last forever. Now you're asking me to jump into another one, with potentially even more problems than the one I just got out of."

"Ashley, I'm not Butcher! Damn it, stop comparing us! I won't walk out on you. I love you."

He reached for her, but she slipped out of his grasp. Knowing if he touched her she wouldn't be able to think, she escaped from the sofa, pacing the room. "You just don't understand. You can't. You've never lived through the agony of a dying marriage or the pain of a divorce. I have to be one hundred percent sure this time. I just have to be! I don't want to fail again. I'm not sure I could survive that."

Zane shook his head, obviously confused by her reluctance. "Ashley, I'm trying to understand, but it's hard. Everything seems so simple to me. I love you. You love me. How can we fail?"

Ashely stopped pacing and turned to face him. "You keep insisting love will solve everything, but I've lived long enough to know it won't magically make all of our problems melt away." She knew from the set of his shoulders that her words were hurting him, but their future was too important not to let him know what she felt in her heart. "Kakalina said when the love is stronger than the doubt I'll know I'm doing the right thing. And I still have doubts," she admitted, in a voice choked with tears.

"That's just great!" Zane retorted, hurt fueling his anger. "I give my heart to you, and you trash it.

You love me, but you don't love me enough. Damn it, I deserve better than that!"

She reached out to him, pleading for him to understand her fears. "I'm just not ready. I need time . . . time to be sure that what we feel will last forever. Can't you understand that? Why can't we just go on the way we are?"

"No!" The anger, the hurt, made his voice harsh. "That's not enough for me anymore. I love you. That means I want a home. I need a commitment from you—not for a day or a week. Forever." Tears matching her own glistened in his eyes. "If you can't give me that you don't really love me, and I guess what we had wasn't as wonderful as I thought."

"Zane, don't say 'what we had,' as if it's over. I do love you. I need you." Ashley went to him, needing his touch to ease the pain ravaging her heart. But he backed away. "Make love to me," she pleaded, "until the doubts go . . ."

"No! Don't touch me!" The hurt was plain in his face. "I feel like you've used me," he accused her. "You and your damn fantasies! What did you want —just some big strong stud to teach you about sex?"

"Zane, no, it isn't like that."

"Oh, no? It sure as hell sounds like it to me. I'm good enough for a hot roll in the hay, but I'm not good enough to marry. Thanks a lot, Ashley. You've made my day. I hope you enjoy sleeping with that purple dragon because you won't find me in your bed again, ever!"

Before she could stop him, Zane slammed out of her house . . . and out of her life.

CHAPTER SIXTEEN

As Zane's motorcycle roared angrily off into the night Ashley felt like her heart was being torn apart by the sound. She loved him! How could she have let him go? Hot tears scalded her eyes as she stared at the closed door, but with determination she blinked them back. She wasn't a fool. She knew just loving someone didn't magically dissolve all the problems. So how could she beg him to stay, knowing she was probably setting herself up for more heartbreak?

Zane had reached something deep within her, something Butcher had never touched. Losing him could produce an agony she might not survive. But maybe he was right, maybe it could work out. . . . No, it couldn't when—

"Stop it, damn it!" she muttered out loud. The endless spiral of questions did nothing but drive the hurt deeper into her soul, where somehow she knew it would always live. It might fade with time, but it would never die.

With weary steps Ashley picked up the brandy snifters and took them to the kitchen. When she went back into the living room and saw the unicorn peeking around the corner of the sofa, she couldn't keep the tears away any longer. Ashley cried into Jezebel's soft fur, cuddling the stuffed animal against her. Hours later, finally exhausted, she fell asleep on the sofa.

The phone jarred her awake early the next morning. Thoughts of Zane swept through her mind as she grabbed the receiver, but fresh tears gathered when she heard Jake's cheery hello.

"Is there anything wrong, Ashley?" Jake asked with concern. "Your voice sounds funny."

"No, I'm fine," she lied, pulling herself together. "I was just thinking about our first issue."

"That's why I called, boss. What's my first assignment?"

Ashley closed her eyes, willing herself to think of work and not of the man who'd slammed out of her life the night before.

"Sorry to take so long, Jake. Actually I haven't given it much thought, but since this will be the first issue it would probably be a good idea to introduce the readers to the first string. Why don't you get out to the practice field and get an action shot of each player?"

"Offensive and defensive?"

"Sure. That should make a nice photo spread to kick off the issue. Did you have any trouble getting your release from the *News*?"

"No. They wanted the standard two weeks, but when I explained to Ray about your new project he didn't insist. Oh, by the way, he asked me to tell you good luck. Where shall I deliver the pictures after they're developed?"

"Better bring them out to my house. Clyde's having offices decorated for us in his building, but until they're ready, my living room is our headquarters."

"Hey, I've got a great idea. I'll bring Kakalina and Jake Jr. along and we can all—"

"No!" Ashley snapped as a stab of pain drove

into her heart. Seeing Kakalina and Jake so happy with their child was something she just couldn't cope with after what she'd been through.

"Ashley, what's wrong? You love holding Jake Jr."

"Jake, I'm sorry. I didn't mean to snap at you. It's just . . . uh, it's just that I think I'm coming down with a cold and I don't want the baby to catch it."

"Kakalina will sure appreciate that. He's been a little irritable with colic, and a cold wouldn't help. I'll see you later this afternoon when I bring the pictures."

The instant she hung up the phone, Ashley got her typewriter and brought it to the dining room table. Work might be her only salvation. Maybe it could fill the void in her life that at that instant felt as wide and as deep as the Waimea Canyon. Maybe if she filled her mind with stats and stories she wouldn't have time to think of Zane. Maybe she wouldn't miss him, and miss the hours he'd filled her body with his love. Maybe.

Ashley pulled out the Kings press guide and started creating catchy captions for the pictures Jake would take. After ten frustrating minutes and twenty corrections, she scowled at her typewriter in disgust. "A word processor sure spoils you," she muttered, twisting the cap off the correction fluid again to correct another typo. She'd just dealt with the offensive line when her doorbell rang.

Her first thought was that it was Zane, and she raced to answer it. Her radiant smile faded at the sight of the stranger in overalls standing outside. "Are you Ashley Buchannan?"

She nodded. "I've got a delivery for you from Mr. Winston," he said. "Where do you want me to put all the junk?"

"Junk? What junk?" she asked, wondering what in the world Clyde would be sending her.

"Lady, I just deliver the boxes. I don't inspect them." He held out a card. "His secretary told me to give you this."

As he walked back to the truck Ashley ripped open the envelope. Clyde had written, "I thought you'd be most comfortable with the kind of equipment you used at the *News*, so I'm having the identical system delivered, along with the furniture to hold it. Best wishes to my new editor."

Ashley was unpacking the computer and printer when Jake arrived and came bounding into the room. "What happened between you and Zane?" he asked. Her smile froze. "I kiddingly asked him if he was still shacking up with my boss, and for a minute there I thought I was a goner! Remind me never to make anyone that big and strong mad." Jake requested fervently.

"I don't want to talk about it!"

"Okay, okay, don't take my head off." Jake tossed a manila envelope onto her table. "Here are the pictures. What's my assignment for tomorrow?"

With an effort Ashley forced her mind back to business. "You're going to love it, but Kakalina may never speak to me again. I want you to spend the day with the cheerleaders, from their practice session to their dress rehearsal on the field. I want our readers to see the sweat and effort that goes into their polished performance. I'll do the interviews for the accompanying article separately."

"A day with a bunch of the most beautiful women on the island." Jake kissed her on the cheek. "You're the greatest boss any guy could ask for."

"I bet Kakalina won't agree," Ashley joked.

Jake's smile of anticipation disappeared. "Are

264

you sure you're going to be all right? To put it bluntly, you look like hell."

"I don't want to talk about it, I don't want to think about it, I just want to work. Okay?"

He patted her awkwardly on the shoulder. "You got it. No more questions. But if you ever need to talk to Kakalina about what happened between you and Zane, you know she'd be here in a minute." Ashley didn't say anything, so he let it go. "After I help you get the computer and printer set up, I'm going home to dream of kicking legs and shaking bo—" He grinned. "Ah, make that shaking *pom-poms*."

"Better not tell Kakalina about those dreams, or I'm afraid she'll put you on the sofa permanently," Ashley advised.

She should have applied the words to herself. Each night she worked herself to exhaustion, finally falling asleep over her pile of papers . . . on the sofa. It was all she could do to walk past her bed, the bed where she and Zane had made such exquisite love, to get her clothes from the closet. Every time she thought of sleeping in it, alone except for her purple dragon, the tears returned.

Friday she piled interview on top of interview, with players, coaches, even some of the players' wives, praying there would be no time to hurt. But the aching sense of loss never left her. Ashley was back at home late in the afternoon, transcribing one of the interviews, when her doorbell rang again. As if she'd learned nothing from the disappointment of the day before, she rushed to the door, hope making her feet almost fly across the carpet.

For the first time since Zane left a delighted smile crossed her face, as she saw the huge bouquet of island flowers the delivery man was holding. What a beautiful way to make up, she sighed, grabbing the card before the man even had time to hand her the bouquet. But because her hopes had soared so high, when she read the words on the card the despair felt like a sword had been driven into her soul. The words turned the pain into a raging torrent as she read, "I've talked to Zane. I'm sorry. Clyde."

"Put them on the floor," she ordered, nearly choking on a sob. "Put them anywhere. I don't care."

After the deliveryman left, Ashley picked up the bouquet. Hardly seeing where she was going she stumbled out onto the beach with the flowers in her arms. The tropical sun blazed brightly, yet to her the day seemed shadowed. She stood at the edge of the surf and cast blossom after blossom into the sea, as if trying to say good-bye. Or was she begging the goddess of the sea to intervene, so no good-bye would ever have to be said? Ashley was so confused she didn't know what drove her to destroy Clyde's bouquet.

Sunday she awoke on the sofa with a splitting headache, and knew perfectly well why. The thought of watching the Kings play turned her stomach into a mass of knots. She had to go, though. It was her job. But she trembled, remembering all the little things she'd see again—the way Zane's blond hair curled out from beneath his helmet, the breadth of his shoulders, the way he looked in the huddle. It took every ounce of willpower to turn the key in the ignition and drive to the stadium.

Dave greeted her with a smile when she entered the press box. "I've always known you reminded me of some lovely animal, and now I know which one.

A cat. Monica throws you out of the window and you land on your feet in front of Clyde Winston. Congrats." He held out his hand. "I mean that."

"Thank you." She lowered her voice. "How are things at the *News*?"

Dave glanced around to make sure no one could hear. "Grim," he admitted. "When Monica got the news about your new job I thought she was going to tear the place apart. And, speak of the devil, I hope you've got a bulletproof vest on under that dress, because here comes the she-devil now." Having given her the warning Dave quickly scuttled away, as if Ashley were a total stranger.

At first Monica looked like she was going to march right past her as if she were invisible, but then she stopped. With a look that would have stopped a clock, she coldly observed, "I hear you've gone over to the enemy."

Ashley refused to let the older woman bully her. Giving Monica her sweetest smile, she cooed, "I had no choice. For some strange reason he was the only one who'd give me a job. You don't have any idea why I had such a rough time, do you, Monica?"

For once Monica was left with nothing to say. With a huffy snort, she walked on past Ashley and slammed the door, making the glass rattle.

Ashley knew the game would be a nightmare, but even in her worst fears she didn't think it could hurt as much as it did. The first time Zane ran onto the field the sight of him actually made her dizzy.

Dave heard her soft moan and looked over at her with concern. "Ashley, you're white as a ghost! Do you need to lie down? Can I get you a glass of water?"

"No, I'm all right. I just got too much sun yesterday, that's all," she lied.

Instead of getting better, each time she saw him the pain multiplied, until by the end of the game she could hardly fight down the waves of nausea it created within her.

What made it worse were the injuries. Twice Kings wide receivers hit the ground and didn't get up. As she watched them carry the second player off the field on a stretcher, she imagined it was Zane. Like an instant replay, she remembered the same scene with Butcher and relived the awful aftermath that shattered the life she'd known. *No!* She hadn't been wrong the night Zane left. She couldn't, she just *couldn't* risk living through that kind of hell again. He might say football wasn't his life, but she knew better. She'd done the right thing. She'd walked away before her love for him had spun such a web she'd never escape—except by crashing to the ground when that web, the web of love, unraveled.

All of these thoughts possessed her, shutting out the world, until from what seemed like an endless distance she heard someone call her name. Slowly, as if coming up from the depths of the ocean, she surfaced with a murmured "Uh, um, what do you want?"

"What do I want? I've asked the same damn question three times and the lady wants to know what I want," Dave muttered. "One week away from the paper and already she's going spacey!" He leaned nearer, and almost shouted her name.

With effort Ashley focused on him. "Did you ask me something?"

Dave tossed his pencil up in disgust. "I've asked you *three times*. Are you going down to the Kings locker room? I planned to play the gentleman for once and escort you."

Suddenly images bombarded her—images of Zane rising from the whirlpool, images of Zane clad only in a towel . . . images of Zane without the towel. Ashley cleared her throat. No hint of the passionate emotion she felt colored her answer. "No," she said. "I have enough on the game. That's the joy of being the editor of a weekly. The deadlines don't crowd in quite as quickly."

During the next few days Ashley discovered what hell was really like. Like Tantalus in the myth, she could see, but she couldn't have. For hours she sat at her desk with the photo Jake had taken of Zane in front of her. She picked it up. She threw it down. Once she was tempted to crumple it and throw it away, but realizing the poetic justice, she didn't. It started with a photo, she mused, let it end with a photo. She almost managed to keep her emotions in check as she typed the caption for the picture. But the effort had been too great, and as soon as she'd finished she ran outside to the beach and dived into the ocean to rid herself of the spirits, the feelings, that would give her no rest.

By Tuesday of the next week, Ashley knew she was in trouble. She'd been writing her heart out, but there was no way she could write enough stories to fill the type of Weekly Clyde wanted. She reached for the phone. Clyde had said she could hire the staff she needed. Well, now was the time. She had the photographer, she needed another writer to take part of the burden off her shoulders. The number she dialed rang.

"Dave, this is Ashley. Can you talk?"

"Well, let's put it this way. Monica's gone nuts, but I don't think she's started wiretapping yet."

"I need help," she admitted. "How would you

like to be the sports analyst for Clyde Winston's new brainchild?"

"Are you kidding?"

"No. It would mean a lot of work during the season, but in the off-season we plan to publish only once a month," she said, setting the trap. "That would mean enough time off for you to work on that novel you're always talking about."

"Where do I sign?"

"Wait, it gets better. Mr. Winston assured me he'd top any salary Monica is offering."

"Ashley, my beautiful cat, you've just bought yourself a sports writer. Ray's going to croak, but my resignation will be on his desk quicker than you can blink an eye!"

Ashley settled back in her chair, and for the first time since the flowers were delivered she smiled, reaching for the phone again. "Mr. Winston, please. It's Ashley Buchannan calling."

After endless clicks she got him. When they'd exchanged pleasantries, she explained, "I've got the first half of *Kings Weekly* put together, but it's scattered all over my living room. How about if you come to dinner tonight and preview the initial effort?"

"A home cooked meal?" Clyde said with longing. "You couldn't keep me away. I'll see you at seven."

Not more than a minute after Ashley replaced the receiver the telephone jangled shrilly again. Assuming it was Clyde with some question, she grabbed the receiver with a cheery "Do you want to know what I'm serving, so you can bring the proper wine?"

Monica's icy voice cut through her polite chatter. "What I want to know is how the hell you have the nerve to raid my staff. First Jake, and now Dave. You'll be lucky if I don't bury you."

"Once your threats would have worried me, but not now." An idea glimmered unbidden in Ashley's mind. She smiled. "Besides, there's something more important we have to discuss than your idle threats. I know we have not been the best of friends, but since I left the *News* I've received information about Clyde Winston that you might find interesting. I live miles out of Honolulu, but I think it might be in your best interests to come out and talk with me tonight, say around seven thirty?" Monica didn't say anything. "Don't worry about dinner. I'll throw something together here," Ashley added.

If she couldn't be happy, at least maybe she could see that two other people were. For the first time in a long time, Ashley whistled as she went to the kitchen to start cooking.

Her doorbell rang at seven on the dot. Clyde was standing outside with a bottle of French champagne. Suddenly she realized Monica probably wouldn't even come in if she saw Clyde's limousine out front.

"Why don't you pour the champagne so we can toast the first issue of *Kings Weekly*," she suggested quickly, nodding at the crystal wineglasses on the table. "I want to have a word with your chauffeur. The tide runs high here, so I think he should move the car around to the back of the house, just to be safe."

When she returned, they sipped the sparkling champagne and reviewed all the work Ashley and Jake had done, discussing the addition of Dave to her small staff. Clyde scanned the last article. "It's even better than I'd hoped," he said, raising his glass. "To the best writer in Honolulu."

271

Ashley blushed. "I don't know if I deserve that, but I'm pleased you're pleased." At that moment, the doorbell rang, and she went to answer it. Ashley tried to block Monica's view of the interior as she opened the door to let her in, but as she'd expected, the instant Monica saw Clyde she exploded. "What kind of dirty trick is this?"

Clyde had sprung to his feet. He was equally angry. "Ashley, you know I can't abide—"

"Shut up both of you! I'm doing the talking," Ashley snapped with such authority both were shocked into silence.

Ashley took Monica's arm and guided her to one of the sofas. She looked from one to the other. "Through no fault of my own, I've ended up in the middle of your feud—and I *don't like it!* So I decided to get you two together to get this matter settled once and for all."

Ashley hesitated but when she saw the expression in Clyde's eyes as he looked at Monica and the way Monica was blushing, she knew she'd been right. "You two have been fighting for twenty years. Well, whether you realize it or not, anger is the flip side of love. When I heard Butcher was getting remarried I felt nothing but compassion for his new bride. At that moment, I knew it was finally over. If there's no feeling, the love is dead. It isn't dead for you, or the passion wouldn't still be raging so hotly between you."

Ashley turned to Clyde. "When you hired me for this job you admitted there were things in your past you regretted, but couldn't do anything about. Unless I'm very wrong, I think you were talking about trading Monica for a grove of macadamia trees. I hope getting you two together like this will give you the chance to admit that mistake, to admit that

272

neither of you has ever stopped caring. If you want dinner, there are plates warming in the oven."

With that Ashley turned and left the house, leaving them alone. As she walked down to the beach she strongly suspected neither had even noticed she'd gone. Curling up on the sand, she crossed her fingers and waited.

An hour later, Clyde called her. She went back into the house and found them in each other's arms, kissing with such passion she marveled that they didn't start a fire. When they came up for air Ashley couldn't believe the change in Monica. Gone was all the brittle hardness. In its place was a starry-eyed glow that reminded her of a teenager deep in her first summer romance.

There were tears of joy in Monica's eyes as she pressed Ashley's hands. "We've been such fools, wasting all those years. How can we ever thank you?"

A sad smile touched the corners of Ashley's mouth. "Seeing you both happy is enough thanks. Now go. I'm sure you've got better things to do than talk to me."

They started for the French doors, Clyde's arm never leaving Monica's waist. "Which car shall we take?" he asked.

Monica smiled up at him. "Whichever one will get us to your bedroom first."

New tears came to Ashley's eyes as she stared after them. She was glad she'd done it, yet their happiness only made her own heartache worse. Twenty years from now, would she admit she'd been as big a fool as they to let Zane slip from her life because of fear and doubts she had no answers for? Her tears splashed onto the keyboard of her word processor as she began another night of working until she was too exhausted to think . . . or feel . . . or want.

CHAPTER SEVENTEEN

Wednesday afternoon, after talking with the Kings team doctor about the condition of the two wide receivers who'd been injured, Ashley flipped on her word processor to write her story. She'd just finished the first draft when the phone rang. She no longer leapt for it as she had the first few days after Zane had left her, but she couldn't stop the twinge of hope from flickering in her heart as she reached for the receiver.

It wasn't the voice she longed to hear, a longing that flowed far deeper than even she realized. "Hi, Ashley, this is your favorite inside source calling," she heard Sammy say. "Man, oh man, have I got a story. And this one will be of special interest to you."

Ashley tried to summon up some enthusiasm, something that was harder and harder to do each day. "Great, Sammy," she replied, "let me grab my pad and pencil and you can give me all the juicy details." She reached for her legal pad. "Okay, I'm all set. Let's have it."

"You know that the Kings are desperate for a wide receiver, since two went down in Sunday's game, right? Well, the Jets have one available, and guess who the grapevine says they want in return?"

"I hope it's Razor Williams. I wouldn't mind seeing him go at all."

"Nope. I'm afraid it's that guy you've been keeping company with, Zane Bruxton. With Bubba Pirrs back to full strength the Kings can afford to . . ."

Sammy rambled on, but Ashley didn't hear a word. The thing she'd feared most was really happening. Zane was being traded! Mercifully Sammy cut the conversation short.

Ashley felt a cold numbness as she sat back down in front of her word processor to type the end of the story she'd been working on. "Because of these injuries it is rumored that Zane Bruxton will be sent to the New York . . ."

Her hands froze over the keys as the shattering implication of what Sammy had told her finally hit her with the power of a sledgehammer. She might never see Zane again! He'd be gone from her life forever!

Just as suddenly, she knew what Kakalina had meant when she said, "you'll know it's right when the love becomes more important than the doubts."

Leaping up from the chair, she experienced such a surge of joy she felt almost faint. She couldn't grab the phone quick enough. The moment he answered, she said, "Sammy, I've got to talk to Zane—now! I don't care if he's on the practice field. Call him. Tell the coach it's an emergency. Lie. Do anything. Just get him for me!"

"Ashley, will you simmer down and listen. I can't get Zane because he isn't here."

Desperation made Ashley almost curt. "Where is he?" she demanded. "I've got to find him!"

"Well, unless you sprout wings and fly, I don't think you can make it."

"Make what?" she asked, her voice rising in exasperation.

"Make it to the airport. Remember? They're playing Denver this week, and the coach wants them there early to get used to the altitude. I'm bringing the equipment in the cargo plane. It's not leaving until—"

"Thanks, Sammy," she cut him off. "I've got to go."

Ashley said a silent prayer as she floored the accelerator. Roaring into the airport parking lot, she left her car in a loading zone and dashed inside. Frantically she scanned the departure schedule, smiling elatedly when she found the flight. She might just make it. She ran for the gate, arriving just in time to see the plane taxi down the runway and soar into the cerulean blue of the Hawaiian sky.

Tears of disappointment brought a lump to her throat. But then a delightful idea how to welcome Zane home popped into her head, and her happy smile returned. She found a public phone and dialed Kakalina's number.

When her friend answered, Ashley said, "I've called to ask you a favor. Or I guess I should say I need a favor from your folks. Here's the plan."

When she was finished, Kakalina laughed. "You can't be serious? This is a joke, right?"

"No, I'm very serious. It's important. Please ask them," Ashley begged.

"Anything for a friend, even if I think she's a little nuts," Kakalina teased. "And don't worry, I'm sure they won't mind. In fact, they're planning on coming over Friday to see Jake Jr."

"That will be perfect. That'll give me a couple of days to get everything set."

Saturday morning Ashley arrived at Zane's apartment building in a borrowed pickup truck. The guard at the service entrance took one look at what she had in the back and shook his head. "Lady, you gotta be crazy!"

Ashley, her heart filled with joy, just smiled serenely. "Maybe I am, but will twenty bucks buy your help?"

"Hell, lady, for twenty bucks, I'd cart that stuff on my back. Oh, by the way, I talked with Mrs. Brown as you suggested, and while we normally don't let strangers into an apartment without the tenant's permission, she assured me Mr. Bruxton wouldn't mind."

When he'd made the last trip up to Zane's apartment he stood at the door, scratching his head. "My wife is never going to believe this!"

Ashley went merrily on with her work, not paying one bit of attention to him.

Sunday afternoon the minutes seemed like hours as Ashley watched the Kings beat the Broncos by seven. It got worse as she waited for Zane's plane to land. After what seemed like an eternity Ashley finally heard Zane's key in the lock. She glanced quickly around, making sure everything was perfect.

Zane snapped on the light. He blinked, obviously not believing what he was seeing. His living room was knee deep in sweet-smelling hay, and Ashley, in one of the muumuus he'd given her, was lying in the middle of it. Pinned to the wall was a huge banner that read, "How about a roll in the hay that lasts a lifetime?"

When she saw his shock, Ashley was afraid for an instant that he didn't want her. But she was wrong . . . very, very wrong.

With a whoop of joy, Zane tossed his suitcase

aside and in three strides was at her side. As he dropped to his knees beside her, he gently reached out a hand to touch her cheek, as if hardly believing she really was there waiting for him, and not just some creation of his imagination.

Ashley opened her arms to receive him, and she didn't have to offer twice. But before he sank down into her soft embrace, he grinned that impish grin she loved. "It's hard to believe you're really here. I want to make sure."

With one yank he ripped the muumuu open down the length of her body. His smile widened, finding her completely naked beneath. "Yes, you're here, all of you. And obviously ready for me."

"Don't make me wait," she whispered.

"I won't!" Zane promised fervently, his hands already at the zipper of his slacks.

The time apart had hurt too much for slow love-making now. As soon as he'd kicked aside his clothes, Zane took her, driving hard into her body with a conquering force they both craved. They loved with savage intensity, as if possessed by the need to burn away their agonizingly lonely memories with their passion. Over and over they rolled in the hay, becoming one, each trying to show the other the depths of their love.

It was after dawn when Zane cuddled her close and they slept. Hours later, Ashley stirred in his arms.

His eyes fluttered open. "I wasn't dreaming," he said, and smiled. "You really are here."

"For now and for always, if you want me," she whispered.

"If I want you? Didn't I show you last night how much I want you, over and over, every way I could imagine?"

"Mmm, yes." She stretched like a contented cat. "It was rather a convincing performance."

His smile faded and his eyes grew serious. "What made you change your mind? I've been going through hell, thinking I'd lost you, damning myself because I couldn't make you love me enough."

She traced the dark shadows under his eyes. "I'm surprised we didn't meet. I've been in hell too."

He ran his hand down her body as if memorizing every curve. "I think we need to talk," he suggested. "But if we stay like this it'll be right back to the R and R for sure."

Reluctantly Ashley agreed. "But we've got a problem," she added. "You tore the only dress I brought."

"I can fix that." Zane grinned, rising from the hay. He went into his bedroom and returned with a Kings jersey in his hand. "Here, put this on. It should cover the essentials."

Ashley slipped it on over her head. He was so much larger than she was, it fell almost to her knees.

Zane winked. "You look kind of cute in that." He came nearer, smiling. "And I love the idea I can do this," he said as he ran his hand up the soft inner part of her thigh, "anytime I want."

Ashley felt the fire start anew, the sweet sensations swirling at his touch. "Aren't you ever satisfied?" she murmured.

"Not when it's you." With a sigh he took his hand away. "Why did I ever insist we needed to talk?"

"Because we do. We have the rest of our lives for loving."

Zane kissed her on the mouth. "Sounds wonderful, doesn't it?"

Without hesitation, she insisted, "Yes, it does, even if it means we do that loving in New York."

He frowned. "Why would we be doing it in New York?"

"Haven't you heard the rumor about the Kings trading you?"

"Sure. But I told them to forget it. No way am I going to play for the Jets, or any other team."

Ashley stared at him in astonishment. "You can't do that. They'd never let you get away with it."

"Want to bet?" He took her hand and led her through the hay to the sofa. When she was nestled against him, he explained, "Ashley, I kept telling you football wasn't my life. You just didn't seem to hear me. When the Kings started talking trade I simply told them I was not leaving Hawaii, and if that meant getting put on waivers, then so be it."

"But I don't understand."

"It's simple. Uncle Clyde is rich, I'm not. Football was always a means to an end to me. It was never my life. The only reason I signed a pro contract in the first place was to have enough money to be able to get my master's and go on to do doctoral research at the oceanographic institute. Believe it or not, I really am interested in plate theory. Between my bonus for signing and the salary I can now do that very comfortably. So when they mentioned the trade, I told the Kings if they want me to play for them fine. If not, it just means I can start my research full-time sooner than I'd planned." He smiled that impish smile. "I hope Bubba likes the Big Apple, cause that's where he's going. Better him than me!"

Ashley raised her head to look at him. "There are so many things you said, that I didn't hear. You

281

always told me how much your studies meant to you. I guess I just didn't listen."

"I know. But it really wasn't your fault." He kissed her gently on the forehead. "All your perceptions were tainted by what happened between you and Butcher."

"I'm glad we're not going to New York, but I'm also glad that trade rumor surfaced," she confessed, tears blurring her eyes. "The thought of losing you was what finally made me realize the love I held for you in my heart was a whole lot more important than any problems we might have."

"I tried to tell you that over a week ago."

"I know. Can you love such a stupid fool?"

Zane smiled roughishly. "I sure can. And I intend to, any way I can think of. But before I start trying out some of my more wicked ideas on your body, I've got a question. Not that I didn't enjoy our roll —or I should say, *rolls*—in the hay, but I would like to know where you got it? This is Honolulu, not Texas."

"You may not know it, but on the island of Hawaii there are a lot of cattle ranches. Kakalina's parents own one of the largest. Since I knew they use a helicopter to herd the cattle, I asked them to toss in a couple bales the next time they flew over to see Jake Jr."

"Now I've got another question. How are we going to clean it up?"

Ashley slipped her hand into his. "Together, the way we're going to do everything else for the rest of our lives. Come on, we might as well get started," she urged, jumping to her feet.

Suddenly everything went blurry. She stood swaying, trying to bring Zane's concerned face into focus.

He rose quickly, putting his arm around her. "Ashley, what's wrong? You're white as a sheet! You aren't sick, are you?"

Suddenly the truth dawned on her. Her smile blazing, she murmured, "Zane, I think we have a little problem."

"How can you say we have a problem when you're standing there with such a radiant smile you'd shame the moon?"

She stood on tiptoe and kissed him on the mouth —softly, gently, with gratitude.

He blinked. "You've never kissed me like that before."

"I've never thought I was carrying your baby before," she confessed, her hands unconsciously going to her stomach.

For a stunned instant he just stared at her. "My . . . my baby?" Hurt dimmed his blue eyes. "Is that why you came back to me?" he whispered.

"Oh Zane, no! It's not that way at all," Ashley said pleadingly. "I decided I wanted to be with you forever before I ever had a glimmer I might be carrying your child. You have to believe that! I wouldn't—"

"Shh, love." He laid a finger against her lips. "I believe you. I don't even know why I asked that stupid question. Those gorgeous eyes of yours can't lie, and right now they're shining with such love that I feel like the luckiest man in the world."

"Do you mind if we start our family right away?" she asked hesitantly.

"Mind?" he shouted. "I love it! And I love you!"

Sweeping her up in his brawny arms, he spun her round and round, chanting, "We're going to have a baby, we're going to have a baby."

Suddenly Zane stumbled to a stop. "Oh, my God, we're going to have a baby!!"

Carefully setting her on her feet as if she were the most fragile thing he'd ever touched, he ran his hand anxiously over the spot where his child lay. "You don't think I . . . I mean, holding you like that didn't hurt—"

"Zane stop." She laughed. "I'm just having a baby. I'm not a fragile piece of china. Believe me, you didn't hurt the baby with your exuberance."

His blue eyes suddenly sparkled with another question. "Speaking of exuberance what about—"

"Let's put it this way," she interrupted, sliding her arms around his neck. "It'll be months and months before we have to be careful."

"And then?"

"And then"—she chuckled knowingly—"we'll just follow the advice of the wise sage who once said, 'Where there's a will, there's a way.'"

Zane grinned. "I'm good at finding ways."

Ashley's smile answered his. "I *know*."

Become a winner at love, work, and play.

A distinguished, practicing psychologist, Dr. Kassorla describes the differences between winning and losing personalities. She first pinpoints the skills and attitudes that carry winners to the top, and then illustrates how *everyone* can develop such skills and use them successfully in love, work, and play. Dr. Kassorla also includes enlightening, instructive interviews with winners from many fields: Malcolm Forbes, Diane von Furstenberg, Jack Lemmon, Bruce Jenner, Bob Woodward, and many more.

You won't be the same after *you* go for it!

12752-1-30 $3.95

Dr. Irene C. Kassorla

Rebels and outcasts, they fled halfway across
the earth to settle the harsh Australian
wastelands. Decades later—ennobled by love
and strengthened by tragedy—they had
transformed a wilderness into fertile land. And
themselves into

The Australians

WILLIAM STUART LONG

THE EXILES, #1	12374-7-12	$3.95
THE SETTLERS, #2	17929-7-45	$3.95
THE TRAITORS, #3	18131-3-21	$3.95
THE EXPLORERS, #4	12391-7-29	$3.95
THE ADVENTURERS, #5	10330-4-40	$3.95
THE COLONISTS, #6	11342-3-21	$3.95